MRS. JEFFRIES
RIGHTS A WRONG

EMILY BRIGHTWELL

BERKLEY PRIME CRIME
NEW YORK

BERKLEY PRIME CRIME
Published by Berkley
An imprint of Penguin Random House LLC
375 Hudson Street, New York, New York 10014

Copyright © 2017 by Cheryl A. Arguile
Penguin Random House supports copyright. Copyright fuels creativity, encourages diverse
voices, promotes free speech, and creates a vibrant culture. Thank you for buying an
authorized edition of this book and for complying with copyright laws by not reproducing,
scanning, or distributing any part of it in any form without permission. You are supporting
writers and allowing Penguin Random House to continue to publish books for every reader.

BERKLEY is a registered trademark and BERKLEY PRIME CRIME and the B colophon
are trademarks of Penguin Random House LLC.

Library of Congress Cataloging-in-Publication Data

Names: Brightwell, Emily, author.
Title: Mrs. Jeffries rights a wrong/Emily Brightwell.
Description: First edition. | New York: Berkley Prime Crime, 2017. |
Series: A Victorian mystery; 35
Identifiers: LCCN 2016056070 (print) | LCCN 2017002328 (ebook) |
ISBN 9780399584206 (softcover) | ISBN 9780399584213 (ebook)
Subjects: LCSH: Jeffries, Mrs. (Fictitious character)—Fiction. |
Witherspoon, Gerald (Fictitious character)—Fiction. |
Women detectives—England—Fiction. | Housekeepers—England—Fiction. |
Murder—Investigation—Fiction. | Police—England—Fiction. |
BISAC: FICTION/Mystery & Detective/Women Sleuths. |
| GSAFD: Mystery fiction.
Classification: LCC PS3552.R46443 M733 2017 (print) |
LCC PS3552.R46443 (ebook) | DDC 813/.54—dc23
LC record available at https://lccn.loc.gov/2016056070

First Edition: May 2017

Printed in the United States of America
1 3 5 7 9 10 8 6 4 2

Cover illustration by Jeff Walker

continued . . .

Mrs. Jeffries on the Trail

Who killed Annie Shields while she was out selling flowers so late on a foggy night? It's up to Mrs. Jeffries to sniff out the clues.

Mrs. Jeffries Plays the Cook

Mrs. Jeffries finds herself doing double duty: cooking for the inspector's household and trying to cook a killer's goose.

Mrs. Jeffries and the Missing Alibi

When Inspector Witherspoon becomes the main suspect in a murder, Scotland Yard refuses to let him investigate. But no one said anything about Mrs. Jeffries.

Mrs. Jeffries Stands Corrected

When a local publican is murdered and Inspector Witherspoon botches the investigation, trouble starts to brew for Mrs. Jeffries.

Mrs. Jeffries Takes the Stage

After a theatre critic is murdered, Mrs. Jeffries uncovers the victim's secret past: a real-life drama more compelling than any stage play.

Mrs. Jeffries Questions the Answer

Hannah Cameron was not well liked. But who wanted to stab her in the back? Mrs. Jeffries must really tiptoe around this time—or it could be a matter of life and death.

Mrs. Jeffries Reveals Her Art

A missing model *and* a killer have Mrs. Jeffries working double time so someone else doesn't become the next subject.

Mrs. Jeffries Takes the Cake

The evidence was all there: a dead body, two dessert plates, and a gun. But Mrs. Jeffries will have to do some snooping around to dish up more clues.

Mrs. Jeffries Rocks the Boat

Mirabelle had traveled by boat all the way from Australia to visit her sister—only to wind up murdered. Now Mrs. Jeffries must solve the case—and it's sink or swim.

Mrs. Jeffries Weeds the Plot

Three attempts have been made on Annabeth Gentry's life. Is it because her bloodhound dug up the body of a murdered thief?

Mrs. Jeffries Pinches the Post

Harrison Nye had dubious business dealings, but no one expected him to be murdered. Now Mrs. Jeffries and her staff must root through the sins of his past.

Mrs. Jeffries Pleads Her Case

Harlan Westover's death was deemed a suicide, but the inspector is determined to prove otherwise. Mrs. Jeffries must ensure the good inspector remains afloat.

Mrs. Jeffries Sweeps the Chimney

A dead vicar has been found propped against a church wall. And Inspector Witherspoon's only prayer is to seek the divinations of Mrs. Jeffries.

continued . . .

Mrs. Jeffries Stalks the Hunter

Puppy love turns to obsession, which leads to murder. Who better to get to the heart of the matter than Inspector Witherspoon's indomitable companion, Mrs. Jeffries?

Mrs. Jeffries and the Silent Knight

The yuletide murder of an elderly man is complicated by several suspects—none of whom were in the Christmas spirit.

Mrs. Jeffries Appeals the Verdict

Mrs. Jeffries and her belowstairs cohorts have their work cut out for them if they want to save an innocent man from the gallows.

Mrs. Jeffries and the Best Laid Plans

Banker Lawrence Boyd had a list of enemies including just about everyone he ever met. It will take Mrs. Jeffries' shrewd eye to find who killed him.

Mrs. Jeffries and the Feast of St. Stephen

'Tis the season for sleuthing when wealthy Stephen Whitfield is murdered during his holiday dinner party. It's up to Mrs. Jeffries to solve the case in time for Christmas.

Mrs. Jeffries Holds the Trump

A very well-liked but very dead magnate is found floating down the river. Now Mrs. Jeffries and company will have to dive into a mystery that only grows more complex.

Mrs. Jeffries in the Nick of Time

Mrs. Jeffries lends her downstairs common sense to this upstairs murder mystery—and tries not to get derailed in the case of a rich uncle–cum–model train enthusiast.

Mrs. Jeffries and the Yuletide Weddings

Wedding bells will make this season all the jollier. Until one humbug sings a carol of murder.

Mrs. Jeffries Speaks Her Mind

When an eccentric old woman suspects she's going to be murdered, everyone thinks she's just being peculiar—until the prediction comes true.

Mrs. Jeffries Forges Ahead

A free-spirited bride is poisoned at a society ball, and it's up to Mrs. Jeffries to discover who wanted to make the modern young woman into a postmortem.

Mrs. Jeffries and the Mistletoe Mix-Up

There's murder going on under the mistletoe as Mrs. Jeffries and Inspector Witherspoon hurry to solve the case before the Christmas Eve eggnog is ladled out.

Mrs. Jeffries Defends Her Own

When an unwelcome visitor from her past needs help, Mrs. Jeffries steps into the fray to stop a terrible miscarriage of justice.

Mrs. Jeffries Turns the Tide

When Mrs. Jeffries doubts a suspect's guilt, she must turn the tide of the investigation to save an innocent man.

Mrs. Jeffries and the Merry Gentlemen

When a successful stockbroker is murdered just days before Christmas, Mrs. Jeffries won't rest until justice is served for the holidays . . .

continued . . .

Mrs. Jeffries and the One Who Got Away

When a woman is found strangled with an old newspaper clipping in her hand, Inspector Witherspoon will need Mrs. Jeffries' help to get to the bottom of the story.

Mrs. Jeffries Wins the Prize

Inspector Witherspoon and Mrs. Jeffries weed out a killer after a body is found in a gentlewoman's conservatory.

Berkley Prime Crime titles by Emily Brightwell

THE INSPECTOR AND MRS. JEFFRIES
MRS. JEFFRIES DUSTS FOR CLUES
THE GHOST AND MRS. JEFFRIES
MRS. JEFFRIES TAKES STOCK
MRS. JEFFRIES ON THE BALL
MRS. JEFFRIES ON THE TRAIL
MRS. JEFFRIES PLAYS THE COOK
MRS. JEFFRIES AND THE MISSING ALIBI
MRS. JEFFRIES STANDS CORRECTED
MRS. JEFFRIES TAKES THE STAGE
MRS. JEFFRIES QUESTIONS THE ANSWER
MRS. JEFFRIES REVEALS HER ART
MRS. JEFFRIES TAKES THE CAKE
MRS. JEFFRIES ROCKS THE BOAT
MRS. JEFFRIES WEEDS THE PLOT
MRS. JEFFRIES PINCHES THE POST
MRS. JEFFRIES PLEADS HER CASE
MRS. JEFFRIES SWEEPS THE CHIMNEY
MRS. JEFFRIES STALKS THE HUNTER
MRS. JEFFRIES AND THE SILENT KNIGHT
MRS. JEFFRIES APPEALS THE VERDICT
MRS. JEFFRIES AND THE BEST LAID PLANS
MRS. JEFFRIES AND THE FEAST OF ST. STEPHEN
MRS. JEFFRIES HOLDS THE TRUMP
MRS. JEFFRIES IN THE NICK OF TIME
MRS. JEFFRIES AND THE YULETIDE WEDDINGS
MRS. JEFFRIES SPEAKS HER MIND
MRS. JEFFRIES FORGES AHEAD
MRS. JEFFRIES AND THE MISTLETOE MIX-UP
MRS. JEFFRIES DEFENDS HER OWN
MRS. JEFFRIES TURNS THE TIDE
MRS. JEFFRIES AND THE MERRY GENTLEMEN
MRS. JEFFRIES AND THE ONE WHO GOT AWAY
MRS. JEFFRIES WINS THE PRIZE
MRS. JEFFRIES RIGHTS A WRONG

Anthologies

MRS. JEFFRIES LEARNS THE TRADE
MRS. JEFFRIES TAKES A SECOND LOOK
MRS. JEFFRIES TAKES TEA AT THREE
MRS. JEFFRIES SALLIES FORTH
MRS. JEFFRIES PLEADS THE FIFTH
MRS. JEFFRIES SERVES AT SIX

This book is dedicated to
Linda Ruth Domholt and Sandra Nanette Caldararo—
my two wonderful sisters who have
"righted many wrongs" in this world!

MRS. JEFFRIES
RIGHTS A WRONG

CHAPTER 1

Thomas Mundy forced himself to smile as he stepped through the double doors of the Wrexley Hotel. He glanced at the two elderly women sitting at a table in front of a huge potted fern and sipping whiskey out of cut crystal glasses. The hotel wasn't top-drawer, but it was close enough for his purposes—it attracted the class of respectable widows and widowers who were his specialty. Blast, it galled him that he had to leave just when he had the pigeons right where he wanted them. He swept off his black silk top hat and tucked his gold-headed walking stick under his arm as he approached the two women. Although in a hurry, he wasn't going to burn his bridges. This was only a temporary retreat, and if his luck held, his pigeons would still be ripe for plucking when he returned to London.

"Mrs. Blanding, Mrs. Denton, you're both looking lovely this evening."

"You're too kind, Mr. Mundy," Elvira Blanding said, tittering behind a diamond-bejeweled hand. Thomas forced his gaze away from the sparkles on her skinny, blue-veined hand and glanced at her twin, Eleanor Denton. They were slender women in their late sixties, identical in every way except that poor Elvira's salt-and-pepper hair was so thin you could see her scalp. Both were widows, wealthy, unworldly, and so ready to back any cockeyed scheme he mentioned that fortune itself seemed to be cheering him on. But he didn't have time to chat. After what had happened tonight, he had no choice; it was either leave town or face some very uncomfortable consequences.

"Do join us for a drink." Eleanor Denton tapped the rim of her whiskey glass. "Elvie and I were just talking about how excited we are about investing in your Brazilian venture. I do believe I shall try to like coffee a bit more, considering that I'm now going to be part owner of a plantation."

Thomas contrived to look disappointed. "I do wish I could, Mrs. Denton—you know how I adore your company—but unfortunately, I've a late business meeting with the comte de Valois. Apparently, he's heard about the Brazilian opportunity and wants to talk to me about investing. Business before pleasure, I'm afraid."

"Oh dear, that is disappointing, but I suppose it can't be helped. Shall we see you tomorrow, then?" Eleanor asked.

"Of course, of course. Perhaps we can breakfast together." He edged toward the reception counter, where he hoped the clerk would have his key ready.

"We'll be in the dining room at our usual time," Elvira added.

"I look forward to seeing you both. Until the morrow, ladies." His luck held when he reached the counter and the clerk handed him his room key. Mundy kept to a dignified pace on the broad staircase until he was out of sight; then he took the steps two at a time. His sense of urgency increased as he reached the third-floor landing. This was where the cheaper rooms were located. The carpet was threadbare in places, some of the wallpaper was peeling, and a bit of the crown molding was missing from a number of spots along the ceiling. But the corridor was bright, as new electric lights had recently been installed. Mundy didn't mind the décor; he'd chosen this floor and his room because they had the easiest access to the back stairs, and tonight, that would come in very handy.

He raced toward his door, holding his key at the ready. He'd stayed alive and out of jail by listening to his instincts, and right now they were screaming at him to be on the night train to the Continent. He was sorry that he'd wasted those few precious minutes with the old ladies in the lobby.

He shoved the key into the lock and gave the door a quick kick. It tended to jam, and he wasn't in the mood to be careful. Then he heard the squeak of a floorboard. Mundy froze for a second and then looked around carefully.

But he saw nothing. The doors along the corridor were closed, and there was no one lurking at the exit to the back stairs. He let out the breath he'd been holding. Stay calm, he told himself. You can't panic. You weren't followed. You're safe enough now. All you have to do is gather your things and get to the station in time for the night train. As he shoved into the room, he mentally started listing everything he needed to do.

Mundy dumped his things onto the chair and, not wanting to take time to fool with lighting either of the small lamps, he left the door open to let in the light from the corridor. He skirted around the bed to the wardrobe. Taking out his case, he flung it open onto the bed and then started yanking out his clothes.

He tossed a pair of trousers and a brocade waistcoat inside and then snatched two shirts off their hooks and flung them onto the pile. His belts and jewel case came along next, with both his formal cravats and a business tie. He picked up a pair of shoes and then yanked open the other side of the wardrobe. Kneeling, he grabbed the small carpetbag from the bottom of the wardrobe, opened it, and checked the contents. He was so engrossed in his task, he didn't notice the sudden increase in light as the door was pushed farther open and someone slipped inside.

The visitor glanced around the room, making sure they were alone before picking up the walking stick from the chair and then slowly closing the door, until only a tiny shaft of light was still visible.

As the light dimmed, Mundy realized he wasn't alone. He dropped the carpetbag onto the floor as he scrambled to his feet. His eyes widened in shock. "You! What are you doing here?"

"You promised you'd never come back." The visitor moved slowly around the foot of the bed toward Mundy. "You swore it on your mother's life, remember?"

"My mother was already dead the last time we met." Mundy relaxed. At least his unwanted guest wasn't the one he really feared. This individual was more of a nuisance than anything else. Nonetheless, it was a nuisance that had to be dealt with quickly if he was going to make that train. "So that made any past promises null and void. What do you want? I'm in a bit of a hurry." He turned back to the wardrobe and grabbed a heavy, expensive blue suit off the back hook.

"Going somewhere?" The intruder moved quickly, coming up behind Mundy as he struggled with the heavy clothing. He lifted Mundy's walking stick and smashed it hard against the back of his silky black hair. "I don't care how long your mother's been dead. A promise is a promise."

The suit fell out of Mundy's fingers as the blow stunned him.

"Frankly, I don't think you'll be going anywhere." The intruder glanced toward the door before bringing the heavy cane down again, this time even harder. "I told you not to come back. You should have listened to me."

But Mundy was past hearing anything. He'd already crumpled to the floor.

His assailant gave his head a third whack for good measure and then knelt down to make sure his victim was dead. "I do hate people who break promises to me."

"The inspector seemed out of sorts this morning," Mrs. Goodge, the cook for Inspector Gerald Witherspoon, said to the housekeeper. "He left half his breakfast on his plate, and you know how much he loves kippers." She was a stout elderly woman with wire-rimmed spectacles and a headful of gray hair that she kept tucked under her floppy cook's hat.

Mrs. Jeffries put the household expense ledger on the table next to a stack of papers. "Out of sorts is precisely how he's feeling. Lady Cannonberry is still in Kent. He misses her dreadfully." Hepzibah Jeffries, the widow of a Yorkshire policeman, was a plump woman of late middle age with graying auburn hair, dark brown eyes, and a sprinkling of freckles across her nose. As was her custom, she wore a brown bombazine dress and comfortable brown high-topped shoes.

Mrs. Goodge pulled her mixing bowl out from beneath her worktable and put it next to the sack of flour. "Kent? What's she doing there?"

"What she generally does when she's called out of town—nursing one of her late husband's relatives." She heaved a sigh as she stared at the small mountain of household bills and receipts she needed to enter in the ledger. She hated paperwork, but it had to be done.

"Which one is it this time?"

"His aunt Catherine." Mrs. Jeffries pulled out her chair and sat down.

"Good gracious, isn't that old woman dead yet? She's got to be in her late nineties, and she's had so many ailments, all of which were supposedly fatal."

"She's ninety-eight, and from what the inspector told me after he read Ruth's letter, she's still going to need more nursing. He's very down at the mouth because Ruth won't be back until next week at the earliest."

Ruth, or Lady Cannonberry, was both their neighbor and the inspector's "special friend."

A clatter of footsteps came from the back stairs. They both turned to it as Phyllis, the housemaid, led Constable Griffiths, a policeman from the inspector's station, into the kitchen. Fred, the household's black and brown dog, got up and stared at the stranger, but after sensing that the newcomer was welcome, he flopped back onto his warm spot next to the cooker. He didn't, however, go to sleep. He slept only when it was his people in the kitchen.

"Constable Griffiths came by to deliver a message," Phyllis explained. She was a slender, attractive young woman in her early twenties with dark blond hair, porcelain skin, and sapphire blue eyes.

Griffiths, a tall, gangly man, held his policeman's helmet under his arm as he nodded politely. "I'm sorry for coming to the front door, but the gardener had the gate blocked, and I was in a bit of a hurry. As Miss Phyllis explained, I've a message for you from the inspector."

He gave the housemaid a quick glance, and instead of blushing and looking away, she smiled. Mrs. Jeffries and Mrs. Goodge exchanged knowing looks. When Phyllis had come to them more than two years ago, too scared to say "boo" to a goose in a barnyard, she'd been a plump young girl with a pale face as round as a pie tin. But she, like everyone else in the household, had changed greatly because of their activities, and now she was a confident young woman who could handle an admirer with aplomb and grace.

"Do you have time for a cup of tea, Constable?" Mrs. Jeffries asked. There was only one reason the inspector would send one of his men there. Witherspoon had been called to a murder, and she was determined to get as much information about it as possible. "I know it's only October, but it's quite chilly outside."

Mrs. Goodge had also figured out the situation and added her two cents' worth. "Have a nice cuppa, Constable. I've a freshly baked Madeira cake in the larder. You look like you could use something to warm you up."

Griffiths hesitated. "I shouldn't, I really shouldn't, but I've been on an early shift, and I've not eaten since the wee hours of the morning. I can't pass on a chance for a slice of your cake."

"I'm sure the inspector won't mind if you take a few minutes to fill your stomach." Mrs. Goodge waved toward an empty chair and started toward the hall, but Phyllis cut her off. She, too, had figured out what the constable's sudden appearance meant. "I'll get it, Mrs. Goodge."

"Thank you, Phyllis. That will be very helpful. The kettle's already on the boil, so it'll only take a moment."

Mrs. Jeffries picked up the ledger, the bills, and the receipts and swept them onto the pine sideboard as the constable took a chair. She kept up a steady stream of pleasantries and conversation until the food was ready and the others were at the table.

"Here you are, Constable." Mrs. Goodge cut a huge slice of cake and passed him his plate.

He took a bite, chewed, swallowed, and then his bony face broke into a blissful smile. "Mrs. Goodge, this is wonderful. Even my Nan can't make a cake like this."

"I'm glad you're enjoying it, Constable. You young lads work so hard. Now, why don't you give us the inspector's message?"

"And don't leave out any details," Phyllis added. She gave him a shy smile when he looked at her. "I'll bet the inspector was called away on something ever so important. I so love hearing about his work, but he's such a humble man." She reached over and touched his arm. "I've noticed that all of you policemen are like that, so very modest about your work."

Mrs. Jeffries ducked her head to hide a smile. Surely Phyllis was laying it on a bit thick?

Griffiths blushed. "That's kind of you, miss, but we're only doing our duty. Mind you, the inspector is known for hiding his light under a bushel. He's solved more murders than anyone in the Metropolitan Police Force."

They knew that, but what Constable Griffiths didn't know was that a large part of the inspector's success was due to the enormous amount of help he received on each and every case. His entire household as well as several of their friends used their considerable resources to track down clues, verify alibis, and sniff out every kernel of gossip about both the victim and the suspects.

"The only one who doesn't seem to know that is the inspector." Phyllis laughed prettily. "He never mentions it. But do tell, what's happened today?"

Griffiths took another quick bite. "He got called to the Wrexley Hotel."

"And where's that?" the maid asked innocently.

"On the Queens Road in Bayswater," Griffiths explained. "There's been a murder. Quite a messy one, too."

"Gracious, who was killed?" Mrs. Goodge asked.

"A man named Thomas Mundy was murdered in his room last night. It sounds pretty brutal, too. He was coshed on the head, supposedly with a cane or a walking stick, and left for dead." He grabbed his cup and quickly downed half the tea.

"A walking stick as a murder weapon? Goodness, I've never heard of such a thing." Mrs. Jeffries clucked her tongue. She wanted to keep him talking. It was important to find out as many details as she could.

He shrugged. "People get bashed about with all manner of strange objects, Mrs. Jeffries, and we don't know for a fact that it's really the murder weapon, but that's what the fixed point constable reported when he called the inspector to the scene. Mind you, there was a bit of confusion at first. The Queens Road in Bayswater is one of the boundaries of our division, so the superintendent wasn't certain the case belonged to us. But the dividing line is the middle of the street, and then Constable Hughes pointed out the Wrexley is on our side of the road."

"So it's definitely in the inspector's division?" Mrs. Jeffries pressed. She didn't want Witherspoon having more problems with jurisdictional jealousy. There were those in the Metropolitan force who claimed he "hogged" all the murders, despite the fact that the inspector never asked to go outside his own district. It was his superiors at Scotland Yard who always sent him to other divisions.

When it came to murders, police divisions were as jealous as old cats if a detective or an inspector from another division nosed in on their territory. Mrs. Jeffries blamed those awful Ripper murders for this change in attitude. Jack's heinous crimes had shown that murders sold newspapers, and for many an ambitious policeman, that was the fastest way to find oneself in an office at New Scotland Yard. Like it or not, getting one's name associated in the public mind with solving serious crimes tended to make one's superiors take notice. So it wasn't surprising that each division wanted to be sure its officers got a chance at the most important cases.

"It's ours, and from what we already know, it's goin' to be a messy one. The fixed point constable had blood on his shoes." Griffith took another large bite of cake.

"Oh dear, that must have been dreadful." Mrs. Goodge struggled with her conscience. It wasn't right to be so excited about some poor soul losing his life, but then she realized she wasn't excited about the death, but about the investigation. "Who found the body?"

"The maid. She found him this morning when she went in to clean his room."

"That must have been quite early?" Mrs. Jeffries glanced at the carriage clock on the pine sideboard and saw that it was almost eleven.

"I don't know exactly when they found him, but the first constable got there at half nine and sent to the station immediately for the inspector."

"I don't suppose anyone had any idea how long the man had been dead?" Mrs. Jeffries asked.

"I don't expect the police surgeon's been there as yet," Griffiths replied. "They sent for him when the inspector sent a constable back to the station for more men."

"How sad for the poor gentleman," Phyllis said softly. "Imagine having someone come into your room and take your life."

"Murder's never nice, is it?" Griffiths smiled at the maid and then looked at Mrs. Jeffries. "The inspector asked me to tell you he'd not be home till late and to keep his dinner in the warming oven for him." He nodded at the cook. "Thank you for the tea and cake. I'll probably be working a long shift today because of this incident, and it'll keep me from bein' hungry. I'll get going, then." He glanced at Phyllis.

"I'll see you to the door, Constable," she said. She kept up a steady stream of chatter as they walked down the hall. Mrs. Goodge and Mrs. Jeffries were quiet as they cleared up the tea things.

A few moments later, Phyllis raced into the kitchen. "Do you want me to get Wiggins first or try to contact Smythe?"

Wiggins, the footman, was currently at the ironmongers getting new hinges for one of the dry larder cupboards. Smythe, the coachman, was at Howards, the local stable that housed the inspector's horses and carriage.

Inspector Witherspoon wasn't your average policeman. He'd inherited a huge house and a substantial amount of wealth from his late aunt, Euphemia Witherspoon. But he'd kept his position as a policeman because he'd not been raised to be a gentleman of leisure. Add to that, he frequently said that being on the police force and solving crimes made him feel as if he was doing good in the world.

"Wiggins should be on his way back by now." Mrs. Jeffries headed for the coat tree and grabbed her hat and cloak. "So go to Howards and tell Smythe we need him right away." She looked at the cook. "Mrs. Goodge, let Wiggins know to be at the ready. As soon as Smythe gets here, send the two of them over to the Wrexley Hotel to see what they can find out. If we're lucky, they might pick up some information before we meet this afternoon. I'll go to Betsy."

"Do you want me to go anywhere after Howards, or come straight back?" Phyllis asked as she trailed after the housekeeper to the coat tree. "What about Luty and Hatchet? Do you want me to go there after I talk to Smythe?"

Mrs. Jeffries popped her hat on, slung her cloak over her shoulders, and headed for the back door. "Yes, tell them what little we know and ask them to be here at four this afternoon. We've got ourselves a murder."

"This has been such a shock, Inspector. We've never had a murder here." Ezra Cutler, the manager of the Wrexley Hotel, dabbed at his wide forehead with his handkerchief. But despite his efforts, there was still a faint streak of perspiration along the rim of his curly brown hair, and he'd missed a drop that dangled on the edge of his handlebar mustache. He was a short, slightly rotund man wearing a brown suit and a very worried expression. "The Wrexleys, they're the owners, are dreadfully upset about this incident. They want this whole matter cleared up as quickly and quietly as possible."

"Yes, I'm sure they do," Inspector Gerald Witherspoon replied. "And that is precisely what the police are trying to accomplish. Now, if you don't mind, I'll need to ask you some questions." He was a man of medium height with thinning brown hair, deep-set hazel eyes, and pale skin.

Cutler's face paled. "You'll do it out here, won't you? I don't think I can go back into that room. There's blood everywhere—"

"You won't have to," Witherspoon interrupted. He was somewhat sympathetic to the man's plight. He was a bit squeamish himself. "I'm only going to ask a few preliminary questions, and then you can go back downstairs. When we're done here, I'll come to your office. Will that suffice?"

He heaved a sigh of relief and nodded.

"Who found Mr. Mundy?"

"Elsie Scott. She's a chambermaid. She brought clean linens up this morning."

A tall constable with a ramrod-straight back and a ruddy complexion stepped out of the dead man's room. "What time?" Constable Barnes asked. He'd slipped inside to have a quick look at the body but had been following the conversation.

"Half past eight. We try to bring up the clean linens when the guests are at breakfast," he explained. "They don't like being disturbed when they're in their rooms. I'd noticed that Mr. Mundy wasn't in the dining room, but that wasn't unusual for him—he often breakfasted elsewhere."

"Are the linens changed every day?" Witherspoon asked. His experience in other cases had taught him that seemingly trivial details could often be important. Knowing which staff came at what hour might turn out to be very significant. It could also prove useful when he constructed what he called his "timeline" of the crime.

"Linens are changed when a guest checks out, of course, and for the guests who are here for any length of time, we change them on Tuesdays, Thursdays, and Saturdays."

"The chambermaid brought his linens up, knocked on the

door, and then went in when he didn't answer?" Witherspoon wanted to be sure he understood the exact sequence of events.

"That's what she would have done, yes. We don't allow the staff to go barging into a guest room without knocking," Cutler said defensively. "But Elsie was so hysterical when I saw her, I could barely understand what she was on about. All I could get out of her was that Mr. Mundy's head was covered in blood and he looked dead. Naturally, I rushed up here to have a look, and then I immediately sent for the police."

"Did you check to make sure he was dead?" Barnes asked.

"Well, he certainly looked dead enough to me," Cutler snapped. "And I've no idea how to determine whether someone has a pulse, so I did what I thought best and sent for you lot."

"Which was precisely what you should have done," Witherspoon said quickly. "That'll be all for now, Mr. Cutler. Please make sure that both your staff and your guests will be available later."

He jerked back, and the motion caused the bead of sweat to finally roll off his mustache and down his chin. "You want to speak to our guests? Really, Inspector, must you bother them? I'm sure the Wrexleys won't approve."

"Be that as it may, we have to speak to everyone. One of your guests might have seen or heard something that will help us solve this case quickly," the inspector explained.

"But the Wrexleys—"

"The Wrexleys will appreciate our getting on with it," Barnes interrupted.

Witherspoon gave him a quick, grateful smile. "Mr. Cutler, we'll be down shortly to ask our questions. In the meantime, can you please keep people off this floor until we've finished?"

Cutler looked like he was going to cry. "Keep them off this

floor?" he repeated. "For how long? This is turning into a nightmare. We're going to have complaints, and the Wrexleys hate complaints."

"I understand that, and I assure you we'll be as quick as possible. But we do need this floor empty until the police surgeon has examined the body and we've searched Mr. Mundy's room," Witherspoon replied.

"Alright, please let me know as soon as our guests can gain access to their quarters. I'll be in my office." He nodded sharply and headed down the corridor, muttering just loud enough for them to hear that this incident was causing him a world of trouble.

Witherspoon stepped through the doorway, stopped, and looked at his surroundings. The room was decently decorated, but not as opulently as one would expect from the trappings in the lobby. His eyes took in walls covered in gold and green striped wallpaper, a cane-backed straight chair next to the door, wood floors with a slightly faded Oriental rug at the foot of the bed, and two old-fashioned gas lamps on a small table against the wall opposite the foot side of the iron bedstead. A traveling case topped with rumpled clothing sat at the end of the mattress. "Mr. Cutler said there was a lot of blood. Is it all over the floor? Do I need to be careful where I step?"

"It's not everywhere, sir. You know civilians—they tend to panic when they have to deal with a body." He pushed past Witherspoon and crossed the room, stopping in front of the open wardrobe. "To my way of thinking, the man's been dead a good ten or twelve hours. Come see for yourself, sir. The air is damp enough this time of year, yet the blood surrounding his head wounds is already dried. There's only a bit of ooze left on it, sir."

Witherspoon swallowed uneasily and fought off a wave of nausea. During his years as a detective, he'd seen dozens of corpses—gunshot casualties with half their heads gone, bodies turned blue from drowning, stabbing victims gutted so badly you could see their internal organs—and in all that time, he'd never overcome his squeamishness. He never would.

He took a deep breath, straightened his spine, and crossed the room. He would do his duty and make certain this victim received justice.

Barnes spared him a sympathetic glance. "I'm not a police surgeon, sir, but even I can tell he's been hit more than once. It looks as if there're at least three blows to the head. Someone wanted this man dead."

Witherspoon leaned to one side to get a look at the back of Thomas Mundy's head. Blood, hair, and tissue were matted together, but not even the gore could hide the three very clear indentions in the victim's skull. "It certainly looks that way." Witherspoon knelt down, wedging himself between the open wardrobe door and the body. The dead man had been rolled onto his side. He wore a dark blue suit, a blue and gray checked waistcoat, a blue cravat, and a white shirt, all now splattered with dried blood.

The constable knelt on the opposite side of the corpse, with his back up against the side of the bed, and they began their examination of the body. The suit and waistcoat were well made, the shoes of good quality and polished properly, and on the man's hand was a large onyx ring in an ornate gold setting.

"It doesn't look like robbery was the motive here; otherwise, the assailant would have taken the ring," Witherspoon said.

"And he'd have taken this, too, sir." Barnes held up a silver chain at the end of which dangled a pocket watch. "This was in his trousers pocket. No robber would leave such valuables, sir."

"So you think the assailant came for the express purpose of murdering Mundy?"

"That's what it looks like so far, sir." Shifting his weight so he could get up for a moment, he grimaced as he momentarily lost his balance but saved himself by jamming his hand on the floor behind him and resting his back against the side bed frame.

"Constable, do be careful. You'll hurt yourself."

Alarmed, Witherspoon started to get up, but Barnes waved him off. "Not to worry—I'm fine, sir. Just my old knees giving me a spot of bother." He grinned sheepishly as he tried to gain traction by shoving his hand flat onto the floor with his fingers splayed beneath the bed. "What's this? There's something under here, sir." Moving carefully so he wouldn't bash his knee into the corpse's nose, he eased to one side and felt around beneath the bed.

"What is it, Constable?"

Barnes pulled out a long black object with a gold head and stared at it for a few seconds. "It's a cane, or more precisely, a walking stick, sir. I think this is our murder weapon. I know the constables searched the room, sir, but as they all know your methods, they must have put it back where they found it."

Both men got to their feet. Barnes held the stick toward the window for a better look. "See for yourself, sir. The head is covered with blood and hair, and there's more caked on the top of the shaft. It's much heavier than it should be." He gave it a shake and then handed it to Witherspoon. "There's something in the head."

"Oh dear, you're right. There's blood and some rather awful bits all over this thing. It is quite heavy." He held it by the shaft, taking care to keep his fingers well away from the top, and examined the head.

"Could be lead weights," Barnes suggested. "I've known several East End lads who put weights they stole off butcher's scales into the top of walking sticks or canes. Makes them handy weapons. Mind you, sir, none of them sticks had gold heads, but could be that this fellow"—he glanced down at Mundy—"was as much a crook as those lads."

"That's certainly possible." Witherspoon studied the top. "Or it could be a family heirloom. The head seems to be an engraving of two lions' heads placed back to back. We'll take a closer look once we've finished here." He put the stick down next to the open case. "Let's search his things and the room. Then we'll have the whole lot sent to the station."

"Take care, Wiggins," Smythe warned. "Most of these con-stables goin' to and fro know us by sight, and I'd hate to have to explain to the inspector what his coachman was doin' here in the middle of the day." He was a tall, heavily muscled man with dark brown hair that was now going gray; harsh, jagged features; and brown eyes. Once Phyllis had told him they had a murder, he'd met up with Wiggins at the house and they'd come to find out what they could. They'd been hiding in the recess between a small office building and an estate agent's, watching the Wrexley for twenty minutes now, but they had seen nothing of interest.

"I've got me collar up and me hat pulled down—that'll 'elp a bit." Wiggins was a brown-haired, blue-eyed young man in his early twenties. "This isn't doing us any good. Maybe I should go 'round to the mews on the side of the hotel. That's the back entrance, and that's where the staff will be 'anging about."

"The inspector might have put a constable on duty there," Smythe pointed out.

"I'll see him before he sees me." Wiggins grinned.

Smythe nodded. "Right, then, I'm goin' to head to that pub we passed and see if the news about the killin' has spread that far. You come get me when it's time. Mrs. Jeffries wants us back for the afternoon meeting."

Wiggins crossed the road and went around the edge of the hotel into the mews. He was relieved to see a constable hadn't been posted and, as he'd hoped, two young lads in maroon and gray uniform jackets and matching trousers were outside on the steps.

Wiggins put on a cheerful smile as he approached. He knew what to do—he'd done this lots of times before. "'Ello, lads. You both work in this 'otel?"

The taller of the two, a blond-haired boy, about fifteen, looked Wiggins up and down. "Yeah, we work there. What of it? If you're lookin' for a position, don't bother. They aren't hirin', and you're too old anyway."

"I'm not lookin' for work—I've already got a job." Wiggins wasn't put off by the lad's manner; the youth was just showing off. "And that's where you two come in—maybe you can 'elp me."

"Help you what?" the other boy said. He was short and so chubby that he strained the front buttons of his jacket.

"My newspaper sent me 'round. They got word some bloke 'ad been murdered here."

The boys looked at each other. Then the one with blond hair said, "We're not supposed to talk about that. Mr. Cutler said we're to keep our mouths shut."

"I'll not tell if you don't."

"It's not your job that'd be lost, now, is it?" the chubby one said, and glanced at the closed door. "And jobs is scarce these days."

Wiggins understood their reluctance to talk, but he had to keep trying. "True, but if I don't 'ave something for my guv, he'll 'ave my guts for garters. Come on, help a feller out. I can't go back empty-handed. Leastways, tell me the name of the victim. I promise you'll not be mentioned in the article." He'd found that once people started to talk, they often couldn't stop. "I can make it worth your while. I'll give ya the price of a pint if ya talk to me."

The one with blond hair gave the door another quick glance. "A bloke named Thomas Mundy was bashed on the head last night. Killed him. Elsie found him this mornin' when she took the linens up to his room. Said it were a right gruesome sight, it was. We've had the coppers 'round all day. They're goin' to be questioning the whole staff and the guests."

"So the police don't know who done it?" Wiggins pulled a pencil stub and a small notebook out of his jacket. His memory was excellent, but he'd learned to play the part, and newsmen took notes.

This time it was the chubby one answering. "Nah, they've not got a clue. Mind you, I'm not surprised someone done the bloke in. I knew there was something shady about him right from the start."

"You did not," the blond snorted. "You didn't like him because he's a skinflint and only gives you a sixpence for running his stupid errands."

"What kind of errands did 'e have you run?" Wiggins asked quickly.

Chubby shrugged. "The sort we always run, you know, to

the telegraph office or to Thomas Cook's for a train schedule or to the newsagent's to fetch him a paper."

"The hotel doesn't have newspapers for the guests?"

"Not from New York or the Midlands."

"Where was the last place he sent you to?"

"It was me he sent," the blond boy said. "And it was yesterday afternoon. He sent me to Cook's for the boat train schedule."

"Do you know where he was planning to go?" Wiggins asked.

He snorted again. "Mundy wasn't one for chattin' with the help. The only people he was friendly with was the other guests, especially the old ladies. But, like I said, he sent me for the boat train schedule and that means he was goin' to Paris."

"How much longer must I keep the third-floor guests away from their rooms, Inspector?" Cutler ushered Witherspoon into his office behind the reception counter and then took his seat behind a desk. An open ledger was in front of him. Along the wall were shelves of file boxes, stacks of plain paper, envelopes, more ledgers, and several boxes, one of which was labeled "Old Keys." Cutler motioned for the inspector to take the chair opposite him.

"It shouldn't be much longer. The police surgeon is doing his examination now. As soon as the body is removed, your guests can have access to the floor."

Cutler's eyes widened at the mention of the body. "Oh dear, you will have your men use the back stairs to bring Mr. Mundy down, won't you? The Wrexleys will have a fit if he goes through the lobby."

"My men wouldn't think of bringing the body through the

21

lobby," Witherspoon assured him. "Provided, of course, the back stairs are wide enough to accommodate the stretcher."

Cutler sagged in relief. "Furniture goes up and down all the time, so that shouldn't be a problem. Now, Inspector, I know you must have questions."

"What nationality was Mr. Mundy?" Witherspoon asked.

"English," Cutler replied. "He told one of the waiters he'd been in the United States for a number of years, but he was from Leicestershire."

"Do you know where in Leicestershire?"

"I'm not sure. It might have been Nottingham, or it might have been Leicester City. No, neither of those are right. Mundy might have told me, but if he did, I don't remember. Why? Is it important?"

"We're trying to find Mr. Mundy's next of kin," the inspector explained. "We found nothing among his things that pointed to any relatives, so I was hoping you might have more detailed background information."

"I'm afraid I can't help you. We don't pry into our guests' personal lives."

"Is there anyone here who was particularly acquainted with Mr. Mundy?"

"Mrs. Denton or Mrs. Blanding might know more about him. They're two of our guests and were quite friendly with Mr. Mundy."

"How long has he been at the hotel?" Witherspoon asked.

Cutler looked at the ledger in front of him. "He arrived on September fourth, just a little more than a month ago."

The inspector's brows rose in surprise. "That's rather a long time for a hotel stay."

"Not really, Inspector. We cater to both travelers and residents. We've a number of guests who obtain a special rate for long-term stays of a month or more."

"And Mr. Mundy was one of those guests?"

"Correct, as are Mrs. Denton and Mrs. Blanding."

"What was Mr. Mundy's occupation?"

"He worked for a consortium of American businessmen who were looking for investment opportunities in both England and elsewhere in the British Empire." Cutler smiled faintly.

"Did this consortium have a name?"

"Not as far as I know," Cutler replied. "Again, you might try asking Mrs. Denton or Mrs. Blanding. They could tell you more about Mr. Mundy's business. The ladies come twice a year for a few months each time. I believe one or perhaps both of them were getting ready to invest in one of Mr. Mundy's projects. I overheard Mrs. Denton tell Mrs. Blanding that she had a 'good feeling' about investing with his group."

"When was this?"

"Just yesterday. I make it a point to chat with our guests at teatime, and I'd just finished talking with Colonel Brody when I overheard the two ladies. Mrs. Denton tends to speak rather loudly—I suspect she might be losing her hearing. As a matter of fact, they spoke to Mr. Mundy when he came in yesterday evening. He stopped and chatted with them before getting his key from reception and going upstairs."

"What time was this?"

"Half past seven. I know because I was leaving. Mr. Stargill—he's the night manager—had just come on duty."

"Did Mr. Mundy go out again last night?"

"I've no idea. As I said, Inspector, I was on my way out. You'll need to ask Mr. Stargill, but he won't be here tonight until seven."

"But you said you left at half past last night?" Witherspoon reminded him.

"I usually leave at seven, but last night I stayed late because Mr. Stargill asked if he could come a bit later. He had a late-afternoon appointment and couldn't get here at his usual time," Cutler explained. "We try to accommodate each other when the occasion calls for it."

Witherspoon made a mental note to verify this with Mr. Stargill. "Did Mr. Mundy ever indicate to you that he was in fear of anyone?"

Cutler raised an eyebrow. "My dealings with Mr. Mundy were limited to handing him his bill and the exchange of pleasantries. I never spoke to him about anything substantial."

"Did he pay his bill promptly?"

"He did."

"In cash or with a check?"

"Cash, Inspector. He always used cash. He even paid his evening bar bill with cash."

"Did he have a lot of visitors?"

"Not that I noticed," Cutler replied. "But Mr. Stargill mentioned that recently there'd been several people inquiring after him in the evenings. But you'll need to ask Mr. Stargill about that."

"Is there anything else you can tell me about him?" Witherspoon sighed inwardly. "Anything you saw or heard or might have noticed. The man has been murdered, and sometimes even the smallest detail which doesn't seem important can be instrumental in catching a killer."

Downstairs, Constable Barnes was trying to get a coherent statement from Elsie Scott. They sat across from each other at the housekeeper's table just inside the linen closet. "It's quite alright, Miss Scott. I understand how shocking it must have been for you to find Mr. Mundy."

Elsie Scott's gray eyes flooded with another bout of tears. Her curly black hair was ruthlessly pulled into a tight bun behind her chambermaid's cap. Her pale face was blotchy, and her hands shook as she tried to stem the flood of tears. "I'm sorry to be such a ninny, sir, but I can't seem to get myself under control. I went to that room and there he was. At first I thought he'd just fainted, but then I saw all that blood. I hate the sight of blood, sir. It makes me right sick."

"I'm sure it does." Barnes decided to try another tactic. "Let's start again, shall we. What time did you go upstairs?"

"I started my round at half past eight, sir. Mrs. Beaumont— she's the head housekeeper—gave me my stack of linens, and I went up to the third floor. That's the top, sir, and we always start at the top and work our way down." She took a deep breath and seemed to calm down a bit. "I checked my list before I started and saw that Mr. Mundy's key wasn't at reception, so I decided to start with the room across the hall—that's Mr. Cassidy's room—but I knew he was gone because he's a salesman, and he's always gone right before nine. So I did his room, changed the linens, and tidied up. Then I went across the hall and knocked on Mr. Mundy's door."

Barnes looked up from his notebook. "You said that Mr. Mundy's key wasn't at reception?"

"That's right, sir. It wasn't there. I checked before I went upstairs because Mr. Mundy doesn't like the staff bargin' into his room when he's there. I did it once when I thought he was gone, but it weren't my fault—I'd knocked good and proper like we're supposed to. Yet when I went in, he got ever so cross, so

I always check to see if his key is gone, and it was, which meant he was still in his room. But I still needed to clean it, sir."

"I understand. Please go on."

"I knocked hard, sir, but he didn't answer, so I used the passkey and went inside. Then I saw that the bed was made and that there was a traveling case open on it, and I thought that was odd. Guests don't make their own beds, and Mrs. Beaumont would have told me if Mr. Mundy was checking out, so I wondered, why was his suitcase there? Then I noticed the wardrobe was standing open. I came a bit further into the room, and I saw his legs sticking out from the far side of the bed. I just stood there for a minute, wondering what I should do."

"What do you mean? Do you often find guests lying on the floor by their beds?" Barnes asked.

"More times than you'd imagine," she said. "Sometimes some of the gentlemen have too much to drink. That's what I thought he'd done, so I started to back away, real quiet-like in case he woke up. I didn't want him to get angry." She clasped her hands together, and her eyes filled with tears. "It took a second or two before I realized something wasn't right. Maybe it was the way he was lying, so I thought I'd make sure he'd not slipped and fallen. Truth is, Constable, I don't have very good eyesight, and it was only as I got right up to him that I saw all the blood. I was so scared, I turned and ran downstairs, straight into Mr. Cutler's office. He come right up and then sent Jamie Little—he's a bellboy—for the constable."

"How long did it take you to clean Mr. Cassidy's room?"

"Not more than ten minutes, Constable. So by my estimate, I went into Mr. Mundy's room about a quarter to nine, ten minutes till nine at the latest."

CHAPTER 2

Phyllis put the big brown teapot next to the plate of currant buns and sat down in her usual spot. She looked at the carriage clock on the pine sideboard. "Shouldn't they be back by now? It's a quarter past four, and they knew we were having a meeting."

"Not to worry—if they're late, it's usually because at least one of them has found someone who knows something about either the victim or the murder itself," Betsy said. She was a lovely blue-eyed blonde, slender as a girl and devoted to three things: her family, her friends, and the cause of justice. She'd once been the housemaid, but since marrying Smythe and having their daughter, she now had a home of her own. They had a delightful flat less than a quarter of a mile away.

Born and raised in the worst part of London, Betsy knew firsthand how the world treated the poor and the powerless. But at seventeen, her life had changed forever when, instead of interviewing for the job as a housemaid, she'd collapsed of fever on

Witherspoon's doorstep. Unlike what most men who lived in big fancy houses would have done, the inspector took her in, and Mrs. Jeffries nursed her back to health. She loved them almost as much as she loved Smythe and their daughter, Amanda Belle.

"Let's hope they're findin' out plenty of information. I'm itchin' to git out on the hunt. We ain't had us a murder in months." Luty Belle Crookshank reached for a bun. She was a rich, tiny, white-haired American with a love of flashy clothes and a tendency to be overly blunt. She had met the household during one of their early investigations, when her sharp eyes had noticed a pretty blonde housemaid and a brown-haired footman asking the locals questions about the murder of one of her Knightsbridge neighbors. But she'd held her tongue until she had a terrible problem of her own and had to go to the inspector's household for help. Since then, she, along with Hatchet, her employee, insisted on helping with Witherspoon's cases.

"Nonsense, madam. We had a murder in June, and as it's only the beginning of October, I don't think you can complain overly much," Hatchet retorted. Tall, robust, and as straight-backed as an admiral, he was a white-haired Englishman with a colorful and mysterious past. He wore beautifully tailored black suits and pristine white shirts, and he was an excellent marksman. Luty had found him battered, bruised, and drunk in a Baltimore back alley, and they'd been together ever since. Theoretically, he was her man-of-all-work, but in reality they were devoted friends.

"I do wish Ruth could be here," Mrs. Goodge muttered. "It's not fair that she's stuck taking care of her late husband's relatives."

"Do you think she'll mind missing this case?" Phyllis asked.

"Of course she will," Betsy answered. "She might be the widow of a peer, a suffragette, and a member of the upper class, but she's as devoted to justice as we are."

"More so, I should think," Mrs. Jeffries added. "I've never met anyone who took Christ's admonition to love thy neighbor as thyself so seriously."

"Is that why she insists on our calling her by her Christian name when it's just us all together?" Phyllis nodded her thanks as Mrs. Goodge passed her a cup of tea.

"Yes, she has very egalitarian views, and calling her by her title doesn't seem to sit well with her these days. Now that we've a case, let's keep our fingers crossed that she's able to come back soon. We're going to need her." The housekeeper glanced at the clock. "Let's get started. We can catch the men up when they get here. Constable Griffiths told us the victim's name is Thomas Mundy, and he was killed last night in his room at the Wrexley Hotel. That's on the Queens Road in Bayswater."

"Do we know what time?" Hatchet asked.

"Not a precise time, only that his body was found this morning," Mrs. Jeffries replied. "Please keep in mind that Constable Griffiths was reporting the information he'd heard from the fixed point constable who was the first one to the murder scene. Hopefully, we'll have more details by tomorrow morning's meeting."

"How was he killed?" Betsy asked. "Do we know?"

"Constable Griffiths said he was killed with a walking stick." Mrs. Goodge finished pouring the last cup of tea, this one for her. "He was coshed on the head and found by the maid when she brought up clean linens this morning. But as Mrs. Jeffries pointed out, this was just the first report that came into the station."

Fred suddenly lifted his head, then leapt up and raced down

the back hall. They heard the door open and the click of nails against wood as the dog greeted his friends. "Hello, old fellow." Wiggins' voice carried into the room. "You been waitin' for me." A few moments later, he and Smythe, accompanied by a tail-wagging Fred, appeared in the kitchen.

"Sorry we're late." Wiggins unbuttoned his jacket as he hurried to his chair. "I 'ad a bit of luck at the hotel, and I didn't want to leave while my source was chatting."

"Come and have some tea." Mrs. Goodge already had his poured. "It's cold out there. You, too, Smythe. Get warmed up. We don't need either of you catching a chill right when we've got a case. We're already shorthanded as it is."

"Where's the little one?" Smythe dropped into the chair next to his wife and grabbed her hand under the table. He gave it a squeeze. "Isn't it too late for her to be nappin'?"

Betsy smiled wryly. "Her godmothers decided she needed a bit of playing about in the garden, and they tuckered her out."

Smythe cocked an eyebrow at Luty, then at Mrs. Goodge. "You wore 'er out, did ya?"

The two women adored their mutual godchild. Inspector Witherspoon was the third godparent, and he was equally besotted with her.

"She's not really sleepin'," Mrs. Goodge protested. "I just had a peek at her, and she's just lyin' there, playing with that sweet little baby doll that Luty brought her from France." She wasn't actually playing with the doll, she was bashing it against the edge of the cot, but Mrs. Goodge considered that very good training in case anyone ever tried to harm her little darling. Investigating murders tended to open one's eyes, and the cook was now of the opinion that females needed to know how to protect themselves. Luty agreed with her, and the two women had decided that if they were still alive when their darling got old enough to handle a weapon, they'd make sure she learned to shoot. They also agreed to keep this idea between the two of them.

"Exercise is good for little ones," Luty added. "And we wanted to play with her. We don't git to see her near enough."

"I'll try to remedy that," Betsy said, though in truth, the two women saw the child frequently. They both spoiled her so much, she and Smythe were a bit worried. They didn't want their daughter going through life thinking the world was at her beck and call or feeling she was entitled to more than anyone else. Smythe had it in his power to give his beloved child anything she desired, but that didn't mean he wanted her raised as a privileged little snob. The world thought him a coachman, but he was, in fact, a very wealthy man. However, despite his money, he was determined his daughter would grow up unspoiled and with a healthy respect for others.

Years earlier, he'd gone to Australia and made a fortune. Upon his return to England, he stopped in to see his old employer, the inspector's aunt, Euphemia Witherspoon. He'd found her deathly ill and surrounded by a houseful of servants robbing her blind. Wiggins, who was just a young lad, was valiantly trying to take care of the dying woman. Smythe sent Wiggins for a doctor, sacked the rest of the staff, and prayed for a miracle to save his old friend's life. But it was too late. Even the best medical care couldn't save Euphemia Witherspoon. Before she died, she asked Smythe for a special favor. She made him promise to stay on until her beloved nephew and heir, Gerald Witherspoon, was settled into the house with a staff that was trustworthy and decent.

Smythe agreed, and by the time he was satisfied he'd done right by the woman to whom he owed so much, the household had begun to investigate the inspector's cases and, more important, he'd met Betsy. For him, it had been love at first sight.

"Which of you would like to go first?" Mrs. Jeffries asked.

"I'll 'ave a go," Wiggins offered. "I 'ad a talk with two of the bellboys. Seems our victim, Thomas Mundy, 'as been at the 'otel for about a month now. He's English, but he's been livin' in the United States for a long time."

"Did they know when Mundy had come back from the States?" Luty asked.

Wiggins shook his head. "No, but they thought he was gettin' ready to leave again. He sent one of the lads to Thomas Cook's yesterday afternoon for the boat train schedule to Paris."

"Did either of them know where he was from originally?" Mrs. Jeffries asked.

Wiggins reached for a bun. "I didn't 'ave time to ask them too many questions. The lads were real nervous about chattin' with me. They'd been told by the 'otel manager not to talk to anyone about the murders. I had to give 'em the price of a pint just to get them to tell me anything."

"I know where Mundy comes from," Smythe said. "That's about the only thing that I was able to learn. I don't understand what's wrong with people these days. You'd think that with a murder bein' committed right up the road, the whole pub would 'ave known about it. But there was only two at the bar that knew what 'ad happened. Lucky for me, the barmaid was one of them. She knew a thing or two."

Betsy snorted. "Young and pretty was she?"

"Not as pretty as you, love." Smythe laughed. "The barmaid 'eard about the murder from her cousin who works at the Wrexley as a scullery maid in the kitchen. She'd nipped in for a quick gin and a bit of gossip before goin' home."

"I take it the barmaid knew who Mundy was?" Mrs. Jeffries asked. It was important to determine who might have passed along genuine information and who might have just been talking to make themselves sound important.

"She did. Mundy came into the pub quite often—he liked it better than the hotel bar. A while back, she'd overheard him talking to an elderly gent. He was giving legal advice about something or other, and one of the pub regulars asked Mundy what made him such an expert on the law. He said he used to be a solicitor's clerk in Market Harborough."

"That's in Leicestershire." Mrs. Goodge frowned. She wasn't sure she had any sources with a connection to that part of the Midlands.

"Did the barmaid know anything else?" Mrs. Jeffries prompted.

"Just a couple of bits. She said that when someone challenged Mundy and pointed out a clerk wasn't the same as a solicitor, Mundy got annoyed and claimed that the solicitors in his previous firm were all old men who made him do all the real legal work." Smythe picked up his mug and took a quick sip. "The last thing she mentioned was that one of her other customers kept sayin' that Mundy looked real familiar to him. Like he ought to know him, but he couldn't remember where he'd seen him before. But he wasn't there today, so I'll need to go back and see if I can 'ave a chat with him later."

Wiggins waved his hand in the air. "Before anyone else says somethin', can I finish?"

"Of course," Mrs. Jeffries said quickly. "Sorry, Wiggins, we thought you were done. Tell us the rest."

Wiggins told them about the bellboys running Mundy's various errands and their complaints that he was cheap with tips. Then he told them the last bit of information he'd learned and, to his way of thinking, the most important. "Finally, one of the lads told me that as he was leavin' work two days ago, he saw something strange. All the staff leaves by the back door out into the mews. When he come out and went around to the street, there was a well-dressed lady standing across from the front of the hotel. Now there was lots of guests goin' in and out of the Wrexley, so Lester, that's the lad's name, thought she was waitin' for someone. All of a sudden, she darted across to his side of the pavement and hurried off. He didn't think anything of it until he realized the lady was followin' Thomas Mundy."

Phyllis eyed him skeptically. "If there were lots of people moving about, how did he know she was following Mundy?"

Wiggins fixed her with a hard stare and crossed his arms over his chest. "That's a silly question . . ."

"It's not silly," she shot back. "Your source claimed there were guests going in and out, plus there'd be people walking past to do their shopping or get to the station. We've tried following people before and, truth to tell, it's hard to trail after someone, and if we were doing it, I don't think anyone watching us could tell. So how did he know?"

Mrs. Jeffries didn't want to interfere, but Phyllis was asking a legitimate question and making a good point. Yet there was something else going on between these two, something that was threatening to become a problem. Of late, Wiggins' attitude toward the maid was very different from when she'd first come to the household. As a chubby, rather frightened young girl who jumped at her own shadow, she had been so scared of losing her position, she had refused to help them investigate the inspector's cases. Wiggins had been very protective of her, understanding her fear and treating her like a younger sister. Recently, something had changed, and Mrs. Jeffries wasn't sure what it was. But right now, they both needed to calm down.

"Let the lad tell us," Mrs. Goodge interjected. "He knows what he's about, and he's not likely to let a source fool him with a tall tale."

"Yes, Wiggins, do go on." The housekeeper gave Phyllis a quick smile. "But I understand exactly what you mean. Trailing someone is very difficult indeed."

Satisfied, he nodded. "At first 'e didn't know anyone was followin' anyone, but the three of them was all walking in the same direction with Mundy in the lead. Lester was at the back, dawdlin' because it was a nice day and he 'ad a bit of coin in his pocket. The lady was in the middle. Then he noticed that Mundy had a habit of stopping every few minutes or so and turnin' to look behind him, and when he stopped, the lady would scurry behind a letter box or pretend to be staring at a shopwindow. He said this went on all the way to the station."

"What happened then?" Mrs. Jeffries asked.

"Mundy went into the station, and the lady stood there for a few minutes and then went in herself. Lester just went on home."

Unlike some of the bigger hotels in London, the Wrexley hadn't been fitted with a lift, so Witherspoon and Barnes climbed the stairs to the first floor. The corridor was much the same as the third floor, only here the carpet was in excellent condition, there were no gaps in the crown molding, and there were twice as many electric lights. The two elderly twins had a suite on this floor.

"I've put Constable Evans in charge of getting statements from the staff." Barnes scanned the door numbers as they walked down the hallway. "The trouble is, most of the employees who are here now weren't on duty last night, so I doubt any of this lot will have seen anything useful."

"Mr. Cutler says the night staff come on duty at six, but the night manager won't be here until seven."

"Good." Barnes grinned. "We'll get a chance to speak to them without the boss hanging over their shoulder. People tend to speak freely when they're on their own. Poor Miss Scott was in a state when I first started talking to her, but she got hold of herself and gave me the entire sequence of events. She entered Mundy's room at approximately eight forty-five this morning and had the good sense to get the manager right away. Finding Mundy's body upset her enough that there was a lot she didn't notice."

"Good work, Constable. Perhaps once the shock wears off, the girl will remember something else that might be useful." They stopped at a door three-quarters down the hallway. He knocked lightly.

"If you're the police, you may come in. If you're not, then please go away," a voice shouted in response.

Barnes opened the door, and they stepped into a sitting room with forest green and gold patterned wallpaper, heavy green and gold striped curtains at the two windows, and a bright green, blue, and gold Indian carpet.

Two women stared at them from high-backed chairs. A table covered with a maroon fringed shawl and topped with half a dozen photographs in ornate silver frames separated the ladies. A gold settee, side tables, cabinets filled with china figurines, and an armoire, which took up an entire wall, completed the furnishings.

Witherspoon blinked—the two ladies looked very much

alike. Both wore heavy black widow's weeds and small gray lace caps. Despite the mourning clothes, one of them wore a long string of pearls around her neck and an emerald brooch on her high collar while the other had three diamond rings on her long, bony fingers.

"We've been waiting for ages," one of the women said. "What took you so long?"

"You'll not catch poor Mr. Mundy's killer like this," the second lady added. She picked up a cane from beside her chair and pointed to the settee. "Sit down. I'm Elvira Blanding, and that's my sister, Eleanor Denton."

"I'm Inspector Witherspoon, and this is my colleague, Constable Barnes," the inspector said as they took their seats. Barnes pulled out his little brown notebook and sank onto the cushions, wincing as his backside made contact with the hard wood beneath the thin cushion.

"I'm sure you know why we're here," he began, only to be interrupted by Mrs. Denton of the exquisite pearl necklace.

"Of course we do, and we want to make certain whoever killed poor Mr. Mundy hangs for it."

Witherspoon nodded. "When was the last time you saw Mr. Mundy?"

"Yesterday evening," Mrs. Denton replied. "Elvira and I were having a drink in the lobby when he came in—we have one every evening before retiring. He stopped to say hello . . ." Her voice trailed off, and she brushed at her cheeks.

Mrs. Blanding reached across the table and patted her sister's arm. "Now, now, Elie, don't get upset. Poor Thomas is in a better place now."

"I know, I know, he's with the Lord now, God rest his soul. But if I'd known that was the last time we'd get to see him, I'd have insisted he have a drink with us. It wouldn't have hurt for him to be just a bit late to his appointment. People shouldn't be doing business that time of night anyway." Mrs. Denton pulled a white lace handkerchief out of her sleeve and blew her nose.

"He had a business appointment last night?" Witherspoon asked.

"That's what he told us." She wiped her nose again. "He was supposed to meet an investor."

"Do you know the name of this investor?" Barnes asked.

"Of course we do," Mrs. Blanding replied. "Thomas confided in us. He was meeting with the comte de Valois. Like us, the gentleman was interested in investing in Thomas' Brazilian venture."

Witherspoon noted that both ladies were now referring to the victim as "Thomas" and not "Mr. Mundy." "Brazilian venture? What kind of venture?"

Mrs. Denton leaned forward. "Coffee, Inspector. Thomas' consortium was buying a huge coffee plantation in Sao Paulo."

"The comte was going to invest as well," Mrs. Blanding added. "You should talk to him. I'll wager he was the last person to see poor Thomas alive."

"Do you know what time they were to meet?" Barnes asked.

"Not exactly." It was Eleanor Denton who replied. "But it must have been close to the time we saw him, and that was about half past seven, perhaps seven forty-five."

"He didn't say where they were meeting, either," Mrs. Blanding said.

"How long have you known Mr. Mundy?" Witherspoon pushed his spectacles up his nose.

"Since the day he arrived at the hotel." Mrs. Blanding sighed heavily and glanced down at the floor. "He'd just finished at the reception desk when I dropped my cane. He saw that I couldn't reach it, so he hurried over and very kindly retrieved it for me. That evening, he stopped by our table in the lobby to say hello as we were having our drink. I introduced him to Eleanor, and we invited him to sit down. Since then, we've become good friends." She glanced at her sister. "We're both widowed and lucky to have each other, but still, one gets a bit lonely, and he was such a jovial sort of man. Always making us laugh with his stories and tales about the exotic places he'd been in the course of his work."

"I can't believe it's only been a month since we met him." Mrs. Denton shook her head sadly. "He was such a nice man. I'm going miss him terribly."

"How did you come to be interested in investing with his consortium?" Barnes asked.

"It wasn't easy. We had to pry the information out of him," Elvira declared. "We kept asking him about his work, and he'd just murmur that he raised investment capital for business ventures. Finally, though, I persuaded him to give us a few more details. After he confided in us, we decided that we'd like to hear more."

"And he suggested you might like to invest in a coffee plantation in Brazil?" Barnes said.

"No, he did not. We had to ask him if he'd consider us as investors. At first, he was against the idea. He kept saying he didn't want us to risk our capital. But I made it very clear that despite what most men think, we were perfectly capable of making business decisions for ourselves. So he showed us the prospectus, and we decided that while it might be a bit risky, the money to be made might be substantial."

"That's right," her sister added. "It was our decision completely. He didn't talk us into it or anything like that. We'd like to have a bit more money to make us comfortable in our old age."

"When you saw Mr. Mundy, did he seem worried or upset?" Witherspoon asked.

Mrs. Denton shook her head. "Not that I could tell. He was in a hurry, that's all. He didn't want to be late for his appointment with the comte de Valois. He disappeared up the stairs, and that was the last time we saw him."

"You didn't see him when he left for his appointment with the comte?" the inspector asked.

"No." She fingered her string of pearls. "As I said, Inspector, we never saw him again. Thomas frequently used the back stairs to the mews when he was pressed for time. It's a shortcut to the station, so he didn't come through the lobby."

Barnes looked up from his notebook. "How long did you stay in the lobby after Mr. Mundy went upstairs?"

Elvira Blanding glanced at her twin. "I'm not sure, but it was probably a good half hour, wouldn't you say, Elie?"

She thought for a moment. "It was longer. I'd say we were there for another forty-five minutes. Remember, we each had a second whiskey, and then Mrs. Ottley stopped by our table and chatted for a few moments."

"Who is Mrs. Ottley?"

"She's a guest here, like us. She comes every year to spend time in London. Why is this important? I've already told you we didn't see Thomas again."

"I understand you didn't see *him*." Barnes smiled as he stressed the last word. "What I'd like to know is if anyone else caught your eye last night? You were still in the lobby, and both of you seem to be intelligent and observant women. I was hoping that perhaps one or both of you had noticed someone who looked a bit out of place."

"Or even suspicious," Witherspoon added.

Mrs. Denton looked pleased. "Well, I'm not certain," she began, only to be interrupted by her sister. "There was that man who came in right after Thomas went upstairs, and he didn't stop at reception—he went right up the stairs. I'm sure he's not a guest here; I've never seen him before."

"What did this man look like?" Witherspoon asked.

"He was quite ordinary-looking, Inspector," Mrs. Blanding replied. "Short, rather stout but decently dressed. I imagine that was the reason no one stopped him from going upstairs. But I'm certain I've never seen him before and that he isn't a guest here."

"What color hair did he have?"

"What there was of it was a grayish blond."

"Grayish blond," Witherspoon repeated. He wasn't sure what that meant.

"It's difficult to describe, but it was the sort of gray that comes to people who once had dark blond or light brown hair. It was hard to tell as he didn't have a lot of it left."

"He was bald?" Barnes interjected.

"Thinning," Mrs. Denton put in. "I remember him now. He was carrying his hat, and I recall noticing that his hair was so thin, you could see the electric light reflecting off the top of his scalp."

"Is there anything else you can tell us about this man?" Witherspoon glanced at Barnes, who gave a nearly imperceptible nod indicating he had no more questions for the ladies.

But neither woman had anything left to tell them, so they took their leave. When they stepped out of the hotel suite, the electric lights flooded the corridor in brightness. Witherspoon squinted slightly, glanced at Barnes, and realized the man was tired. The brackets around his mouth and eyes were sharp, and his shoulders slumped in fatigue. "Go home, Constable. I can speak with the night manager, and we've enough constables to interview the rest of the evening staff."

"If it's all the same to you, sir, I'd like to stay and finish up. My wife isn't expecting me till late." He knew the inspector was being kind and that at his age, hiding his fatigue was impossible. But despite his weariness, he wanted to press on. It was now a matter of pride as well as duty.

Witherspoon fought the urge to pull rank and order the constable to go home, but he'd not humiliate his colleague and friend that way. "Alright, if you're sure, but I don't mind telling you it has been a long day, and I for one am exhausted." He stopped under the light and pulled out his pocket watch. "Let's call the constables together and see what they've found out from the day staff. Perhaps by then the evening shift will be arriving."

William Stargill, the night manager, waved Witherspoon and Barnes into the office. Tall, balding, and with a dark handlebar mustache, he looked sturdy enough beneath the lines of his suit to handle any emergency that might arise in the next ten hours or so. "Do come in and sit down." He waved at the chair that Witherspoon had sat in earlier, and the inspector was gratified to see that he'd brought a second chair in for the constable.

Stargill went back behind his desk, sat, and then fixed the two policemen with a mournful stare. "This is a dreadful business, absolutely dreadful, and the sooner you can get to the bottom of it, the better off we'll be. We've had several guests pack up and leave today, and once the evening papers are out, I'm afraid more of them might decide to go. The Wrexleys are most upset. We've had three telegrams from them already."

"We're trying our best, Mr. Stargill, and I'm truly sorry for the effect this murder is having on your business." Witherspoon gave a brief, apologetic smile. "Now, when was the last time you saw Mr. Mundy?"

Stargill's chair squeaked as he leaned forward and rested his elbows on the desk. "Last night as he went up the stairs to his room. I'd just gone into my office after speaking with Mr. Cutler, and the door was still open. I happened to glance out as he passed by."

"Did you see anyone follow him upstairs?" Barnes flipped open his notebook. He didn't want to put words in the man's mouth, but it would be very helpful if Stargill had got a look at the fellow the ladies claimed followed Mundy.

"No, but I wasn't paying him any attention, Constable. I was in a hurry to do the books, you see, and my mind was on reconciling the daily receipts."

"This is a large hotel. Does the reception staff know all the guests by sight?" the inspector asked.

Stargill smiled wryly. "We like to think so, but the reality is that is impossible."

"So anyone could have followed Mr. Mundy upstairs, and if that person were nicely dressed, there's a good chance the reception clerk wouldn't know that person wasn't a guest?"

"That's correct."

"Mrs. Blanding and Mrs. Denton saw a short, stout man with thinning hair follow Mr. Mundy upstairs. Is there a guest here who fits that description?"

Stargill thought for a moment. "That could be Mr. Ericson or Mr. Palmer, but the ladies know both those gentlemen."

"No, this is someone they didn't recognize," Witherspoon replied.

"I can't think who it would be, but it's possible that it was someone who'd checked in before I came on duty last night." Stargill shrugged. "Have a word with our night clerk. He's a clever young chap, and not much gets past him. He might be able to identify this person."

"I understand you got here a bit later than your usual time yesterday evening," Witherspoon said.

"I did. I had a personal matter to attend to, Inspector. I took my eighty-three-year-old aunt to Paddington Station and saw her safely aboard the six-thirty train to Bristol. The traffic was so congested, I didn't arrive here until almost half seven." Stargill looked amused. "Why? Am I a suspect? I assure you, Inspector, I don't make it a habit to murder our guests. Especially not the ones who pay promptly and in cash."

"Mr. Cutler commented that you came in later than usual yesterday," Witherspoon explained. "And as there was a murder here, I thought it prudent to ask for an explanation. We're simply doing our job, sir. No offense was intended."

Stargill laughed. "None was taken, sir."

"What else can you tell us about Mr. Mundy?" Barnes asked quickly.

"He paid his bill regularly, treated the staff politely, and was quite popular with the other guests, especially the ladies."

"Popular with the ladies," the inspector repeated. "How do you mean?"

"I don't know how much Mr. Cutler explained about our hotel, but a large percentage of our guests are essentially residential. We've a good reputation for ensuring that unaccompanied female guests are welcomed and, more important, that they're safe in our establishment. Which is one of the reasons this murder is having such a devastating effect on our business. Ladies don't like to stay in a hotel where they're scared of getting their heads bashed in by a lunatic."

"Exactly how many residential guests do you have?" Barnes interrupted.

"Five. We did have six, but Mrs. Metcalf checked out this afternoon. When I say 'residential,' I don't mean they live here permanently—merely that they come and stay a month or two, or even three, several times a year."

"You mean like Mrs. Denton and Mrs. Blanding," Witherspoon said.

"That's right, and like those two ladies, most of our residential guests are older, and some are even what one could describe as elderly. From the moment Mundy arrived, he spent what I thought was far more time than necessary ingratiating himself with these ladies." Stargill's eyes narrowed. "One oughtn't speak ill of the dead, but I didn't trust the fellow, not in the least."

Mrs. Jeffries was waiting at the front door when Witherspoon arrived home. "I'm sorry to be so late," he apologized, and handed her his bowler hat. "I do hope it hasn't inconvenienced any of the household."

The inspector, though well educated, had been raised in very modest circumstances and therefore treated his staff as human beings and not instruments put on this earth to do his bidding.

"Of course not, sir. We knew you'd be later than usual.

Constable Griffiths stopped in and said you'd been called to a murder." She hung his hat on the coat tree and waited while he shrugged out of his coat. "If you'll go into the dining room, sir, I'll bring your dinner up. I'm sure you must be hungry."

"I can wait a few minutes. I'd love a drink before dinner. Let's have one in the study." He headed down the hallway.

She tossed his coat on a peg and hurried after him. Whenever he had a murder case, he always wanted to discuss it over a glass of sherry, and this time was no exception.

While he settled himself in his favorite chair, she went to the cabinet, pulled out a bottle of Harveys Bristol Cream sherry, and poured them both a drink.

She handed him his glass and sat down on the settee opposite him. "I do appreciate how very kind you're being this evening, sir."

He looked surprised. "I don't understand what you mean."

"Now, sir, don't tease. We both know you're delaying your dinner because you know how much I love hearing about your cases." She gave him a grateful smile. As sitting and discussing his murders was his habit, she was certain he'd have had delayed his meal in any case, but it never hurt to grease the wheels, so to speak, and she genuinely appreciated his treating her as an equal. "Now, don't protest, sir," she said when he opened his mouth to speak. "You know it's true. Now do tell, who was the victim?"

"A man named Thomas Mundy." He told her about the specific circumstances surrounding the murder itself and didn't spare her the gory details because of her gender. Mrs. Jeffries had a far stronger stomach than he did.

"And Constable Barnes was sure he'd been hit on the head more than once?" she clarified.

"Three times, the police surgeon confirmed it. We had a quick word with him as well before he took the body to the hospital for the postmortem."

"And the victim's walking stick was possibly the murder weapon," she mused. If that turned out to be the case, it could mean the killing wasn't premeditated. "But most sticks aren't heavy enough to do such damage, are they?"

"Not usually, but the head in this one was exceptionally heavy. Constable Barnes thought weights had been added to the head of the stick. Apparently, that's frequently done among the criminal class."

"And I presume the added weight would be enough to cause substantial damage."

"We'll know for certain tomorrow when we go through everything taken into evidence. The head appears to be made of gold, and I didn't want to damage it by bashing it about at the hotel. Tomorrow it'll be done properly. I'm sure Mundy's heirs will appreciate having his property back in good condition." He sipped his drink. "We found out quite a bit about Mundy. He was in the United States before coming here."

"Was he an American?" She knew he wasn't, but it was always a good idea to ask obvious questions.

Witherspoon shook his head. "English. He was from Leicestershire, but no one at the hotel knew exactly from where in Leicestershire."

Mrs. Jeffries had to bite her lip to keep from telling him she knew Mundy hailed from Market Harborough. Instead, she said, "Do you have witnesses, sir?"

"That's a difficult question to answer. There were a number of guests in the lobby of the hotel when we think the murder might have happened, but apparently, even though it is frowned upon by the hotel, a number of guests at the hotel come and go by the back door that leads out into the mews. It's a shortcut to Queens Road Station, so there's a chance no one saw the murderer."

"The back door?" she repeated. "But isn't it locked after dark?"

"Yes, but even if it was locked, all the killer had to do was wait until another guest stepped outside. He or she could grab it before it closed, then slip inside and up the back stairs with no one the wiser."

"Perhaps one of the staff might have seen someone," she suggested.

"We're going to ask all of them that very question tomorrow," he said. He told her the rest of what they'd learned that day, taking care to repeat everything he'd heard from both the managers as well as the two elderly women.

She listened carefully and only occasionally interrupted with a question. "When you searched his room, sir, did you find any documents that indicated he worked for this group of investors?"

He put his empty glass on the table and got to his feet. "Not that we could tell at first glance, but we took all of his things to the station and perhaps we'll find a logbook or notes that will give us a clearer picture." He yawned. "Oh dear, I think I shall eat a quick dinner, and then it's off to bed for me."

But long after he'd gone upstairs, long after the household had been tucked in safely and the doors locked, Mrs. Jeffries sat at the kitchen table. She didn't like to make assumptions this early in an investigation; they'd been fooled too many times in the past to ever rely on the first few bits of information they learned. Yet she couldn't stop herself from feeling that there was far more to this victim than met the eye.

Barnes took his seat next to Mrs. Jeffries. When they had a murder, it was his habit to come early and escort Witherspoon to the station so they could discuss the case together. But before he went upstairs to the inspector, he stopped in the kitchen for a word with the two women.

It hadn't taken the constable long to determine that Witherspoon received help with his cases, and he'd soon realized where that help came from. When he'd first sussed it out, he'd debated the wisdom of amateurs poking about in official police investigations, but being a wily old copper, he'd soon understood that they were careful, smart, and, most important, could get information out of people who'd sooner spit on a policeman than talk to him.

"There's somethin' odd about our victim," he announced as Mrs. Goodge put a mug of tea in front of him before taking her own seat.

"The inspector told me that the night manager at the hotel didn't like him, that he thought it strange Mundy spent so much time befriending older women," Mrs. Jeffries said.

"And the one thing all the ladies have in common is that they've a bit of money and, for the most part, they're alone in the world," he finished.

"What kind of hotel is the Wrexley?" Mrs. Goodge asked. "I mean, is it the sort of place where rich women tend to stay?"

"It's not top-drawer"—Barnes took a quick sip of his tea—"but it's very nice, the sort of place where a well-off person would be comfortable. They've got modern bathrooms in some of the suites, and they've put in electric lighting in the common rooms and corridors. One of the bellboys told me the owners are goin' to put in lifts before the summer. But it's getting late, and I've a few bits and pieces I want to tell you." He told them about his interview with Elsie Scott and made certain he repeated her statement almost word for word. He also provided a few more details of the interviews with the hotel managers and the twins as well as his impression of what kind of man the victim might have been.

When he'd finished, Mrs. Jeffries told him what they'd learned from Smythe and Wiggins. "So your information is true," she said. "Thomas Mundy was from the Midlands, Market Harborough to be precise."

Barnes grinned broadly as he got to his feet. "I'll figure out a way to get that information to the inspector. It's a good starting point. If he really was a solicitor's clerk, someone will remember him. Maybe it'll even help us find his next of kin."

Everyone was at their morning meeting on time. Amanda Belle giggled as Betsy plopped her in Luty's lap and tried to ignore the wounded look on Mrs. Goodge's face.

"Now wipe that pathetic expression off right now." Luty narrowed her eyes. "You git the little one more than I do, so it's my turn."

"I am not looking pathetic." Mrs. Goodge laughed. "Oh, alright, I tried it on, but it didn't work. You're a hard one, Luty." The two women had a good-natured competition for time with their goddaughter, and they both enjoyed it enormously.

"Let's get started," Mrs. Jeffries said briskly. "I've a lot to report, and I think someone will need to make a quick trip to Leicestershire." She took a deep breath and then spent the next fifteen minutes repeating what she and Mrs. Goodge had learned from the inspector and Constable Barnes.

"Mundy sounds like a confidence trickster—a real con artist," Hatchet murmured.

"That was the impression I got from Constable Barnes," Mrs. Goodge exclaimed. "Only he didn't actually come right out and say it."

"He wouldn't, not this early in the game, but that's what I think as well. Good-looking, middle-aged men don't generally spend a lot of time with old ladies unless they're after something." Smythe looked at the housekeeper. "Are you wantin' me to go to Leicestershire to see what I can find out about Mundy's past?"

Mrs. Jeffries hesitated. She knew that Smythe had an invaluable source of information right here in London, a source that was especially good when it came to learning something useful about the criminal classes. At this stage in the investigation, it would be far better for him to mine that vein rather than try to get some Leicestershire lawyer to talk. "Actually, I was hoping that Hatchet could do that for us." She looked in his direction. "That is if he's willing and Luty doesn't mind."

"I don't mind," Luty said quickly. "I've got sources of my own to tap this mornin', and they'll talk faster if I'm alone." She swayed gently back and forth, causing Amanda to pump her arms in glee. "Accordin' to what the hotel manager said, Mundy paid his bills in cash, but if he's been here for a month, unless he brought a carpetbag full of loot, he must be usin' letters of credit or have a bank account set up somewhere. I know a lot of bankers, so I'll see if I can find out where he kept his money."

"Of course I'll go to Market Harborough." Hatchet looked pleased by the prospect. "Do we know the name of the firm where Mundy might have been employed?"

"No, but it's not that large a town, so there can't be too many solicitor firms. You'll have to come up with a good story about why you're tracking the man down."

"I assure you, that won't be a concern. I'll come up with something on the train."

"Can you leave today?" Mrs. Jeffries asked.

"I can and if I'm lucky, I should be back late tomorrow afternoon. If I'm not, I'll send madam a telegram."

"Excellent." Mrs. Jeffries looked at Phyllis. "I doubt the victim did much shopping, so trying to get any information out of the local merchants might be a waste of time, but there's always a chance he was known in the area. Can you do that?"

"I will. I don't know that neighborhood very well, but I'll do my best, and if the local merchants don't know anything about him, perhaps I can get some of the hotel maids to chat a bit," Phyllis replied.

"I'll do the restaurant waiters and try to speak to the bellboys who come on duty late in the evening," Wiggins volunteered.

"I'll talk to the hansom cab drivers and go back to the pubs—maybe I'll get lucky again." Smythe was also going to pay a quick visit to his best source of information, but he didn't need to announce his intention to the whole room.

"There doesn't seem much for me to do," Betsy murmured.

"Oh, but there is, but you can't do it until the police are gone," Mrs. Jeffries said quickly. "From what we know, Mundy seemed to concentrate on ingratiating himself with several elderly women at the hotel. I'm not sure how to say this, but I'm thinking a lovely young woman with a darling baby in tow having tea in the hotel restaurant might find someone to chat with."

Betsy grinned broadly. "That would be wonderful. I can have tea there several times and pretend I'm making sure the hotel food is good enough for my dear aunt Nellie."

"And I'll send notes out to my sources to see if anyone can remember a solicitor from the East Midlands named Thomas Mundy." Mrs. Goodge frowned. "I don't think it likely, but you never know what you'll learn until you try."

CHAPTER 3

Constable Griffiths nodded respectfully as the inspector and Barnes climbed out of the hansom in front of the Wrexley Hotel. They had come directly to the scene of the murder because one of Witherspoon's "methods" was to question every likely witness as soon as possible. Experience had taught both men that even a few hours after a crime, people could forget important details or, even worse, have their memories tainted by sharing what they'd seen or heard with others. Even though the staff working at this time of day wouldn't have been here when the murder was committed, any one of them might have useful information about the victim; as it stood, they were very short of facts about Thomas Mundy. They had interviewed a good portion of the staff yesterday, but there were many they'd simply not had time to question even with the assistance of several constables. The inspector was determined to get a statement from everyone who worked at the hotel.

"Good morning, sir, Constable." Griffiths reached for the door handle but stopped short of opening it when the inspector held up his hand.

"Good morning, Constable. Was everything normal here last night?"

"Yes, sir. Constable Dutton reported that all was well and that the only people who'd checked out of the hotel were two elderly ladies, neither of whom were acquainted with the deceased."

"Good, that'll make life a bit easier. At least we won't have to chase down any possible witnesses. Any reports from the station?"

"I stopped in on my way here," Griffiths said, "and Constable Grayling confirmed there were weights in the head of the walking stick. Not only that, but a lead pipe had been inserted into the top six inches of the stick as well. A hole was drilled directly into the wood beneath the head. Constable Grayling said whoever had done it originally knew what he was doing, and Grayling ought to know—he was an apprentice carpenter before he joined the force."

"That explains why it was so ruddy heavy," Barnes said.

"And that also means it was most definitely the murder weapon." Witherspoon frowned. "Too bad we don't know whether Mundy carried it because he had reason to fear for his life or just for general protection because he traveled so much."

Griffiths leapt away from the door as it swung open and two well-dressed matrons appeared. Directly behind them came two bellboys loaded down with luggage. Witherspoon and Barnes stepped out of their way as the ladies charged out of the hotel.

"Maybe a good hunt through the victim's personal effects

will help us answer that question." Barnes watched as the bell-boy dumped the luggage on the pavement and then rushed out into the traffic to flag down a four-wheeler.

"Sergeant Malloy said he tried to have a good look through Mundy's effects last night, but he got called away because there were more than half a dozen arrests between late last night and the wee hours of the morning," Griffiths explained.

"Not to worry, we'll have a look ourselves as soon as we finish with the interviews." Witherspoon nodded at the constable and led the way into the hotel.

There were only three guests in the lobby: a woman dressed in a bright green cloak at the reception desk, a gentleman asleep with an open newspaper on his chest, and an elderly lady reading a book at a table by the window.

"Let's have another word with Mr. Cutler," Witherspoon said as he and the constable headed toward the reception counter. "I've a few more questions to ask him."

"I'm sorry, ma'am, but he isn't here," the clerk said.

"What do you mean he isn't here?" the woman snapped. "He must be. We had an appointment."

"I'm sorry, ma'am, but Mr. Mundy is uh . . . well . . ." The clerk, who was hardly more than a lad, flushed a deep red and looked frantically at the two policemen. "Here's the police. They can give you more information."

The lady whirled around and came face-to-face with the inspector. She was a handsome, middle-aged woman with fine lines around her blue eyes and just a touch of gray streaking her red hair. "Who are you?" she demanded.

"I'm Inspector Gerald Witherspoon, and this is Constable Barnes. Are you here to see Mr. Thomas Mundy?"

She studied him for a moment and then said, "I don't see why my appointment with Thomas Mundy is any concern of the police, but if you must know, yes, I am."

"Are you a relative of Mr. Mundy's?" Witherspoon asked.

"No, I'm here to see him on a business matter. Why? What's wrong? Where is he? Have you arrested him? If you have, then you must tell me where you've taken him. I've got to speak to him."

Witherspoon hated this part of his job. "I'm afraid, ma'am, that we've some very bad news for you. Thomas Mundy is dead."

Her eyes widened and her mouth opened in shock. "What do you mean he's dead? He can't be dead. He's got to be here. He's got to give me my money back. He promised, he promised I could have it today," she said, her voice getting louder and louder. "This can't be happening. He has to be here," she screamed.

The manager's office door flew open, and Ezra Cutler rushed out. "What's all this noise? What's going on here?"

"Don't you understand, I'm ruined." She pounded her fists on the reception counter. "Ruined, you hear."

"This lady wants to speak to Mr. Mundy," the clerk replied, having to yell over her. "And the police just told her he's dead."

"I knew I shouldn't have trusted him," she wailed. "I knew he wouldn't give it back to me. I knew it, I knew it, I knew it. I shouldn't ever have given him the money. What am I going to do now?"

"Madam, please get ahold of yourself," Cutler pleaded. She ignored him and kept on wailing. He looked at Witherspoon. "For goodness' sake, Inspector, take her into the dining room before she ruins what business we have left."

"Please, ma'am, you need to come with us. We've got to ask you some questions." Barnes took her elbow and gently tugged her away from the reception counter. She didn't resist as he led her across the lobby and through the doors of the dining room. Luckily, the restaurant was empty save for a very startled waiter who was collecting soiled serviettes and tablecloths. Grabbing the linens, he ran toward the corridor.

Barnes guided her to the nearest table and pulled out a chair. The woman, who now looked as if she'd gone into shock, sat down. He and the inspector took the seats on either side of her.

"This can't be happening." She stared straight ahead. She'd gone very pale, her face almost as white as the tablecloths.

"I'm afraid it's true." The inspector gazed at her sympathetically. "What is your name?"

For a moment, Witherspoon was afraid she wasn't going to answer, but finally, she blinked, took a deep breath, and turned to look at him. "My name is Jennifer Payton."

"Where do you live, Miss Payton?"

"Number twenty-four Harlow Road, Shepherds Bush." She took another breath. "But you don't need to go there. If you need to speak to me, I'll come to you. I live with an elderly relative, and if the police come to the house, it will scare her."

"I understand." Witherspoon nodded. "You're a business associate of Mr. Mundy's?"

She laughed bitterly. "That's one way of putting it. The truth is, Mundy owes me a great deal of money, fifty pounds in all. I lent it to him six months ago, and he promised to pay me back with interest. He was supposed to meet me at seven this morning at Queens Road Station. I waited and waited, but when he didn't show up, I came here." She smiled faintly. "He didn't know that I knew he was staying here. Thomas always thought everyone was stupid, but I didn't trust him, so I made certain I knew where he was staying."

"How did you do that?" Barnes asked.

"Simple, Constable, I followed him."

"When was this?"

"The night before last, after we had an early dinner at Babcock's. That's a restaurant on Oxford Street. He thought he could fob me off with a bit of roast pork and a glass of wine, but I told him he had to pay what he owed."

Witherspoon wasn't sure what to ask next, but he needn't have worried, as she apparently had quite a bit to say.

"He had no idea I was following him. Like I said, he was one of those people who assume the rest of the world is stupid."

"How did you follow him, ma'am?" Barnes asked. "Were you on foot, or did you trail him in a hansom?"

"Both. He went down Oxford Street until right before Marble Arch. Then he grabbed a hansom." She laughed again. "But the traffic was so congested, I managed to keep up with his cab on foot. I almost lost him when he reached the Uxbridge Road, but I'm a strong woman and I kept on going. I was determined to know where he was staying. Once his hansom turned onto the Queens Road, I knew he had to be at the Wrexley. It was the perfect place for a man like him."

Phyllis ducked into the mews behind the Wrexley Hotel and leaned against the wall. Her feet hurt and she was so disappointed, she wanted to cry. She'd tramped all over the neighborhood trying to figure out what, if any, shops would be useful to someone living in a hotel. The trouble was, she knew practically nothing about Thomas Mundy except that he'd been bashed over the head and was originally from the Midlands. But she'd tried her best. Thinking he might be prone to headaches or other ailments, she'd gone into the neighborhood chemist and tried to get the pharmacist to chat, but that hadn't gone well at all. Then she'd gone to the local newsagent's, but the woman there had been downright rude. Last, she'd even asked about Mundy at both the greengrocer's and the tailor's, but they'd not heard of him, either.

She glanced down the mews toward the door of the hotel. She wished she had the courage to open it, step inside, and find someone who'd tell her something useful. Showing up at their afternoon meeting with nothing would be too humiliating. She wasn't going to let him best her on this case. Oh, he'd pretend to be sympathetic if she had nothing to report today, but the minute no one was looking, he'd give her that superior little smirk that made her feel lower than a worm. Everyone thought Wiggins was so ruddy perfect, but that was because they'd never been on the receiving end of his sarcastic little remarks. Funny, they'd been good friends until recently, and she'd no idea what had made him change so much. Right now, she didn't really care; she was simply determined not to let him get ahead of her.

Without stopping to think of the consequences, she hurried to the back door, climbed the two broad steps, and opened it a crack. Peeking inside, she saw a corridor leading to a set of stairs and bisected by another hallway that probably led to the kitchen, the larders, and the storage rooms. She took a deep breath, grasped the handle of her shopping basket tightly, and slipped inside. If anyone questioned her, she'd just say she'd been sent here by her mistress to see what was on tomorrow's dinner menu as her mistress was going to host a dinner here for some overseas friends.

She stopped just inside the door. From her left, she could hear the banging of pots and pans and the jangling of silverware and crockery coming from what she knew must be the kitchen. She crept forward, to the intersection of the two corridors. To her right was a long hallway that ran the width of the building and ended at the foot of the front staircase. Along the wall were half a dozen large wicker laundry baskets, a row of sideboards—two with missing cabinet doors—and half a dozen upturned chairs. Opposite one of the wicker baskets was a heap of dirty tablecloths and linens in front of an open doorway.

Suddenly, she heard footsteps on the back staircase. Phyllis turned on her heel, raced down the hall, and flung herself into the open doorway. She held her breath, praying that whoever it was wasn't coming into the darkened room. She almost fainted in relief as her prayers were answered when the person passed by her hiding place. She poked her head out for a better view and saw him stop at the far end of the hall.

A bellboy, his arms loaded with an assortment of dirty linens, appeared at the bottom of the front staircase.

"Hurry up, Jamie," the waiter called. "Quit larkin' about. You should 'ave been 'ere with the last of the dirty linens five minutes ago. The laundry wagon will be 'ere any minute."

"Sorry," Jamie said with a laugh, "but I didn't want to miss watchin' Mr. Cutler havin' a fit. Cor blimey, I've not had that good a giggle since me aunt Enid got caught eating beef during Lent. Was there a red-haired lady in the dining room with the police? A lady in a green cloak?"

"Yeah, what of it?" the waiter said as the two of them met in front of a wicker basket.

"That's what was givin' me the giggles." Jamie laughed again. "You should 'ave heard her. She was at reception askin' for Mundy, and when Bendal told her she couldn't see him, she screamed like a fishwife. Mr. Cutler come running out of his office, but even he couldn't get her to be quiet." Jamie opened the lid of the basket.

"That's not funny." The waiter dumped the linens into the basket. "It just means that Cutler will be in a right nasty mood. You know what an old woman he is. He hates any kind of disturbance that might upset the Wrexleys. Blast, I wanted to ask him to let me switch shifts tomorrow."

"Don't worry, he'll not be in that bad a state today. The police were there, so he had them take her off to the dining room."

"I know," the waiter replied. "I was there. I saw them with her. I just didn't know she'd raised a fuss in reception."

"Did you hear what the police was askin' her?" Jamie asked eagerly.

The waiter sighed heavily. "The only thing I heard was her admittin' to them she followed Mundy here last night, and I only heard that because I had to go back up to get the load of linens that Stuart had left. I wish someone would tell that little sod to do his job properly. He's supposed to bring his load down here, not leave it by the dining room dumbwaiter."

"She followed him here? You think she mighta done it?"

"How the 'ell should I know? All I know is this ruddy murder has put Mr. Cutler in a mood, and now he'll never let me switch." He slammed the lid down. "You'd best get this to the kitchen and pick up the rest. The laundry wagon is due now."

Phyllis took a deep, calming breath and waited for her heartbeat to slow to normal. She knew what she needed to do and hoped she wasn't too late. As soon as the bellboy and waiter had gone, she hurried away from her hiding place and into the hall. She prayed her luck would hold and that she'd not run into

63

anyone as she made her way to the back door. Luckily, the kitchen was busy, and the waiters and bellboys had scarpered off on various tasks, so she managed to get out without being caught.

Once outside, she raced to the end of the mews, cut across the road, and ran down the street until she found a good spot to watch the hotel. Once again, she flattened herself against the wall of an alcove and hoped that no one noticed her. All she had to do was wait until a red-haired woman wearing a green cloak came out the front door.

"What do you think of her statement, sir?" Barnes asked as he and Witherspoon watched Jennifer Payton stalk out the front door of the Wrexley.

Witherspoon shook his head. "I'm not sure. She admitted she followed Mundy here the night before last, and that alone makes her a suspect, but on the other hand, he owed her money, and it wouldn't have been in her interest to kill the man."

"Not unless she confronted him and he admitted he wasn't going to pay her back," Barnes said. He was a tad more cynical than the inspector, especially when it came to the fairer sex. He was a happily married man, but the constable knew that women were just as capable as men of lying through their teeth when it suited their interests.

"True, but people who owe you money rarely tell you they're not going to pay you back," the inspector murmured. "They usually come up with excuses and put you off so they can gain a bit of time. Honestly, Constable, I don't understand why women lend their life savings to men they barely know."

"But she did know him, sir." Barnes was relieved he didn't

have to come up with a reason for knowing that Mundy hailed from Market Harborough. "She admitted they knew each other twenty years ago when he was a solicitor's clerk and that he'd once helped her out of a difficult situation."

"But twenty years is a long time, and Market Harborough isn't London. People change. Perhaps that was the poor woman's mistake—he wasn't the man she used to know when they were both young. I do wish she'd been a bit more forthright in discussing their previous relationship. It might have some bearing on the current situation," Witherspoon said.

"True, sir, it might, but then again, she was adamant that it was a deeply personal matter and that it had nothing to do with his murder," Barnes said. "And the trouble with forcing a statement out of her in this particular circumstance is that because the alleged incident happened twenty years ago we have no way to check whether she is telling us the truth." Barnes glanced around the lobby, his gaze coming to an elderly woman sitting at a chair in the corner. There was a book in her lap, but she was staring straight at him. After a moment or two, she waved her hand, motioning to him.

"Sir, I think that lady wants to speak to us." Barnes nodded in her direction.

"Well, I was going to have another word with Mr. Cutler, but let's go see what she wants." The inspector led the way across the lobby. "Good day, ma'am. Is there something we can help you with?"

"If you're the two investigating Mundy's murder, it's more like I'll be the one helping you." She pointed her bony fingers toward two straight-back chairs at the next table. "Bring those over here and sit down, please."

The inspector noted that her accent sounded Australian, but

he wasn't quite certain. He studied her while Barnes dragged the chairs over and placed them across from her. Her hair was thick, white, and piled high on her head. She had a long, bony face with hazel eyes framed by thick, bushy eyebrows. She met and held his gaze. He had the impression she was taking his measure as much as he was taking hers. He hoped she wasn't one of those lonely souls that sometimes wandered into the Ladbroke Road Police Station and made up all manner of nonsensical things. "Now, ma'am, what would you like to tell us about this matter?"

"Aren't you going to ask me my name?"

"Of course, ma'am," Barnes answered quickly. He opened his notebook, balanced it on his knee, and set his pencil at the ready. "The inspector was just giving me a moment to get prepared. Now, ma'am, what is your name?"

"Mrs. Laverne Hamlin. I live here. More important for you, I spend most of my days and numerous evenings right here in this spot. As you can see, this is an excellent place to watch the comings and goings of my fellow guests."

Witherspoon nodded encouragingly. "Indeed it is, ma'am, and I take it you've seen something that might be helpful to our inquiry?"

She laughed. "Not directly. I mean, I can't tell you who killed the man, but I can tell you that he was very popular. That redhead making all the fuss wasn't the only woman who'd been here asking for him."

"You know of someone else who was inquiring about Mr. Mundy?" The inspector shifted on the hard seat.

"The night before last, there was a blonde woman wanting to see him. But he was out, and she waited for an hour or two, and then she left."

Barnes glanced at the inspector. "Are you certain it was Thomas Mundy she wanted to see?" the constable asked.

"I may be old, but there's nothing wrong with my ears. I overheard her quite clearly as I walked past the reception counter. I like sitting down here and watching the world go by, but at my age, I've got to move about every little bit to keep my arthritis at bay. She distinctly told the night clerk that she needed to speak to Thomas Mundy."

"Was the lady young or old?" Barnes asked.

"Anyone under the age of fifty looks young when you get to be my age." She chuckled. "I'd say she was in her late thirties or early forties—young middle aged and very attractive."

The constable nodded in encouragement. "Nicely dressed?"

"Fashionably dressed, Constable. She wouldn't have looked out of place strolling down the Champs Elysées, and I ought to know as I spend three months a year in Paris."

"She spoke to the night clerk, not the night manager?" Witherspoon clarified. He was annoyed at himself for not speaking to the young man himself, but instead had let a constable take the clerk's statement.

"It was definitely the clerk. Mr. Stargill had taken three ladies to King's Cross. They were taking the night train to Scotland and didn't want to be out without a male escort," she snorted derisively. "Silly fools—if they're that frightened of the world, they should have stayed in Edinburgh."

"Did the lady give her name to the night clerk?" Witherspoon asked.

"You'll have to ask him. But that's not all I've got to say. Mundy knew that someone was after him. He's been running scared for the past three days."

"Running scared," the constable repeated.

She laughed again. "That's right, I know the signs when I see them. Where I come from, there were plenty of men who passed through, and a lot of them were hoping to get far away from something they'd done or someone chasing them."

"I'm not sure I understand what you mean." The inspector frowned. "Could you be a bit more specific? Exactly how did you know he was, uh, 'running scared'?"

"It wasn't hard to spot, Inspector. The first time I noticed it was three days ago in the dining room. I have a table next to the window so I can look out onto the street. I was sitting there finishing my coffee when I saw Mundy hurrying down the road. He kept stopping and looking behind him, you know, like he was scared there was someone chasing him. I noticed it again later that day. He came to the top of the landing on the first floor, but instead of coming down, he stood by the banister and looked around the lobby. The day before yesterday, I noticed the same thing. Before he came down, he stopped and had a good look around."

Witherspoon didn't think she was deliberately making things up like some of those poor unfortunates they occasionally dealt with, yet he wasn't sure how seriously to take her statement.

Constable Barnes had no such qualms. "How did he look when he finally came down the stairs?" he asked.

"He looked relieved, Constable, at least for a few seconds. Then he'd put on that false smile and make his way over to butter up the twin ladies."

"Butter up?" Witherspoon repeated.

She raised her eyebrows. "Of course, Inspector—why else would a handsome middle-aged man pay any attention to the likes of people my age?"

"Perhaps he enjoyed their company," the inspector argued.

"He was after their money; he was a confidence trickster," she said flatly. "I know—he tried it on with me when he first arrived but soon realized I was neither naive nor foolish."

"What did he do?" Barnes didn't stop writing as he spoke.

"His first day here, he contrived to sit next to me at luncheon, and he struck up a conversation. Now, I'm a friendly sort, so it took a good half hour or so of listening to him before I realized what he was doing. He was as slick as a slippery eel, I'll give him that, but I noticed that no matter what was said in our conversation, he kept bringing the talk around to his business here in England and how excited he was about the investment opportunities his consortium was offering."

Barnes looked up from his notebook, his expression doubtful. "From what the other ladies have told us, Mr. Mundy was quite reluctant to discuss his business interests."

"The other ladies? Oh, you must mean the twin widows. By the time he got to them, he'd learned his lesson and was bein' a bit more careful. Mundy was a sharp one, not the type to make the same mistake twice."

"Did you tell Mrs. Blanding and Mrs. Denton your suspicions that Mr. Mundy was less than honest?" the inspector asked.

"I tried"—she waved a hand dismissively—"but they didn't want to hear it, Inspector. Like me, they're two lonely old women, and they were flattered by his attention. Unfortunately for him, I've a more suspicious nature. But I'm the first to admit, when you get to be my age, having someone interested in you for any reason is a powerful incentive to want to believe them."

Witherspoon nodded. "Mundy approached you without success but apparently had made some headway with the other two ladies. Do you know if he approached anyone else here at the hotel?"

"As far as I know, it was just the three of us," she replied. "Mind you, in the past few days, there's been a steady stream of people sniffing about, wanting to know what the fellow was up to."

"Not just the blonde lady?" Barnes pressed.

"She was one of several." Laverne Hamlin grinned. "There was a nice-looking, middle-aged blond-haired fellow as well. He had the prettiest blue eyes, but that's of no interest to you. He was smarter than the rest. He didn't bother asking at reception for Mundy. But he was here twice, lookin' for Mundy. The first time was out in front. I was coming back from taking my morning walk when I overheard him asking one of the bellboys if Thomas Mundy was at this hotel."

"Exactly when was this?" the inspector asked.

She tapped her finger against her chin, her expression thoughtful. "Let me see now. Mundy was murdered the night before last, and I hadn't gone out that day, my arthritis was hurtin' something fierce, so it must have been the day before he was killed. Yes, that's right, it was Sunday."

"And the second time you saw this man?" Barnes probed. "When was that?"

"The evening Mundy was killed. He was in the dining room. I heard him tell the maître d' that he was dining with Mundy, but he was late, and he asked the maître d' to send someone up to Mundy's room to tell him his guest was here."

"You overheard all this?" Witherspoon pressed.

"I'm not making it up, Inspector. I was standing two feet away, waiting to be seated myself. The maître d' grabbed a waiter and ordered him to go up to room three thirty to tell Mundy his dinner guest was here. But the funny thing was, neither Mundy nor the blond-haired man ate dinner in the hotel that night."

Smythe stepped into the Dirty Duck Pub and stood by the door to give his eyes time to adjust to the gloomy interior. The room was noisy as dockworkers, day laborers, tally clerks, and bread sellers chatted, laughed, and argued over their pints of beer and glasses of gin. The crowd at the bar was two deep, the tables were full, and on the rough benches along the walls there wasn't so much as an unoccupied inch.

Blimpey Groggins, the owner of the establishment, was in his usual spot at a table near the fireplace. He was in deep conversation with two other men, one of whom was dressed like a banker and the other dressed in ordinary but dirty working man's clothes. Smythe moved around the edge of the crowd and caught Blimpey's eye before shoving into an impossibly small spot that had opened at the bar. He ordered a pint while he waited for Blimpey to finish his business.

Blimpey Groggins bought and sold information. He had a network of paid sources all over the South of England—hospitals, shipping lines, railway offices, newspapers, police stations, courthouses, every office at Whitehall—and some claimed he even had people at Buckingham Palace. His information was always reliable and, most important, he was discreet. He knew London as well as his own hand, and he'd share that knowledge with anyone who could pay his fees. He could tell you which titled lady was having an affair and with whom, and which free-spending aristocrat was almost bankrupt.

"He's free now." The barmaid nodded toward Blimpey as she gave Smythe his beer. "Go on over."

Smythe nodded his thanks, picked up his glass, and made his way to Blimpey's table. Groggins was a stout middle-aged fellow with wispy ginger-colored hair, rosy cheeks, and a huge grin. He wore his usual attire of an old brown and white checked suit and an oversized white shirt, and he sported a bright red scarf wound around his throat.

"Nice to see ya, Smythe. I wondered 'ow long it was goin' to be before I saw ya. Sit down and make yourself comfortable."

Smythe flopped onto the stool. "I take it that means you've heard about the murder at the Wrexley?"

"'Course I have." He chuckled. "And I 'ad a feelin' you'd be 'round, so I did a bit of diggin' about your victim. This Mr. Mundy was a bit of a shadowy sort."

"Is that your way of admittin' you 'aven't found out much about him?" Smythe took a sip of beer.

Blimpey merely raised an eyebrow. "Don't be daft. The fellow was cagey about his past, but in this town, it's impossible to hide in the dark forever."

"What 'ave you found out?"

"Mundy's not been in town long, no more than a month or six weeks, but there're already rumors floatin' about. For starters, he's been connected to some sort of scandal from the Midlands."

"He comes from Leicestershire." Smythe nodded. "He might 'ave once worked for a solicitor in Market Harborough. But that was years ago."

Blimpey frowned. "Nah, it's not Market Harborough. It's Hinckley, and the rumors aren't from years ago, but six months ago. I've not got the details, but someone died and Mundy's name kept comin' up."

"This might be important. Can you get the details?"

"'Course I can if you want to pay. But it'll mean sendin' a man up there to have a right good look around."

Smythe hesitated. He could easily afford it, and he didn't mind spending his money in the cause of justice, but they had sent Hatchet to Leicestershire, and he might stumble on this information himself. He shook his head. "Let's hold off on that for the time being. Who else was interested in Mundy?"

Blimpey grinned. "I don't know their names, Smythe. I only set my people on it yesterday when I 'eard your guv caught Mundy's murder. Give me a day or two."

The red-haired woman headed toward the corner. She was moving fast. Phyllis trailed her as closely as she dared, speeding or slowing her steps to keep pace with her quarry. But after walking for a good fifteen minutes and ending up very close to where they'd started, Phyllis realized the woman had either spotted that she was being followed or wasn't going to any particular place. When the redhead reached the corner opposite Kensington Gardens, Phyllis decided trailing her had been a waste of time. But the woman stood between her and the fastest way home, so Phyllis threw caution to the wind. She went to the corner, stopping next to the redhead. The woman ignored her, and Phyllis congratulated herself on not being spotted. Then the lady stepped into the busy roadway, directly in the path of a fully loaded Belsen's Brewery wagon. Oblivious to the heavy traffic, she turned and faced the horses bearing down on her.

"Get out of the way, you stupid cow," the driver screamed as he yanked on the brakes.

Without thinking, Phyllis leapt into the street, grabbed the woman's arm, and yanked her backward just as the team thundered past. She pulled hard enough to send them both onto their backsides in the gutter.

For a moment, the world seemed to move in slow motion. Phyllis glimpsed the relieved expression flashing across the face of the wagon driver and saw two well-dressed matrons pointing at them. An eel seller who'd been pushing his cart on the pavement raced over to them. "Bloomin' Ada, you ladies alright?" He extended a fishy-smelling hand toward Phyllis. "I saw what you did—you saved your friend's life."

"Thank you." She took the proffered hand and rose to her feet. The redhead stayed on the ground, staring at a spot near her shoe, and said nothing.

"You're very kind," Phyllis said with a smile.

He glanced uneasily at the redhead. "Uh, is she alright?"

"She'll be fine. She just needs a moment or two. The shock, you know. Thank you kindly for your help, sir."

He gave her a friendly nod, looked uncertainly at the redhead, and then headed back to his abandoned cart.

"Get up," Phyllis ordered. "You're making a spectacle of yourself." The two matrons weren't the only ones staring at them; a young woman pushing a pram and two elderly men gaped at them as well.

"What do I care?" she snapped. "I didn't give you leave to interfere in my life."

Phyllis spotted a constable at the end of the block and knew if she didn't get the woman out of the street, the police would do it for her. There was a good chance she might know this constable, and she didn't fancy having to explain to the inspector why she'd been found with a half-crazed lady he'd questioned in his latest murder.

"Well, I did interfere." She reached down, grabbing both

her arms, and pulled her to her feet. "Come on, there's a café around the corner. You can tell me your tale of woe there."

"A café won't do me any good, not with the day I've had," she snorted in derision. "I want a whiskey."

"Right, then." Phyllis picked up the shopping basket she'd dropped. "We'll find us a pub."

"There's one 'round the corner." The redhead pointed across the road. "It's a decent enough place."

Neither of them spoke as they crossed the busy Uxbridge Road and made their way to the Rose and Crown. Stepping inside, Phyllis ignored the curious looks from some of the men along the bar and led her charge to a table on the far side of the room. She pushed her onto a stool. "Stay here. I'll get you a drink."

Gathering her courage, she lifted her chin and marched to the bar. "I'd like two whiskeys, please." This wasn't her first time in a pub—she'd been in one before when they were on a case—but she was far from comfortable here. The barmaid gave her a friendly smile and poured their drinks. "That'll be a shilling." She pushed the glasses across the counter. Phyllis dug a coin out of her pocket, paid, and picked up their drinks.

She put the glass in front of the woman and saw that her gaze was still unfocused and her mouth slightly open. "Take a drink," Phyllis ordered as she sat down.

Picking up the glass, the redhead took a swallow, then shuddered slightly before downing all of it. She blinked and gave Phyllis a slight smile. "Thank you, I needed this. I'm sorry, I know I'm being rude, but you see, I've no idea what I'm going to do."

"What's your name?" Phyllis asked gently. "Just start with that."

"Jennifer Payton."

"Where do you live?"

"Now that's a good question." She shook herself and looked up. "Right now I live with my cousin in Shepherds Bush, but if I can't pay back the money I borrowed from her, she'll put me on the street. I'm out of time. You see, I didn't think she'd need to use the money. For God's sake, she's had it hidden away for years. She kept it stuffed in the back of an old cushion, but now she's sayin' she's going to use it to take her niece on holiday."

"Does your cousin know you borrowed the money?"

Jennifer shook her head and then looked down at her empty glass. "Not yet. But she will soon. She has to buy their tickets in a couple of days."

"You need this more than me." Phyllis shoved her whiskey across the table. "Take it—I don't really like the taste. What did you do with the money?" It was getting late, and though she had sympathy for the woman, she wanted to move this conversation along. Now that she had something to tell the others, she wanted to be back at Upper Edmonton Gardens for their afternoon meeting.

Jennifer reached for Phyllis' glass and took a quick sip. "I lent it to a man who'd once done me a big favor. He promised to pay me back double as soon as he got settled, but he didn't and now he's dead."

"Dead," Phyllis repeated. "What happened to him?" She knew perfectly well what had happened to him.

Tears sprang into her eyes. "Why do you care? Why'd you bother pulling me back from that wagon? Thomas Mundy's the lucky one. He's gone and doesn't have to worry about keepin' a roof over his head or food in his stomach. I wish it was me that was dead. I'd be better off."

"Don't be daft. No one is better off dead," Phyllis snapped impatiently. "Stop feeling sorry for yourself and talk to me. You tried to throw yourself in front of a brewery wagon. Surely your cousin wouldn't want you to do that just because you borrowed money from her."

"Borrowed." The laugh she gave bordered on hysteria. "That was a ruddy lie. I didn't borrow it. I pilfered it when she'd gone up to bed one night. I just didn't want to admit it, even to myself. The truth is I stole money from my own flesh and blood, from the woman who took me in when I had nothing, and because I was greedy, I gave it to a liar who promised to pay me back double. But now the bastard's dead, and so are my prospects for keeping a roof over my head."

"This Thomas Mundy was murdered?"

"That's right, and the saddest part of all is I wish I was the one who'd killed him."

"But you didn't, did you?" Phyllis probed.

"No, but I don't think the police believed me when I told them I hadn't done it. I'm a nobody who lives off the charity of a relative. The police will want to solve this case, and I stupidly told them the truth." She gave a harsh laugh. "Mind you, I didn't tell them everything."

"Why not? I mean, if you're innocent, won't it help the police to catch the real killer if you tell them everything you know?"

Jennifer smiled cynically. "I didn't just fall off a hay wagon. I could tell by the way they were askin' their questions that they thought I was lying. All I wanted to do was to get away from them. I'm so stupid. I should never have told them I followed him back to the hotel the night he was killed."

"So you got a bit frightened—I'd be scared, too." Phyllis decided it might be worth being a bit late to the meeting. "Why don't I get you another drink and you can tell me all about it."

She got to her feet. "I've had some hard times in my life, too, and sometimes, talking about it helps."

Jennifer stared at her warily for a moment. "Why are you bein' so nice to me? You don't know me, we're strangers, and from what I've seen, no one in this city lends you a helping hand unless there's somethin' in it for them."

"Don't be so suspicious. Not everyone is out to do you a misery." She started to the bar. "Now, do you want that whiskey or not?"

Jennifer relaxed and nodded. "Yeah, I do, but I still don't understand why you'd care about the likes of me. No one else has in a long time."

"Let's just say, I know what it's like to worry about keeping a roof over my head and a bit of food in my stomach." Phyllis kept her eye on Jennifer as she ordered the whiskey; she wanted to make sure the woman didn't bolt for the door. If she did, there wouldn't be much she could do about it short of knocking her down and dragging her back to the table.

But Jennifer Payton stayed put and even gave Phyllis a shy smile when she came back with her drink. "Thank you. I know I sound like an ungrateful old cow, and you're bein' ever so nice. I'm sorry."

"It's alright." Phyllis sat down. "Now, why don't you tell me what you didn't tell the police. Maybe it's not as bad as you think."

"I don't know why I never find anything valuable or get a decent tip," Letty Hazlitt complained as she and Wiggins crossed the Notting Hill High Street. She was a slender girl with tendrils of curly brown hair slipping out of her chambermaid's cap, blue eyes, and a square jaw. "Of course, Mr. Cutler doesn't like us accepting tips, and we're always supposed to turn everything we find in to the office, but that's easy for him to say—he makes a good wage. He ought to try living on what they pay us. Mind you, a lot of the guests know how hard we work and give us a bit here and there."

Wiggins politely took the young chambermaid's elbow and guided her through a gap in the stopped traffic. She'd been talking—well, complaining—nonstop since they'd left the Wrexley. He'd made a terrible mistake, but it was too late now for him to get back to the hotel to find someone else who'd talk to him. Blast a Spaniard, now he'd have nothing to report this afternoon, but he wasn't to know that this girl was an empty-headed chatterbox who didn't know a ruddy thing about Mundy or his murder. He'd spent the entire morning trying to make contact with a waiter or a bellboy or anyone else connected to the hotel, but it was hopeless. A cold front had blown in from the east, and that meant that no one had wandered out onto the back steps for a quick break or some fresh air. As he couldn't go into the hotel proper, he'd tried a couple of pubs but had learned nothing. He'd thought his luck had changed for the better when he'd arrived back at the Wrexley just as four chambermaids had finished their shift. Three of the girls had hurried off toward the front of the hotel while Letty had gone down the mews toward the station. He'd made contact and even congratulated himself on his cleverness when she'd agreed to let him walk her home.

"Some people are generous enough to tip for good service." He let out a sigh of relief as they made it to the pavement. She'd said she lived just off the High Street, so surely it couldn't be much farther. Cor blimey, it was just his bad luck to get stuck like this.

"I'm never as lucky as the others. Just last week, Jamie, he's a bellboy, got tipped a half crown by this American lady. A half crown, can you believe it? 'Course, he didn't say a word to Mr. Cutler like he should have because he didn't want to have to give it back, and Mr. Cutler is real strict about us not taking advantage of foreigners." She pointed to the street directly ahead. "I live on that street, halfway up. Mind you, it's not just tips I miss. You'd never believe all the things we find, and not just in the rooms, either. The guests are always leaving things about the place. Losing them and such."

Wiggins picked up his pace as they swung around the corner. "You mean the help keeps the things people leave behind?"

"Not always." She shrugged. "For the most part, things get turned in, and Mr. Cutler or Mr. Stargill has to write a letter to the owner. Not everyone is as honest as I am." She sniffed disapprovingly. "Just last week, Tommy Dukes found a lace handkerchief in the hallway. It was a really nice one, too, and I know he kept it, because all of a sudden, Angela Banks had it, and Tommy is right sweet on Angela. And day before yesterday, the day that fellow you asked about got murdered, Elsie Scott found a nice gold button on the back stairs when she was takin' Mrs. Ottley up a lunch tray, and I know she kept that, too."

"Why would anyone keep an old button?"

"It wasn't just an old button—it was a right fancy one, and she'll be able to sell it. But that's not the worst. Last week, Amy Clover found a pearl hatpin, and I know she kept that, too. I overheard her tellin' Elsie the hatpin would do as a birthday gift for her gran. But I never find anything. It's just not fair."

Wiggins almost asked her why she was moaning about never finding anything valuable if she was so honest, but he held his tongue.

Letty stopped suddenly and nodded toward a three-story redbrick town house that had seen better days. "That's where I live. Thanks ever so much for walking me home." She smiled shyly and looked down at the ground. "It's not often that a nice-looking fellow pays any attention to someone like me. Would you like to come in for a cup of tea? We've got the ground-floor flat, so you'd not have to walk up the stairs. My gran's home, so we'd be properly chaperoned. She's never met someone like you."

"Like me?"

"You know, a newspaper reporter."

CHAPTER 4

Ezra Cutler sighed heavily, pulled a handkerchief out of his breast pocket, and wiped the perspiration from his hairline. He was in his office with Witherspoon and Barnes.

"I'm afraid I can't help you, Inspector. I've no idea who the people that Mrs. Hamlin claimed to see might be. I don't recall anyone inquiring about Thomas Mundy while I was on duty." He leaned forward over his desk and pointed at his door. "Please understand I'm rarely at reception. Most of my time is spent here, in the office, and if I don't keep that door closed, I get very little work done. If the guests see me, they assume my time is there for the taking."

Barnes put his pencil down on the corner of Cutler's desk, flexed his cramped fingers, and then picked it up again. "Would your desk clerk have told you if there had been several people inquiring after Mr. Mundy?"

"Bendal is an excellent worker, and if he thought there was

anyone making unusual inquiries about a guest, yes, of course he'd mention it to me. The night clerk is also a person of good character and would most certainly have said something to Mr. Stargill if he thought there was a problem. But you've got to understand, our guests tend to be of the class that has substantial social and business obligations, so even if several people inquired after a specific guest several times during a short period, the clerks wouldn't necessarily think there was anything amiss. However, don't take my word for it. Go ahead and speak to both of them."

"Our constables have already taken statements from both young men," Barnes said. He'd had a quick word with Constable Griffiths and been assured that both clerks had been properly interviewed yesterday. Cutler was right; both clerks *had* stated several men and women had been asking to see Thomas Mundy on the day of his murder. But that wasn't unusual as people often came to call upon the man, so they'd thought nothing of it. "But we'll speak to them again." And this time, we'll make sure to ask very specific questions and get some decent descriptions, he added silently.

"Please try to do it when we're not busy," Cutler pleaded. "The Wrexleys are not happy. Your presence is playing havoc with our guests and our business. They want to know how much longer you'll be here."

"At least another day or two." The inspector smiled apologetically. "There are some of your staff left to interview and several we'd like to question again."

"Oh dear, that is bad news. The Wrexleys will be most upset, but I suppose you must do your job. Now, if you've no more questions for me, I'd like to get back to work."

"We're done, sir," Witherspoon said. Barnes closed his notebook, and both men rose to their feet. As soon as they were out of the office and out of earshot of the people in the lobby, Barnes said, "If it's all the same to you, sir, I'd like to interview Bendal, the reception clerk, again. This time, I'll try to get descriptions. I'm afraid our lads fell down a bit on the job when they took the previous statements."

"I'm sure they did their best." Witherspoon nodded. "But I'm glad you're taking charge, Constable. You've so much more experience than most of these lads. We'll have a word with the night clerk before we leave this evening. He should be here by six. I'm going into the dining room. I've made arrangements to interview the rest of the kitchen workers. There aren't many left. Can you do the hotel staff that weren't interviewed yesterday?"

Inspector Witherspoon smiled at the young man sitting opposite him. They were at a dining table as far away from the kitchen as possible. He didn't want their conversation overheard. It was important that all the witnesses make their own statements based on what they knew, not on what they might have accidentally overheard. "On the night Mr. Mundy was killed, did you see anyone coming in or out of the back door who shouldn't have been there?" Witherspoon asked.

The waiter, a skinny young lad named Joey Finnigan, looked puzzled by the question. He had pale skin, brown hair worn slicked against his skull, and a prominent Adam's apple protruding over the high collar of his white jacket. "That's difficult to say, sir. The guests aren't supposed to use the back stairs, but they lead out onto the mews and it's a shortcut to the station, so they do it anyway, so there were a lot of people goin' in and out. We do our best, but we're not supposed to be rude to the guests, and well, when we see it happening, we just look the other way, if you know what I mean."

The inspector knew all too well what he meant. "I understand that. I'm not asking if you confronted any of the guests because they were breaking the rules. What I need to know is whether you *noticed* anyone who wasn't a guest or an employee going up or down those stairs the night Mr. Mundy was murdered."

"Like I say, sir, we tend to look the other way when it's someone not workin' here, but I saw a man earlier, but not at any time near when Mr. Mundy was killed. It was in the afternoon."

"This other man, I take it he wasn't a guest here at the hotel?"

Joey pursed his lips. "No, he wasn't a guest."

"What did he look like?"

Joey stared at Witherspoon for a second and then looked toward the kitchen. "I didn't get much of a look, sir. You see, I was late that day, and I nipped into the little stairwell under the back steps because I wanted to slip on my jacket without anyone seein' me and realizing I was ten minutes overdue. They're right strict about us bein' 'ere on time, sir. So I was tucked under there gettin' into my uniform when I heard the back door open, but the funny thing was, his footsteps weren't loud and that worried me, sir. Like I said, sir, the guests don't care if we see and hear them comin' and goin'. So I wondered who it could be and why they seemed to be tiptoein' about the place. But I was a bit late in lookin', and when I stuck my head out, all I could see was someone disappearin' up the staircase. I didn't get a proper look at them."

"Was there anything about this person you can recall? Anything at all?"

Joey shook his head. "Sorry, sir, but all I seen was the bottom of his coat sleeves and his trousers. They was dark, sir, but I couldn't say for sure what color of dark."

"If you do remember anything, please let me know."

"Is that it, then? Can I get back to work?"

"Of course. I believe there's one more waiter we haven't spoken with. Can you send him along?"

"That'd be Jimmy Potts, but he won't know anything. He does breakfast and luncheon. He's never here for dinner."

Witherspoon smiled politely. "That may be true; nonetheless, please send him over."

A few moments later, a fair-haired young man with broad, ruddy cheeks approached the table. "I'm Jimmy Potts, sir. You wanted to speak to me?"

"Please sit down, Mr. Potts." Witherspoon waved at the chair.

"It's right exciting, isn't it." Potts sat down. "I mean, it's sad that Mr. Mundy was murdered. I don't know what you want to ask me. I wasn't even here when it happened. I come in early to help the chef with the kitchen, and I'm gone by three o'clock most days."

"I understand. However, I'd still like to ask you some questions. On the day of the murder, did you notice anyone, anyone at all, coming or going through the back door?"

He looked confused. "Lots of people come in and out that way."

"What I meant to ask was did you see anyone who shouldn't have been there? Anyone suspicious or anyone who you didn't know?" Witherspoon explained quickly.

"Ah yeah, I see what you're askin'. Well, there was Mr. Hart. Mind you, he comes to the hotel now and then, but I'd not seen him in some time. He was there that day. I saw him comin' in the back door when I was taking the breakfast linens downstairs. It were odd, him usin' the back door. He usually comes in the front way, talking a mile a minute and wavin' at all and sundry so people would notice him."

"What time?"

"It would have been about eleven o'clock, maybe as late as eleven fifteen. But that was hours before Mr. Mundy was murdered."

Witherspoon ignored the comment. "Do you know Mr. Hart's Christian name?"

"He's Mr. Ronald Hart. Chef says he's goin' to run for Parliament one of these days. Chef loves politics and is always goin' on and on about this and that. Most of the time none of us listen to him, and Joey thinks Chef's one of them radical anarchists, but the truth is, Joey wouldn't know an anarchist if one come up and bit him on the bum."

"Has Mr. Hart been a guest here?"

Jimmy laughed. "Nah, we're not good enough for the likes of him. But he's come in two or three times. Chef claims Mr. Hart is doin' a bit of boot lickin' so he can get Mr. Reed's spot on the council. He says Mr. Reed is ill and not long for this world. Some of the men on the county council like to lunch here, and in the last month or so, Mr. Hart's been lunchin' with them. Chef doesn't like Mr. Hart. He thinks he should have stayed in Leicestershire and gotten on the county council there."

"Leicestershire? Is Mr. Hart from Leicestershire?"

"Chef told us that the Hart family has a big estate right outside Market Harborough. Chef knows about things like that. He says he likes to keep an eye on them that likes exploitin' the workers. Mind you, Chef oughtn't to say anything—he's not above makin' us waiters do all the scut work that he don't want to do."

"And you saw Mr. Hart on the day that Mr. Mundy was killed?" Witherspoon asked.

"I did, but like I said, it was hours before the murder."

"Let's git this meetin' started. I gotta git home and get ready to go to a ball tonight," Luty declared. "Half the bankers in London is gonna be there, and I don't want to be late."

"But Hatchet still isn't back." Mrs. Goodge put a plate of scones next to the teapot. "You just said you got a telegram from him, and he'll not be back until tomorrow at the earliest."

"What's him bein' here or not got to do with me going out on the hunt?" Luty demanded.

Everyone at the table stopped talking and looked apprehensively between the two elderly women. Luty was fiercely protective of her independence and hated anyone implying she couldn't take care of herself.

Mrs. Goodge crossed her arms over her chest and met Luty's gaze. "You'd be on your own, that's all I'm sayin'. Like it or not, Luty, neither of us is a spring chicken. I'd not like to think of some ruffian trying to rob you because you're an unescorted woman. Don't give me that nonsense about takin' your peacemaker with you, either. We both know you're a crack shot, but we also both know you can shoot fast enough to defend someone else, but I'm not so sure you'd be willing to take a life to defend yourself."

In one of their more recent cases, Luty had used her Colt .45 to save a life, not take one.

"Mrs. Goodge, I understand you're concerned for Luty—," Mrs. Jeffries began, only to be interrupted.

"I ain't goin' on my own," Luty protested. "Since Hatchet's

been gone, half my household is trailin' after me like a bunch of puppies. But if I had to go alone, I could do it just as easy as sittin' in this chair, and I could shoot to defend myself if I had to, but you're right about one thing—I'd not like to have to pull the trigger. Takin' a human life is serious business."

Mrs. Goodge eyed her suspiciously. "Who is going with you?"

"Andrew, he's the footman, and Harry, the underbutler. They're big strappin' lads, so I ain't scared to stick my nose outside just because it's dark. Now, can we git on with the meeting?"

"Yes, that's an excellent idea," Mrs. Jeffries said quickly. She cast a quick glance at the cook, who was still watching Luty with a skeptical expression. But Mrs. Goodge had obviously decided she'd said enough, because she sat down and began pouring the cups of tea.

"Who would like to go first?" Mrs. Jeffries asked.

"Mine won't take long." Wiggins reached for a scone. "I've not learned much. It's bloomin' hard to find someone from the Wrexley who'll talk now that it's got so cold. Hardly anyone so much as stuck their head out that back door, and I couldn't go in because the inspector and all the constables are still there."

"I managed to find someone." Phyllis gave him a smug smile. "It wasn't hard."

"I didn't say I'd not found out anything," he retorted. "I just said it wasn't much. There's been lots of times when you've shown up for our meetin's without havin' anything to report."

"We've all done that," Betsy said quickly. She cast a quick, worried glance at the maid. What had got into Phyllis? It wasn't like her to be so scornful. But like Mrs. Jeffries, she, too, had noticed that the relationship between Wiggins and Phyllis had changed. "And I for one will be doing it again today. As Wiggins said, we can't go nosing about the Wrexley as long as the inspector is about the place."

Wiggins shot Phyllis one final glare. "Can I get on with my report? As I was sayin', I didn't find out much, but I did learn a bit." Blast a Spaniard, he'd let her goad him into giving a report he didn't really have; the bits and pieces he'd heard from that chambermaid were less than useless. But he couldn't back down now. "Turns out that some of the staff at the hotel don't always follow the rules. Guests lose things, not just in their rooms but in the hallways, the stairwells, and the public areas. When the staff finds something, they're supposed to turn it in to the office, but accordin' to my source, they sometimes keep it. In the last day or so, one of the maids found a gold button on the back staircase and a bellboy found a lace handkerchief in the hallway and another maid found a pearl hatpin. All of them kept what they found." He knew he was stretching the truth. He'd implied all these objects had been found *after* the murder, when the chambermaid had admitted they'd all been found *before* the killing. But he was desperate not to look a fool, especially in front of Phyllis. Besides, if they'd been found hours or even days before the murder, they couldn't possibly have anything to do with the crime.

"That means the killer might have dropped one or more of these items," Mrs. Jeffries said. "In which case, they might be very important evidence. Can you find out more information from your source?"

Wiggins cringed inwardly. Cor blimey, what in the blazes had he done? He'd mucked this up good and proper. But he'd always been a quick thinker. "I'm not sure, Mrs. Jeffries. She got a bit suspicious about all the questions I was askin'."

"Then ask someone else at the hotel," Betsy suggested. "It

sounds like all of them bend the rules a bit, so maybe you can get the details about these items from another employee. Mrs. Jeffries is right, if these things were found at any time near the murder, one or even more of them might belong to the killer. Was the handkerchief monogrammed?"

"My source didn't say." Wiggins wished he'd kept his ruddy mouth shut. "But that's a good idea, Betsy. I'll have a word with one of the bellboys."

"Take 'em to the pub," Smythe added. "It'll only cost you the price of a pint or two. If Wiggins is finished, can I go next? It won't take long."

"I'm done," Wiggins muttered.

Smythe took his turn. "I couldn't find any hansom drivers that had anything useful to say. There's too much traffic comin' and goin' to that hotel. But one of my other sources told me about a scandal that was linked to the dead man. Turns out that about six or seven months ago, someone in Hinckley died, and Thomas Mundy's name was bandied about by the gossips. My source didn't know how deeply Mundy might 'ave been involved with this death, but his name kept comin' up."

"Where's Hinckley?" Luty asked.

"In the Midlands," he replied. "My source didn't have any other details, couldn't even say if it was a man or a woman who died. I'm thinkin' that as Hatchet is up there for another day or so, you should let him know. Hinckley isn't that big a town, and if the gossip has spread to London, Hatchet might be able to find something out."

"I'll send him a telegram on the way home." Luty glanced at the clock on the pine sideboard and frowned. "I don't mean to hurry you along, but time's movin' on and I want to git to that ball."

"I'm done."

"I've nothing." Mrs. Goodge looked at the housemaid. "So it's just Phyllis left. Did you learn anything?"

"'Course she did," Wiggins muttered.

Phyllis ignored him. "I had a nice chat with a lady named Jennifer Payton." She gave Luty a fast, apologetic smile. "Sorry, Luty, this is going to take a few minutes. I hope that's alright."

"Go ahead. Much as I want to talk to them bankers, I don't want to miss anything important."

"There was a woman making a fuss at the Wrexley Hotel." Phyllis was very careful about the way she reported her meeting with Jennifer Payton. She was quite truthful about how she'd sneaked through the back door of the hotel but was deliberately vague about her part in pulling the woman out of the road and their going to a pub. But once she began telling them what Jennifer had told her, she took care to make sure she repeated Jennifer's words accurately. "But the oddest thing she mentioned was the way Mundy behaved when they parted outside Babcock's. She'd already made up her mind that she was going to follow him, so she pretended to leave and went around the corner. She waited a few seconds and then looked out to make sure he was still in her line of sight. She said he had a smug smile on his face. Then all of a sudden, his expression changed."

"Changed how?" Mrs. Goodge demanded.

"He looked shocked and then scared. I asked her how she knew, and she said she just did, that she'd survived this far in life by learning how to read people."

"What happened then?" Mrs. Jeffries asked.

"Mundy started moving fast down Oxford Street. She followed him all the way past Marble Arch to Hyde Park, and she said once he was there, he kept looking behind him as if he was scared he was being followed."

"He *was* bein' followed," Wiggins said, his expression sour. "Jennifer Payton had dogged him all the way to the park."

"He wasn't scared of her," Phyllis argued. "Besides, she made sure he didn't see her. She's not a stupid woman, and I believe her. She said it was obvious from the way he treated her that he considered her just a nuisance. He was dead scared of someone else. Someone he'd seen when they came out of the restaurant."

"She couldn't know what was goin' on in his mind." Wiggins snorted in derision. "That's the trouble with women—they always think they know everything."

"She didn't have to guess about him bein' as scared as a rabbit. Once we started talking, she started to remember some of the details. There was a man there by the restaurant—she remembered seeing him when they came outside. He was just standing there on the street, watching the door."

Luty stopped just inside the huge arched door that led to the Pattisons' ballroom. The orchestra was playing a Viennese waltz, and she stopped for a moment to watch the guests whirling across the dance floor. But she had work to do, and much as she enjoyed a good tune, she needed to get on with it.

She eased behind an overgrown potted fern so she could survey the situation without being bothered. She'd already cornered two of her bankers, Tobias Wade and Frank Harcourt, at the buffet table, but between bites of roast beef and sliced ham, it became obvious that neither of them knew anything about Thomas Mundy. So she'd handed her plate to a passing waiter and headed for the ballroom.

There was one more man who might be able to help her, and she hoped he'd be here. He wasn't the most sociable of fellows, but Geraldine Pattison had told her he'd been invited. Luty used her hands to hold the fern fronds apart so she could get a good look around the huge room. Her gaze moved slowly from the dancers to the people standing in small groups along the edge of the dance floor or sitting on the elegant chairs the Pattisons had provided for the elderly chaperones. Her hopes dimmed as she studied one bunch after another and saw neither hide nor hair of him. "Well, Nell's bells," she muttered softly. "Looks like this is goin' to be a wasted evening."

"Oh, I don't think so," a soft voice came from her left.

Startled, Luty let go of the fern fronds so quickly that one of them bashed her in the nose. She turned and found herself face-to-face with a dark-haired woman. She wore a bright red gown fitted close in the bodice and cut low enough to make a man take a second look but high enough so that she wouldn't be labeled "loose." She wore a diamond choker and matching earrings. An elegant hairstyle framed her lovely features, and though no longer in the first blush of youth, she was still very beautiful. Luty knew who she was, and apparently, she knew who Luty was.

"From what I've heard, Luty Belle Crookshank is far too smart a woman to waste anything as precious as time."

"I'm not sure that's a compliment." Luty cocked her head and took her measure.

"But it was," she insisted with an impish grin. "I don't waste time, either. Forgive me for being so bold, but I've been so wanting to meet you."

"That's right convenient—I've been hankerin' to meet you, too. You're Chloe Attwater." Luty extended her hand.

"Oh my goodness, you know who I am?" She took the proffered hand and laughed. "How wonderful. Come and sit with me for a few moments. I'd love to talk with you. We'll have some champagne."

"That's an offer I won't refuse." She glanced over Chloe's shoulder and saw the person she'd been hunting for come heading their way. But he wasn't looking at Luty; his gaze was on her companion.

Luty hesitated. Dang, what was she to do? He was her last hope when it came to finding out whether Mundy was doing any banking in London, but on the other hand, Chloe Attwater might be a useful source of information, too.

But the decision was taken out of her hands. "Do forgive me for interrupting, Luty, but I was afraid you'd disappear if I didn't corner you immediately." John Widdowes' words were directed at Luty, but he didn't take his eyes off Chloe. "And I hope you'll forgive me as well, Mrs. Attwater."

He was a middle-aged man with dark honey-colored hair graying at the temples, a burly build that was made of muscle, not fat, and a ready smile. He was also one of the founding members of Widdowes and Walthrop, Merchant Bankers, and rich as a maharaja. Luty and he had become friends when she'd gone to him for information on several of the inspector's previous cases.

Luty snickered. She'd never have thought in a month of Sundays she'd see that love-struck expression on this man's face. He was a tough, no-nonsense businessman who'd earned his wealth and his place in society the hard way; he'd worked for it. "Come on, John, you know I'd just about forgive you anything."

"You know my name?" Chloe said, staring at him curiously. "You look very familiar. Have we met?"

"Not formally." John's smile grew wider.

"Oh dang, where are my manners," Luty interrupted. She needed to get this show on the road and find out something useful. She wanted to get home and see if Hatchet had replied to the telegram she'd sent on her way here. "Mrs. Attwater, this is my friend John Widdowes."

"How do you do, Mr. Widdowes." She nodded politely.

"Please, call me John," he insisted. "I'm delighted to finally make your acquaintance, Mrs. Attwater. I've been hoping to meet you."

Her eyebrows rose. "Really? Should I be flattered or frightened?"

He laughed. "Luty can vouch for me. I'm a decent enough fellow. I've heard about you, Mrs. Attwater. People call you a free thinker and an intelligent woman."

"And you wanted to find out for yourself whether that was true," Chloe interrupted. "Fair enough, it's true. I am very much a free thinker. I support publicly funded education for both sexes as well as a woman's right to vote and to hold political office. If the truth be told, I've heard about you as well. From what I understand, you don't suffer fools gladly, and you give to what some would call 'radical causes.'"

"Guilty as charged." He looked enormously pleased. "And I have a sneaking suspicion that you and I probably support the very same 'radical causes.' I, too, believe in universal suffrage, and, frankly, from what I know of politics, I suspect that if women were in charge, things might be done a bit more efficiently."

Luty poked John on the arm. As interesting as this conversation was, she had things she needed to find out. "Can we go sit down? My feet are hurting, I'm thirsty, and if we don't find a table for three, one of these old bores is goin' to join us, and then I won't be able to find out a danged thing."

"Of course." Chloe pushed past John. "Let's go into the buffet room. We'll have that champagne."

John offered his arm to Luty as they followed Chloe out of the ballroom. "On the hunt, I see."

"Danged right," Luty retorted. "And apparently, so are you."

Witherspoon was dead tired when he got home. He unbuttoned his coat and swept off his bowler.

"You look exhausted, sir." Mrs. Jeffries reached for his garments and hung them on the coat tree. "Would you care for a sherry, or would you like to have your meal straightaway?" She was a bit scattered at the moment. Phyllis and Wiggins were barely speaking to each other, and she hadn't a clue what to do about the situation. Their meeting had run a bit longer than they'd wanted, which put the cook behind in getting his dinner ready, and to top it off, Mrs. Goodge had received a note from one of her sources announcing he was coming by tonight! All in all, it would be best to get the inspector safely tucked in his study for a couple of glasses of Harveys so that the household could get his meal on the table and get him safely up to bed before there was a visitor in the kitchen.

"A sherry would be lovely." He headed for his study, and she trailed after him. He settled into his overstuffed chair, and she went to the liquor cabinet. Mrs. Jeffries poured them both a glass of sherry. She deliberately left the sherry bottle on top of the cabinet in the hopes that he'd have more than one drink. Tonight, she needed him to be very, very sleepy.

"Here you are, sir." She handed him his drink and took her usual spot. "Now, do tell me about your day. I can see that you've made progress."

He took a quick sip, sighed pleasurably, and stared at her over the rim of his glass. "How can you tell?"

She laughed. "Because you look so tired, sir. You only wear that expression when you've learned a great deal of information. Don't tease me, sir. You know how much I like hearing about your work."

"As usual, you're correct." He took another sip and closed his eyes for a moment. "It was an incredibly eventful day. I'm not sure where to begin. So I'll start from this morning."

"That would be excellent, sir," she agreed.

"Well, the first thing that transpired was we got confirmation that there were indeed lead weights in Mundy's walking stick," he began. "But we've not finished examining all of Mundy's personal effects, so we've no real idea what else we might find out about the fellow. By the time we finished interviewing all the witnesses today, I simply didn't have the heart to drag Constable Barnes back to the station."

Surprised, she stared at him. "No one at the station went through his things yesterday evening?"

"They did their best, but there were a number of arrests last night, and they simply didn't have time to do a proper search. I instructed Constable Griffiths to put Mundy's possessions in the inspector's office so that either Constable Barnes or I could give them a thorough inspection this morning. We meant to get back to the station after we'd finished the interviews today, but honestly, there were simply too many of them. It's amazing how many people there are going to and fro in a hotel. It took hours to get through them all."

"But you spoke to everyone?" she clarified.

"Oh yes, but before I could even begin the staff interviews, the most extraordinary thing happened." He told her about their encounter with Jennifer Payton.

Mrs. Jeffries sipped her sherry as she listened. When he finished, she asked the first of her questions. "Do you believe her, sir?"

Witherspoon stared at his now-empty glass. "I think so. She was quite distraught, and after she freely admitted that she'd followed him from their appointment the night before, I'm inclined to believe she was telling the truth."

Mrs. Jeffries got to her feet and reached for the inspector's glass. "Would you like another, sir?" He nodded, and she went to the cabinet and poured them each a second one. "Did she realize she was admitting to being at the scene of the crime near the time of the murder?"

"Not immediately, but she understood very soon after we started questioning her." He smiled his thanks as she gave him his drink and took her seat.

"You said she lent Mundy the fifty pounds seven months ago. What made her suddenly want her money repaid?" Mrs. Jeffries asked. She already knew the answer, but she wanted to know what Jennifer Payton had said in her official statement.

"She told us that she needed the money she'd lent Mundy to repay a debt to a relative."

"And he'd agreed to repay her immediately?" Again, she wanted to determine how honest the woman had been with her answers.

"That's what he promised."

"Yet she followed him to make sure she knew where he was staying?"

Witherspoon smiled faintly. "She admitted that even though they'd known each other years ago, she didn't quite trust him. Which makes me wonder why she lent him money in the first place."

Mrs. Jeffries knew the answer to that as well. Greed was a very powerful motivator, and Mundy had promised to repay with fifty percent interest.

"She was right not to trust him," Witherspoon continued. "Miss Payton wasn't the only person who seemed to think Thomas Mundy might not be an upstanding citizen." He told her about their interview with Laverne Hamlin.

"So Mrs. Hamlin was convinced that Mundy was, as she put it, 'running scared.' Do you think he knew someone was going to try to kill him?" This was now the third person who had noticed Thomas Mundy behaving with undue caution. The bellboy at the hotel had watched him stop every few feet and look over his shoulder, and Jennifer Payton almost had to run to keep him in view as he raced down Oxford Street. Surely, that had to mean that Mundy knew he was in danger? Or did it?

"It's impossible to know with any certainty." He took another sip. "From what we're learning about the victim, it is beginning to look as if he's had a long career as a confidence trickster. Perhaps being overly careful was a habit he'd developed over the years. Perhaps always watching his back was what kept him out of prison."

Mrs. Jeffries was thinking along those same lines herself. "Unfortunately for him, his vigilance didn't keep him from being murdered. But if he was so careful, why would he let the killer into his room?"

101

"He may not have realized that person was a danger to him," Witherspoon said. "Again, at this point in the investigation, there's a lot we simply don't know. But we did learn quite a bit today." He told her about his interviews with the rest of the staff. Mrs. Jeffries listened carefully, hoping that she could recall the information properly so she could share it at their morning meeting. But as he continued, she realized she was simply going to have to write everything down before she went to bed. There was too much for her to remember.

Chloe Attwater led them to a table partially hidden by a row of potted evergreens. "I thought we'd have more privacy here," she explained. She smiled at a passing waiter carrying a tray of champagne, and he immediately changed course and headed in their direction. She waited till the young man had served each of them a glass and retreated before she spoke. "I almost didn't come tonight. I don't generally like social functions of this size."

"I prefer smaller functions as well," John said, "but I'm glad I made an exception in this case; otherwise I'd not have met you, nor would I have had an opportunity to visit with Luty."

Luty threw caution to the wind. She wasn't sure how much she *ought* to admit, but if she was going to find out anything tonight, she had to risk speaking up. She'd learned to listen to her instincts, and right now, they were telling her that this woman was someone who could be trusted. Besides, she'd been a suspect in one of the inspector's most recent cases, and as far as Luty could tell, Chloe had kept the details of certain aspects of that investigation to herself.

"I'm glad you both came, because I'm needin' some information, and I was hopin' you"—Luty looked at John—"would be able to help me."

He took a sip of champagne. "If it's about your inspector's latest murder, I'm not sure I'll be of much use. I never met Thomas Mundy."

"I did," Chloe said softly. "He lived in San Francisco for a time. That's why I wanted to meet you, Mrs. Crookshank. When I read in the newspaper that Inspector Witherspoon was in charge of this case, I knew I had to tell one of you, uh, I mean someone close to the inspector, what I know about Mundy."

"Call me Luty, please."

"I will, if you'll call me Chloe."

"Exactly what is it you know?"

"Thomas Mundy is a confidence trickster," Chloe said, "but I suspect you already knew that."

"We do. But how do you know him? Did he try one of his schemes on you?" Luty picked up her champagne. She found it doubtful that Chloe Attwater had been taken in by someone like Mundy. The woman struck her as too smart and sophisticated to fall for a glib tale of easy money.

"Not on me, but on one of my friends. Before I came back to England, I lived in San Francisco for many years. So did Thomas Mundy. He set himself up as an agent for a group of investors from New York."

"Which is exactly what he did here in England," John murmured.

"I thought you didn't know anything about him?" Luty charged.

"I said I'd never met him, not that I'd never heard of him," John replied. "But please, do let Mrs. Attwater tell us the rest."

"Call me Chloe." She smiled at Widdowes. "As I was saying, Mundy tried one of his schemes on an elderly friend of mine. Luckily, before he could relieve her of any of her cash, he had to leave town in a hurry. Someone he'd cheated in Los Angeles had shown up in the city, and this person wasn't just looking for his money back. He was out for blood."

"You mean he wanted Mundy dead?" Luty put her glass down.

"That's right, and Mundy must have realized he was in danger, because he struck first."

"Struck first how?" Luty demanded. "Did he kill him?"

"He tried to. The man was found half-dead in an alley off Market Street. He'd been beaten around the head, half his ribs were smashed, and one of his arms was broken."

"Why didn't Mundy finish him off?" John asked. "I'm assuming that Mundy was his attacker."

"He wasn't." She grimaced in disgust. "He hired some thugs to do his dirty work, and, luckily for Daniel Wright, the police showed up before they were able to finish the job."

"That's the man's name?" John asked.

"Yes, and what Mundy did to him was more than just a confidence trick," Chloe said. "Wright was a builder, and he was working on a commercial structure in Los Angeles. He borrowed a hefty sum of money from his fiancée's father to fund the project and kept most of it in cash in his safe. His suppliers, vendors, and workers were paid in cash. Mundy worked hard to earn Wright's trust and quickly became his assistant. He took care of all the paperwork, but Wright took care of the money. Only he had the combination to the safe."

"Had he memorized it?" John asked.

"No, and that was his downfall. He kept it written on a slip of paper in his wallet. Mundy drugged him, got the combination, and stole every last cent. Wright couldn't pay anyone. He lost everything, including his fiancée."

"But it wasn't his fault. He didn't know Mundy would drug him," Luty protested.

"Mundy was clever. When he drugged Wright, they were having a drink at a saloon near the building. When Wright woke up, he found himself in an upstairs bedroom with a, shall we say, 'lady of the evening.' She'd been drugged, too, and she pointed the finger at Daniel Wright and claimed he'd put something in her drink. He was arrested, and there was an awful scandal. He was completely ruined and barely escaped a lengthy prison sentence."

"How do you know all this?" Luty stared at her curiously.

"I made it my business to know. Mundy tried to cheat someone I cared about. Once the rumors started circulating about why Mundy suddenly left San Francisco, it wasn't hard to find out the details." She glanced up and spotted Geraldine Pattison making a beeline for their hiding place. "Oh dear, we've been spotted. Before she gets here, let me tell you the rest. Daniel Wright is here in London. He's staying at a small lodging house in Hammersmith. I have the address, if you want it."

"He's gone to bed, Mrs. Goodge," Mrs. Jeffries said as she came quietly into the kitchen. "And I've told Phyllis and Wiggins to go up as well. I'm hoping a good night's sleep will bring both of them to their senses."

"I don't know what's got into those two. Wiggins used to

be so sweet to Phyllis, treated her like a little sister and was always watching out for her. Now he watches her like a jealous old tomcat." Mrs. Goodge shook her head in confusion. The lad was like a grandson to her, and she'd do anything in her power to make sure he was happy. But on the other hand, she knew firsthand what it was like to be a young woman alone in the world, and she was glad that Phyllis was standing up for herself.

"I don't know, either." Mrs. Jeffries shrugged and glanced toward the back door. "What time is your source arriving?"

"He should be here any minute. His note said he'd try to come by nine fifteen." Mrs. Goodge stifled a yawn. She liked to be in her room with her feet up as soon as dinner was over.

Both women paused as they heard a faint rapping at the back door.

"I'll get it." Mrs. Jeffries hurried out of the room and raced down the hall. She opened the door, and a tall man swept off his hat. "Good evening. My name is Howard Burrell. I believe Mrs. Goodge is expecting me." In his hand was a small parcel wrapped in brown paper.

"How do you do. I'm Hepzibah Jeffries, the housekeeper. Please come in." She stepped to one side so he could enter and then led him into the kitchen.

Mrs. Goodge got to her feet. "Howard, how nice of you to take the time to come. Please sit down. Would you like a cup of tea?"

"If it's all the same to you"—he yanked the brown paper off the parcel, revealing a bottle of fine Irish whiskey—"I thought we might enjoy a drop of this. As I recall, you used to like it well enough."

"My goodness, you remember." She laughed and headed for

the sideboard. "Have a seat at the table, Howard, and I'll get us some glasses."

Mrs. Jeffries caught the cook's eye. "Mrs. Goodge, I'll retire if it's all the same to you." She nodded at their visitor. "Good night, Mr. Burrell. It was nice meeting you."

Mrs. Goodge put the glasses on the table and reached for the bottle he'd thoughtfully opened. She poured them both a shot of whiskey. "Thank you for coming. I know it's hard for you to get out these days. How is Maisie doing?"

Howard smiled sadly. "The same. Some days she knows me, but most of the time, she doesn't. Our daughter is staying with us for a few days. That's why I was able to get out tonight. Her train didn't get in until half seven, and I had to get her settled in with Maisie before I could leave."

Howard Burrell and Mrs. Goodge had worked together many years earlier when he had been the butler and she the cook. Retired, he and his wife lived in Fulham. Unfortunately, Maisie was going senile. Mrs. Goodge had sent him a note asking for his help for a good reason. After leaving the country house where they'd both worked, Howard had taken a position in Leicestershire with a man widely thought to be a well-educated, well-spoken criminal.

"Why have you asked me to come?" he continued. "I know I owe you a lot, and I know what you did for me back when we worked together. You kept your mouth shut so I could keep my job. I know you work for a policeman, but no matter how much I owe you, I'll not answer any questions about my former employer. I know what people say about him, but I'll not say a word against him. He was good to me, and when he saw what was happening with Maisie, he let me retire with a decent pension."

Mrs. Goodge was a bit hurt. "Just because I work for a policeman doesn't mean I'd betray my old friends."

"I'm sorry. I shouldn't have said what I said. You've always been loyal to your friends, and if it hadn't been for you, the Wainrights would have chucked me out in the cold for leaving the wine cellar unlocked."

She laughed. "They were furious when they found that door open and half their precious wine gone. To this day, I'm sure it was their son who stole those bottles. They'd cut off his allowance, and some of that wine was very valuable."

"Probably, but it was me that left the door unlocked, and you told Mr. Wainright that you'd seen me lock it with your own eyes. That saved me. Now, let's start over, and I'll not be such a suspicious old fellow. Why did you send for me?"

"I asked you here to find out if you know anything about a man named Thomas Mundy."

Burrell looked puzzled. "Mundy . . . You mean the fellow who was murdered in that hotel?"

She took a quick sip. "That's right. Mundy used to live in the East Midlands, in a town called Market Harborough. That's close to where you and Maisie worked. I was hoping you might have heard the name before and could tell me something about him."

He tapped the rim of his glass, his expression thoughtful. Finally, he shrugged. "If I'd heard of the man, I've forgotten. But Maisie and I came to London over five years ago when she inherited the flat from her uncle. I'm sorry, but I don't think I can help you."

Mrs. Goodge had known from the start that it would be a miracle if Howard knew anything. Nonetheless, she was still disappointed. "Well, it was still good of you to come and see me." She lifted her glass. "I know you don't have long to visit, so let's just have a nice chat about the old days."

"I'd like that." He lifted his drink and they clinked their glasses. "I'll tell you what—I've still got a lot of connections in the Midlands. I can send a letter or two and find out what sort of gossip there might be about this fellow."

Mrs. Goodge thought quickly. "That would be wonderful, Howard, but you can't let anyone know that you're doin' the askin' for me or the police. You've got to make it look like gossip about a dead man."

CHAPTER 5

Early the next morning, Mrs. Goodge and Mrs. Jeffries met with Constable Barnes, but he didn't add much to what Mrs. Jeffries had already found out from the inspector the night before. She and Cook told him everything they'd learned.

"Fifty percent interest." Barnes shook his head. "That explains Jennifer Payton's real motive for lending Mundy money." He downed the last of his tea and got to his feet. "You've all done well, but I wish we had more information about this death up in the Midlands that Mundy might have been involved with."

"We know it happened six or seven months back and that it took place in Hinckley," Mrs. Goodge added. "Can't you start with that? How many deaths could there be? It's a smallish sort of town."

"Not that small," Barnes replied with a grin. "And if that's all we have to go on, I'll look into it and see if anything catches my eye. But it would be good to have some additional information. Do you think you'll be able to find out more?"

"We're hoping that Hatchet might have heard something about it," Mrs. Jeffries said. "If that's the case, we might have more details by tomorrow, if, of course, he returns home today."

"Good, let's leave it until tomorrow, then." He nodded politely and disappeared up the stairs.

Five minutes later, he and the inspector left by the front door just as Smythe came in the back.

"Where are Betsy and the baby?" Mrs. Goodge demanded.

"Home. It's rainin' out there and the little one has a cold, so Betsy's keepin' her indoors today." He took his usual seat at the table. "But I've got my instructions. I'm to remember everything and report back."

Mrs. Goodge grabbed the kettle from the cooker, turned back to the table, and slipped the lid off the teapot. She topped it up with boiling water. "How bad a cold?"

"It's just a sniffle, but you know Betsy. She says it's better to be safe than sorry."

Yawning, Wiggins strolled into the kitchen. "Cor blimey, I 'ate to be out on the hunt when it's wet. It's right miserable and most people stay inside. It's bloomin' hard to find out any . . ." His voice trailed off as they heard footsteps on the back stairs and Phyllis appeared carrying the inspector's breakfast dishes on a tray.

She came down the stairs gingerly until she reached the bottom, when something caught her attention and she stopped, her gaze on the back door. "I think Luty's here."

"I'll let her in," Mrs. Jeffries offered. "You take the dishes on in. We've a lot of ground to cover today, and we need to get the meeting started quickly."

"Good morning." Phyllis gave Smythe a friendly nod as she crossed the kitchen and put the tray down next to the sink. "Where's the rest of the family?"

"Home. Amanda has the sniffles, so Betsy's keepin' her inside," he replied just as Luty and Mrs. Jeffries reached the archway.

"What, you mean my baby ain't here?" Luty protested. "Nell's bells, I was lookin' forward to seein' her."

"She'll be right as rain tomorrow." He pulled out a chair for the elderly American. "You can see her then." He flicked a quick glance at Wiggins, who had his head down, looking at his tea, but Smythe could see that his eyes moved as he sneaked fast peeks at the maid. So that's it, he thought to himself. He'd noticed there'd been a sea change in the relationship between these two, and he now had a sneaking suspicion he understood what was driving it.

Ignoring the footman, Phyllis took the chair next to Luty while Mrs. Goodge poured the tea.

"If I'd known we was in a hurry, I'da not been so late," Luty said, "but I wanted to wait and make sure Hatchet hadn't sent another telegram."

"Is he still in the Midlands?" Mrs. Jeffries picked up the sheaf of notes she'd set on the sideboard.

"Yup, there was a telegram waiting for me when I got home last night. He said he's on the trail and he'll be back in time for our afternoon meeting."

"Let me bring everyone up to date on what we've learned from the inspector. But you'll need to listen carefully," she warned as she sat down. "I have a lot to tell you."

"So do I. I think I hit the mother lode last night." Luty grinned. "Too bad Hatchet isn't here. It's not as much fun without him here to get his nose out of joint."

Everyone laughed, and when they settled down, Mrs. Jeffries began reading her notes. She went slowly, adding the details she could recall and hoping she wasn't inadvertently leaving out something important. When she got to the end, she took a deep breath. "There, that should do it. Any questions?"

"Cor blimey, sounds like Mundy had bamboozled more than one person. 'Ow many of 'em was at the hotel lookin' for 'im?" Wiggins asked.

"Jennifer Payton and another woman," Mrs. Jeffries said. "But what I find most interesting is Laverne Hamlin's statement about the man who asked a bellboy about Mundy and then pretended to the maître d' that he had a dinner engagement with Mundy."

"An engagement that he didn't keep," Mrs. Goodge reminded them. "He was the one tryin' to find out about the dead man, and he was doin' it on the sly. That means he didn't want anyone connectin' him to Mundy."

"It does sound that way." Mrs. Jeffries thought for a moment. "But if he didn't actually meet with the victim—and according to Mrs. Hamlin's statement, he didn't—then why was he asking about Mundy?"

"Maybe he was the man spotted by the waiter who was under the stairs changin' into his uniform?" Wiggins suggested.

"But that man was there hours before the murder," Luty pointed out. "The truth is, none of this is goin' to make sense with what we know so far. We've got to keep diggin'."

"But it is confusing," Mrs. Jeffries admitted.

"You'll sort it out, Mrs. Jeffries," Phyllis said. "You always do. Too bad we've no idea who these two mystery people might be. It'll be hard for the inspector to find them."

"He'll manage," Wiggins muttered. "And if 'e don't, we will."

"It might not be as hard as you think," Luty interjected. She looked at Mrs. Jeffries. "Did you say that the man the Hamlin woman saw had blond hair?"

"That's how she described him to the inspector. Why?"

Luty chuckled. "Oh Lordy, Lordy, this is killin' me. I'd love to save it till Hatchet got back so I could see the smoke comin' out of his ears, but I know we need to get movin'."

"Luty, stop teasin'," the cook ordered. "You found out something last night, so go ahead and tell us what it is. When Hatchet gets back, we'll brag to high heaven about how clever you've been."

"I'll hold you to that." Luty looked as if she weren't joking. "Alright then, here's what I found out."

"There doesn't seem to be much here." The inspector sighed and dropped the pair of trousers he'd just searched onto the heap of clothes at his feet. He and Constable Barnes were in the duty office at the Ladbroke Road Police Station, searching through Thomas Mundy's personal effects. Witherspoon looked at the open suitcase propped on the floor next to the window. A shaving kit and small leather case were lying inside. "For goodness' sake, we've gone through everything and found nothing."

Barnes reached for a suit coat, the last of the man's clothing, and stuck his hand in the top inside pocket. "His leather traveling case contained some nice cuff links, and that diamond stickpin is worth a pretty penny. Mind you, let's hope his heirs, if we can find one, won't get nasty over the fact that we ripped out the linings on all his things."

"We really had no choice," Witherspoon muttered. They'd gone through his suitcase, his shaving kit, and a small leather travel case, and left the clothes for last. They had examined them one piece at a time and were down to the last few garments. "I shouldn't worry about his next of kin. There was nothing among his things indicating he had any relatives. In which case it'll be up to the law to dispose of all this."

"I don't see how he lived, sir." Barnes slipped his hands inside the jacket and searched the top breast pocket but found nothing. "He paid his bills at the hotel and the restaurant with cash. But we've not found so much as a farthing or a letter of credit or even a deposit book for the ruddy post office. The lads went over his room twice and found nothing. So where's the money? What was he living on?"

"That is what worries me." Witherspoon picked up the last item, a blue brocade waistcoat, and searched the front watch pocket. Nothing. "It could well be that the motive for Mundy's murder was robbery. As you pointed out, he used cash, and perhaps someone noticed that he didn't get it from one of the local banks."

"You mean they figured out he had money in his room, followed him there, and killed him for it?" Barnes slipped his hand into the outside pocket and ran his fingers along the bottom of the fabric until he came to a spot where it was ripped. He rammed his index finger into the tear and felt it brush something.

"That is certainly a possible solution." The inspector flattened the garment against the top of the desk and ran his fingers along the seams before rubbing the fabric from the top to the bottom. "Nothing here, either. But aside from the money question, Mundy obviously wasn't running a business. He had no records, no invoices, no ledgers, nothing."

"I've got something, sir." Barnes wiggled his whole hand into the opening, tearing the fabric in the process, and pulled out a small, folded-up piece of paper. He flattened it out and held it up. "This was in the lining of the coat pocket." He scanned it quickly, his brow wrinkling as he focused his eyes on the small handwritten print. "It looks like a list of names and addresses, sir. There are three of them."

He handed it to Witherspoon, who read through it quickly. "The first one is Marianne Pelletier, the Bainbridge Hotel."

Barnes pointed to the next name. "Ronald Hart, twelve Florian Street, Bayswater. The last one is Daniel Wright, eight Harding Road, Hammersmith."

"Two men and a woman. I wonder why he had their names on a list and why it was hidden in his jacket lining," Witherspoon said.

"I don't think it was." Barnes picked up the discarded jacket and turned the pocket inside out. "There was a hole in this pocket. It's bigger now because I stuck my hand through it, but originally, it was small enough that the paper could have slipped into it."

"Which means it wasn't hidden at all, but even if that is the case, why did Mundy have these names written on the list? This is the second time Ronald Hart's name has come up. The waiter saw him at the Wrexley on the day Mundy was murdered. I think we'd best go have a chat with Mr. Hart, and after that, we'll see if Marianne Pelletier is still at the Bainbridge Hotel."

"What about Daniel Wright, sir?"

"We'll see him last. Hammersmith is further out than the other two."

Barnes nodded and dropped the coat jacket onto the heap. "Which one should we visit first, sir? Bayswater is closer than the Bainbridge Hotel."

"Then Mr. Hart will be our first interview."

It took less than twenty minutes to get to number 12 Florian Street. Barnes paid the hansom cab and then joined the inspector, who waited for him on the pavement.

A small green garden lined with rosebushes and enclosed by a black wrought-iron fence surrounded the five-story redbrick Georgian house. The paint on the door and the window frames was a brilliant white, the brass door lamps were polished to a high gloss, and there wasn't so much as a weed or a pebble on the brick walkway leading to the wide front steps.

"It appears that Mr. Hart is doing quite well." Witherspoon studied the property. "This place must cost a fortune to maintain. There isn't so much as a crumbling brick or a bit of flaking paint anywhere about the place."

"That's true, sir. He must have money. Perhaps that's why he was on Mundy's list." Barnes looked at Witherspoon. "He was a confidence trickster, sir. Perhaps those three names were his next targets."

"That is possible," Witherspoon admitted, "but I've a feeling it's more than that." Slightly embarrassed, he looked away. Mrs. Jeffries was always telling him to trust his "inner voice," and right now, that voice was telling him that the names on Mundy's list weren't just possible victims for one of the man's confidence schemes. But police officers were supposed to deal in nothing but cold, hard facts, not "feelings" or an "inner voice."

"I do, too, sir," Barnes murmured. "Mundy didn't strike me as the type to put the names of his marks in writing. Besides, the fact that both Hart and Mundy are from the same town in the Midlands strikes me as more than a coincidence."

"I agree. What's more, Market Harborough isn't a very large town, so even if Mr. Hart has nothing to do with Mundy's murder, there is a chance he might know something useful about the victim. Of course, if he's never met the man, he can tell us and we'll be on our way."

Barnes pushed open the gate, and they went to the front door. He banged the knocker, and a moment later the door opened a crack. "Yes, what do you want?"

"We'd like to speak to Mr. Ronald Hart." Barnes drew himself up straighter. "Would that be you?"

"Certainly not." The door opened wider, revealing a tall, long-faced man wearing a butler's uniform. His lip curled as he looked the constable up and down. "The master is indisposed and not receiving."

"Who the devil is it?" an angry voice called from inside the house.

"The police, sir. They said they want to speak to you." The butler spoke without taking his gaze off them.

"Is that Mr. Hart who is speaking?" Barnes edged closer.

The butler ignored him. "What shall I do, sir?"

"Ask them what it's regarding."

"It's important, Mr. Hart." Barnes raised his voice so it would carry into the house.

"Important how?"

"It's about a murder, sir." The constable was losing patience and struggled not to let it show.

Apparently, Witherspoon was getting annoyed as well, because he leaned closer to the partially open door. "Mr. Hart," he yelled, "it's about the murder of Thomas Mundy. Now, as we only want to ask you some questions, you can either speak to us here or come down to the station. It's your choice, sir."

From inside, the voice faded a bit. "Oh for God's sake, let them in so I can see what the devil they want. I'll talk to them in the drawing room."

The butler stepped back and opened the door wide. "Come

in, then." His expression left no doubt as to his thoughts on being forced to admit the police. "The drawing room is this way. Follow me."

They stepped across the threshold into a brightly lighted foyer. A carved Queen Anne sideboard topped with a gold-framed mirror stood on one side of the space, and across from it was a round, claw-foot walnut table holding a huge red vase of elegantly arranged flowers in every imaginable color. The walls of the long hallway were covered in a red and cream diamond-patterned wallpaper. A curved staircase led to the upper floors.

They followed the butler down the corridor to a set of double doors leading to an enormous drawing room. Separate sets of matching furniture were grouped together at each end of the room. Sofas upholstered in red, blue, and white flowers were flanked by side tables covered with gold and red fringed table runners. Directly opposite the sofas were matching love seats and wing chairs. On the far wall was a black marble fireplace. A brass lion, two feet tall, stood sentinel on each side of the hearth. A portrait in a gold frame and at least ten feet tall was hung over the mantel. It depicted a sandy-haired man who, dressed in a red military uniform, stood next to a rearing horse.

A man who looked very much like the face in the portrait was sitting on the love seat nearer the door. But unlike the picture, he was dressed in a normal gray day suit and a white shirt. His knees were splayed apart, and he was leaning forward, glaring at them. "Do you know who I am?"

"Hopefully you're Ronald Hart," Witherspoon said calmly. "Otherwise both you and your butler have wasted the police's time."

The man's jaw dropped in shock, and even Barnes was a bit surprised. Witherspoon was rarely aggressive with witnesses.

"How dare you." He sat bolt upright. "You, sir, are nothing more than a public servant who should know his place. One word from me to your superiors and I'll have your job."

"By all means. My immediate superior is Superintendent Scott at the Ladbroke Road Police Station, or if you wish to go over his head, you might contact Chief Superintendent Barrows. He's at Scotland Yard. Now, if you're through threatening me, I'd like to ask you some questions. First of all, can you verify you are Ronald Hart?"

He seemed to deflate a bit. "I am. What of it?"

"Where are you from, Mr. Hart?" Witherspoon asked.

"Why is that any business of the police?" The bluster was back full force. "But if you must know, I'm from Leicestershire. My family has a large estate outside Market Harborough."

"Do you know a man named Thomas Mundy?" Barnes interjected.

Hart looked from one man to the next before fixing his gaze on the constable's uniform. "Do you often speak out in front of your superiors?"

"Constable Barnes is my colleague and a respected member of this investigation. Please answer his question." The inspector shifted slightly. He'd swept his bowler off when entering the house and wished he could shed his coat as well. The room was warm, and it didn't appear that Hart was going to offer them a chair any time soon.

"Yes, I know him. He's from Market Harborough as well. But we certainly didn't move in the same social circles—he was hardly a friend. I believe he lived in one of those dreadful row houses near the foundry, or perhaps it was the pea-flour factory."

"In what capacity did you know him?" Witherspoon asked.

"Whatever do you mean? I don't understand your question."

"You said yourself that you weren't social acquaintances or friends, yet you know that he lived in a row house."

Hart shrugged. "He worked for a local law firm that my late uncle used. He was their clerk, and he came to our home several times with legal papers. I've a good memory, and I once overheard him telling one of our housemaids that he lived in a row house close to the city center."

"When was the last time you saw Mr. Mundy?"

"I've not seen the fellow in twenty years." He folded his arms over his chest, crossed his legs, and leaned back against the upholstery. "He left the country years ago." He frowned suddenly. "Why do you ask? Is he back in London? Has he been using my name, telling people that we're old friends? If that's the case, you must stop him immediately. I won't have someone of his class and character using my good name to feather his nest."

"Not as far as we know, sir." The inspector glanced at Barnes and gave a barely perceptible nod, indicating that he was to ask whatever questions he liked.

The constable smiled slightly as he spoke. "Mr. Hart, I understand you have political aspirations."

"That's right, and I'll not have someone like Mundy claiming a familiarity with me that doesn't exist."

"I should think someone running for public office would do a better job of being informed," Barnes continued softly. "Thomas Mundy was murdered the night before last. It's been in all the newspapers."

Hart looked surprised for a moment and then gave a negligent shrug. "I don't read the gutter press. I can't say that I'm shocked. Mundy was a pushy sort of person, always trying to get above himself. He had a way of attracting trouble, and it appears he hasn't changed. Now, if that's all you've come to ask me, be on your way." He started to get up.

"We're not quite finished." Witherspoon held up his hand. "You claim you've not seen the victim in twenty years, but we've had it on good authority that you were at his hotel on the morning of the day he was murdered. You were seen and recognized when you came in the back door."

Hart's eyes widened. "I don't know who told you such nonsense"—he got to his feet—"but it isn't true. I haven't been to the Wrexley Hotel in months."

"How do you know Mundy was at the Wrexley?" Barnes said. "You claim you hadn't read the papers and didn't even know he was dead."

He looked confused for a second, and then he jerked his chin toward the inspector. "He must have mentioned the name when he started haranguing me with his questions."

"No, I didn't," Witherspoon said. "Now, again, I ask you, were you at the Wrexley the day before yesterday?"

"What if I was?"

"If you were, then I would ask you why you didn't admit it when I asked you the first time."

"I'm not in the habit of explaining myself to simple public functionaries, Inspector."

"Nonetheless, sir, I suggest that you do. We do have it in our power to ask you to accompany us to the station to help with our inquiries."

"You wouldn't dare."

"I would, sir, and I certainly believe that you can make life difficult for me. I imagine I can make it equally difficult for you. The 'gutter press' as you call it would love to print that someone as rich and powerful as yourself refused to cooperate in a murder investigation." Witherspoon stared at him. "And if you are indeed interested in a political career, that won't do your public image much good."

Hart's eyes narrowed in anger, but then he gave an exasperated sigh. "Alright, you've made your point. But I shan't forget this."

"Neither will I," Witherspoon responded softly. "Now, tell me why you were at the Wrexley."

"I went there to meet someone who could help me with my political career. But the gentleman made it clear that no one was to know we'd met."

"Why was it necessary to meet so secretly?"

"It's a bit awkward. There's soon going to be a vacancy on the county council."

"Vacancy? But I don't see how. The council election was last March, and the next one isn't until March of 1898," Witherspoon said. Because of his relationship with Lady Cannonberry, he was now very well informed about politics. He and Ruth spent hours talking about the latest developments in both the local and national political situations. She knew and understood how government worked and who was or was not powerful and influential. She was always sending off letters, writing petitions, and occasionally, even demonstrating in front of Parliament. As she often put it, politicians were all men, and they weren't going to hand women the right to vote without a fight.

"This vacancy would be filled because one of the current council members is very ill." Hart folded his arms over his chest defensively. "And I wanted to ensure that the gentleman in question gave me his support when the time was right."

"Is he resigning?" Barnes asked.

"No, and that is the reason my meeting with this person must be kept quiet."

"If the current councilor isn't resigning, then you must be waiting for him to die? Is that correct?" Witherspoon hoped he didn't sound as horrified as he felt.

"I wouldn't put it like that, Inspector, but the fellow simply isn't long for this world. I'm certainly qualified for the position, and I've the support of the party. But it would be very bad form if word got out that we were having meetings about such a delicate matter. Hence, the need for discretion. Good Lord, if it became public knowledge, that would make me sound monstrous!"

"What did she look like?" Smythe crossed his arms over his chest and fixed the cab driver with a hard stare. He'd spent a good part of the day talking to hansom drivers, and this was the first one who could recall taking a blonde woman to the Wrexley the day before the murder.

The cabbie wasn't in the least intimidated. "She was wearin' a fancy gold and gray plaid jacket with fur trimming. Her hat had fur on it, too."

"What else do you remember?"

He smiled slyly. "Could be my memory isn't as sharp as it used to be."

Smythe reached into his coat and pulled out a coin. "Will this help your memory?"

"It'll help a bit." The hansom driver, a balding, portly man wearing an old herringbone jacket and brown bowler hat, reached for the florin. "It's all comin' back to me. She was a right pretty woman and carried herself like a queen. I noticed that when she got out and walked into the hotel."

"Do you remember where you picked her up?" Smythe asked.

"On the Uxbridge Road. She waved me over when I dropped a fare at the Weeping Angel Pub. She was coming out of the Bainbridge Hotel. That's right next door."

"What time of day was it?"

"I don't know exactly, but I'd had a cup of tea at the cabman's shelter and that was at four o'clock." His brow furrowed as he thought back. "Then I got the fare for the pub, and then I picked up the lady. The traffic was bad, though, so it must have been close to a quarter to five or so when I dropped her off."

"Do you remember anything else?"

He shook his head and turned to his horse. He stroked her face, and she whinnied softly. "Look, I know you've paid me, but honestly, what I told you is all I know about the lady. This old horse here needs plenty of food, and if I don't work, she don't get fed, so unless you're goin' to hire me, I've got to go." Without waiting for an answer, he climbed up onto his seat, picked up the reins, and pulled away from the curb.

Smythe almost called him back because he was in need of a hansom, but then he thought better of it; it wouldn't do to have too many people know that someone other than the police were looking for the mystery woman. He waited till the cab was out of sight before he turned and headed in the direction of the Uxbridge Road.

Phyllis stopped on the corner and studied the shops on both sides of the busy High Street. Now that she had some names to work with, she was happier than she'd been yesterday. But considering the circumstances, she was quite proud of her previous efforts. Despite being scared to death, she'd gone into the Wrexley and then followed Jennifer Payton. But she was grateful that today all she had to do was chat up the shopkeepers and clerks in Ronald Hart's neighborhood. Constable Barnes had given Mrs. Jeffries his address. Phyllis thought the link between Hart and the dead man was flimsy, but it was a place to start. The only other name they had was Daniel Wright, and according to Luty's source, he lived in a lodging house in Hammersmith, which was a bit too far away.

Phyllis walked slowly up the street, looking into shopwindows as she passed. She paused in front of the baker's and noted that there were five women waiting to be served, so she went on past. A grocer's was next door, but it was equally thick with customers.

It wasn't until she reached the chemist's at the end of the road that she tried her luck. But despite there being a young male shop assistant and her having a good excuse at the ready, she learned nothing. Ronald Hart had never so much as set foot in the place.

But Phyllis was determined not to arrive at their afternoon meeting with nothing; she just knew that Wiggins was going to do his best to outdo her, so she crossed the road and stepped into a butcher's shop. It was blessedly empty.

Moving to the counter, she gave the slender, dark-haired young man in a bloodstained apron an apologetic smile. "I'm so sorry to trouble you, but I've got myself lost and I hope you can help me."

"Of course, miss." He returned her smile with one of his own. "Where do you want to go?"

"That's the problem, you see. I've lost the slip of paper that had his address. All I know is the name of the gentleman. My mistress gave me this parcel for him." She pointed to the brown-paper-wrapped parcel she'd put in her shopping basket. "I'll get in ever so much trouble if I don't get it to him. That's why I thought I'd try the shops along here. I was hoping his household might shop here and that someone might be able to tell me where he lives."

"What's the name of this gentleman, miss?"

"Ronald Hart."

The clerk's friendly expression disappeared. His eyes narrowed and his chin jutted forward. "Is your mistress a friend of his, then?"

Phyllis knew anger when she saw it. "No, no, as a matter of fact, it's just the opposite. That's why I was so worried about getting this parcel to him. My mistress doesn't care for the gentleman, and she didn't want any of his possessions left in her home."

"That's his, is it?" He nodded at her shopping basket.

"It is. It's an old book—well, Mr. Hart called it an ancient antique volume." In fact, it was an old book, one she'd found in the rubbish bin behind Mrs. Adams' house early one morning when she'd been out for a walk. As it suited her purpose, she'd taken it home, wrapped it in brown paper, and stored it in her chest. Wiggins and Betsy both had stressed the importance of having a "prop" when on the hunt, and this parcel had stood her in good stead for several cases now.

"Is it valuable?" He stared at the parcel with a speculative, cunning expression on his narrow face.

She shook her head. "No, that's one of the reasons the mistress is so angry. Mr. Hart told her it was valuable and used it as . . ." She pretended to search for the right word, though she knew it perfectly well.

"Collateral," he supplied quickly. "He used it as security for a loan from your mistress."

She smiled in pretended delight. "Oh my gracious, you must be ever so clever! That's exactly what he did."

"I wouldn't say I'm clever, miss," he said, but looked very pleased with himself. "But I do know how Ronald Hart behaves. I'm not surprised he pulled such a mean trick. He's a nasty one."

"He is. I'm not supposed to know what happened." She lowered her voice and leaned toward him. "But it was hard not to hear her. The mistress was ranting and raving and carrying on something fierce when she got back yesterday. Her friend had come to see her, you see, and she was telling Mrs. Grant everything. She said her husband was going to be furious if he found out she'd lent Mr. Hart so much money."

"How did she find out the book was worthless?" He reached under the counter and pulled out a roll of string.

"She'd taken it to be ap-app—" Phyllis pretended to stumble over yet another word. "Uh . . . appraised, yes, that's what she said. But she found out she'd been taken in by Mr. Hart instead. Turns out it was just something he'd picked up at one of the shops on Charing Cross Road."

He popped the string on an empty spindle next to the cash register. "If it's not worth anything, why is she botherin' to return it to Hart?"

"She wanted him to know what she thought of him, so she put a nasty note in it." Phyllis grinned. "I think she might have threatened him, because I heard Mrs. Grant warning her to be careful what she wrote, that Mr. Hart was known to be vindictive, and if she said something he didn't like, he'd get back at her some way."

"That Mrs. Grant is right. Hart's a mean, awful sort of person. He's three months in arrears to us, and we're a small business—we can't afford to take a big loss. He lives in that big house and everyone thinks he's so rich, but if he's that bloomin' rich, why doesn't he pay his bills properly—that's what I want to know."

"Can't you take him to court and make him pay you?"

"I'd like to, but my dad says we don't dare. He said he'd pay us when he pleased and that if we tried to collect through the courts, we'd be sorry." His face flushed with anger, and his mouth settled into a flat, grim line.

"Threatened you with what?" Phyllis wanted to find out as much as possible.

"Hart said he'd tell everyone we sold dog meat here if we set the law on him. Can you believe it? And we're not the only ones he's cheated out of their money. He's in arrears on his bills to half a dozen merchants around here. Most of the shops won't give him goods anymore, but they're like us—they don't want to set the law on him because he's always threatening to sue us for libel or slander or whatnot."

"Let's hope that Marianne Pelletier is still here," Witherspoon murmured as he and Constable Barnes stepped through the front doors of the Bainbridge Hotel. He stopped and surveyed the lobby. French Empire–style sofas, love seats, wing chairs, and cabinets were grouped together for easy conversation near the massive fireplace. The floor was shiny black and white tile, a huge crystal chandelier hung from the ceiling, and a graceful staircase, carpeted in black and yellow diamonds, led to the upper floors. The walls were covered in pale gold patterned wallpaper and decorated with portraits of cavaliers and elegant women in seventeenth-century dress.

A polished wooden counter ran along one side of the room, at the end of which was a long corridor leading to the rear of the hotel. The lobby was quiet and empty save for the tall, gray-haired woman behind the counter who was sorting the post.

She looked up as the two policemen approached, her eyes widening as she saw Barnes' uniform. "May I help you?" she asked.

"We'd like to speak with one of your guests, Mrs. Pelletier," Barnes said. "Do you know if she's here at the moment?"

The woman moved to her left, turned, and studied the rows of keys on the black backboard. "Her key is here. May I ask who you are?" She directed her gaze at Witherspoon.

"As you can see, ma'am, we're the police. I'm Inspector Witherspoon, and this is Constable Barnes."

"I'm Mrs. Johnson, the manager. If you'll wait here, I'll send a bellboy up to her suite and let her know you're here."

"That won't be necessary," Barnes interrupted. "Just tell us her room number, and we'll go up ourselves."

Mrs. Johnson stared at them for a long moment and then nodded. "As you wish. Mrs. Pelletier is on the first floor, room one thirty-two. Please understand, we have a very particular clientele, so I assume you'll be discreet."

Barnes understood perfectly; if by some chance they had to ask Marianne Pelletier to accompany them to the station, the management would prefer they either do it off the premises or hustle her down the back stairs. "Of course, we've no wish to embarrass either Mrs. Pelletier or your establishment. We only want to ask the lady a few questions."

"She could be an important witness," Witherspoon explained. He didn't want Mrs. Pelletier subjected to any awkward stares or ugly rumors just because they'd had to speak with the lady. But he thought it prudent to have a few facts at hand before he interviewed her. "How long has Mrs. Pelletier been in residence here?"

"She's been here a month."

"Do you know how long she's staying?"

Mrs. Johnson put the stack of letters in her hand to one side. "When she checked in, she didn't know how long she'd be with us. She did say she'd need the suite for several weeks and possibly longer. We came to a mutually beneficial arrangement about the length of her stay. I made it clear that as long as we had vacancies, she was welcome to stay indefinitely."

"Where is the lady from?" Barnes asked.

"Paris."

"She's French?" The inspector frowned in confusion. No one at the Wrexley had mentioned the lady was foreign.

"She's English. I believe her late husband was French. Now, if you'll excuse me, I have to get the post sorted." Dismissing them, she picked up the stack and went back to her task.

They climbed the stairs to the first floor and found suite 132 halfway down the long hall. Barnes knocked softly, waited a moment, and then, fearing she'd not heard him, knocked again, this time louder.

The door opened and an attractive, middle-aged blonde appeared. She didn't look surprised to see them. "I wondered if you'd be able to find me." She waved them inside. "Come in, please, and let's get this over with."

They entered a sitting room furnished much like the lobby, with a French Empire–style sofa and wing chair, a black and yellow rug that matched the hotel carpet, and even a smaller version of the same chandelier.

She motioned them toward the sofa. "Please sit down and make yourselves comfortable."

Witherspoon introduced himself and Barnes as he took a seat on the wing chair opposite her. The constable sat down on an armchair next to a side table and took out his notebook and pencil.

"We've come to ask you a few questions, ma'am," Witherspoon began. "You were at the Wrexley Hotel several nights ago, is that correct?"

"That's correct." She gave him an amused smile. "Before we go any further, can you tell me how you found me? I didn't give my name or address to anyone at the Wrexley."

Witherspoon hesitated but then decided that it wouldn't do any harm to tell her the truth. What was more, she might even be able to shed some light on the issue. "Your name and address were on a list of names. Those names were found in the pocket of a murder victim."

She drew a quick breath. "That is surprising. I didn't know that Thomas Mundy knew I was in England, let alone where I was staying."

"So you know we're here about him?"

"Of course, Inspector."

"Have you any idea why your name would have been on that list?"

"I'm not sure." She looked away, her expression thoughtful. "Who else was on the list? Can you tell me that?"

Again, Witherspoon hesitated. Again, he thought that sharing the information might help them determine who had committed the murder. "There were two other names. One was Ronald Hart and the second was Daniel Wright."

"I've never heard of either of them, Inspector. As to why our names were grouped on the same list"—she shrugged—"I have no idea. I've not seen him since I've been in England."

"But you went to his hotel for the express purpose of meeting him," Witherspoon reminded her. "Why?"

"I don't see what my business with Mr. Mundy has to do with the police." She folded her arms over her chest. "It was a private matter."

The inspector decided to try a different tactic. "Where is your permanent residence, ma'am?"

"Paris. My late husband was French, and I've lived there for almost twenty years."

"Why have you come back to England?" Barnes asked.

"I came to take care of some family business," she replied. "And again, my reasons for coming here are of no concern to the police."

"But it is our concern if one of those reasons has anything to do with the late Mr. Mundy, which we feel it does. Your name was on a list we found in the dead man's pocket."

"As were two other names," she retorted. "Are you going to browbeat them as well?"

"We're not browbeating you, Mrs. Pelletier," Witherspoon insisted. "Please, ma'am, we're not here to upset you or to pry into your personal affairs, but a man has been murdered and you might have some very important information."

She said nothing for a moment; then she uncrossed her arms and clasped her hands in her lap. "Alright, I loathed the man, but I don't approve of murder, not even for him. Go ahead and ask your questions."

"How were you acquainted with Thomas Mundy?" Barnes asked quickly.

"I've never met him. He was an acquaintance of my late sister." She took a deep breath. "No, that's not true. He was more than an acquaintance to Phoebe. They were going to be married."

"Your late sister?" Witherspoon repeated.

"My half sister, really, but I helped to raise her, so we were very close. She passed away six months ago. Mundy didn't even come to the funeral." She blinked hard as tears pooled in her eyes. "I thought it was odd that he wasn't there. He'd broken the engagement, but I still expected him to pay his respects. But he didn't so much as show his face or send a wreath. At the time Phoebe died, I was so heartbroken, I couldn't even bring myself to dispose of her things. I hired a solicitor to handle it and went home."

Witherspoon nodded sympathetically. "Did you ever try to contact Mundy?"

She swiped at a tear that had escaped and nodded. "Yes, a few weeks later, I realized how very, very wrong the situation was, and I wanted to ask him why he'd behaved so callously. They might have decided not to marry, but he should have come to her funeral. So I sent a telegram to what I thought was his lodging house. I got no reply, so I sent another telegram to the solicitor handling Phoebe's estate and asked him to make inquiries. I got a reply from him very quickly. He wrote that Thomas Mundy had left town two days before the wedding. I was shocked, Inspector. I knew they'd canceled the nuptials, but I'd no idea he'd left the area."

"You hadn't come to England for your sister's wedding?" Barnes asked.

"I'd just recovered from pneumonia, Constable, and at one point, I was so ill, it didn't look as if I could be there at all, but two days before the wedding, I'd improved enough that my doctor agreed I could make the journey. It meant I wouldn't arrive until the day before the wedding, so I sent Phoebe a telegram telling her I'd be there. As a matter of fact, I was just about to leave my house for the train station when I got the telegram from her telling me the nuptials had been canceled and not to come." She smiled bitterly. "Phoebe didn't mention the circumstances, so I foolishly assumed it had been called off by mutual consent. It was only later that I realized exactly how he'd treated her."

"You said you were close to your half sister and she'd just had a devastating experience . . ." Witherspoon's voice trailed off, and he wasn't sure how to phrase the rest of the question. But she guessed what he wanted to know.

"You mean why didn't I come anyway when she obviously needed me the most?" She laughed bitterly. "I wish to God I had, but unfortunately, I relapsed, and this time, I almost died."

"Are you in England now specifically to see Mundy?" Barnes asked.

"Yes, I am. The solicitor I'd hired sent me a telegram and told me that he'd learned that Mundy was in London."

"How did you find out where he was staying?"

"That was easy, Constable. I hired a private investigator. It took him some time, but he eventually found out that Mundy was at the Wrexley Hotel."

"And you went there to confront him?" Witherspoon pressed.

"I did, but as I said, I never saw him."

"Where were you on the night Mr. Mundy was murdered?" Barnes blurted.

"Here, Constable. I was right here in my suite."

"Can anyone verify that?" The constable glanced at Witherspoon and noted that his superior was watching her intently.

She shrugged. "Perhaps the clerk who was on the desk when I came in that day. I got my key, came upstairs, and took a rest. Then I went down to dinner. I took an early meal, Constable, and then went for a short walk before coming upstairs."

"Did you leave your key at reception when you went for your walk?" Barnes asked.

"No, I was only going for a bit of fresh air. This is a lovely hotel and I'm generally very happy with their services, but I've noticed that reception can be very busy in the early evening, so I put the key in my pocket and went out. I was wise to do so, because when I returned, there was quite a long line at the desk."

The inspector nodded. "I see. I'm curious, Mrs. Pelletier. I understand you were angry at Mr. Mundy for the broken engagement and his absence at the funeral, but what did you hope to accomplish by confronting him?"

"Accomplish?" she repeated with a puzzled frown. But then her expression changed. "Oh dear, I'm so stupid. I haven't told you the worst of it. He didn't just humiliate her by jilting her in front of all her friends and neighbors; Mundy also tricked her out of every penny she had." She gave another bitter, barked laugh. "I wanted to see him rot in hell, Inspector, but I was going to content myself by dragging him through every court in this country and seeing that he spent the rest of his life in prison."

"How did your sister die?" Barnes asked softly.

She said nothing and looked down at the floor. When she lifted her chin, her eyes were filled once again with tears. "She killed herself. She tied two bloody great stones to her ankles and jumped into the Ashby Canal."

CHAPTER 6

Smythe watched as Witherspoon and Barnes came out of the Bainbridge Hotel. He had no idea how they'd found out the mysterious blonde asking about Mundy might be here, but somehow they had. His original plan had been simple: Come here, find a bellboy or waiter, and bribe him into giving him the names of all the attractive blondes. But now it looked like that wouldn't be necessary. He could just as easily wait and let Mrs. Jeffries get the information from the inspector. But bloomin' Ada, he'd wanted to show up at the afternoon meeting with something useful. It was too early to go to Blimpey's. The man was good, but even he couldn't find information that fast. He watched as the two policemen climbed into a hansom, and toyed with the idea of following them. He could do it on foot, but he decided against it. What to do now? He had a couple of hours before he had to head back to Upper Edmonton Gardens, and he wanted to put them to good use. He looked up the road and saw a line of hansoms rounding the corner. A cab shelter—there must be a cabman's shelter nearby. It didn't take him long to reach it.

Half a dozen drivers were drinking tea in front of the small green shelter. Smythe stopped and silently debated which approach would be the most useful. Trying to talk to each individual driver one by one might take too long, but on the other hand, he'd noticed people were less likely to volunteer information if they thought their mates were listening. Still, he had to give it a try. He walked up to the closest cluster of men. "Good day, gentlemen. I'm hoping you can help with a problem."

For a moment, no one said a word. They simply stared at him, half of them looking curious and the other half skeptical. "What kind of problem?" a dark-haired driver with a handlebar mustache asked.

Smythe whipped out a handful of coins. "I'm tryin' to track down a woman who was picked up at the Bainbridge Hotel three nights ago. She was a nice-lookin' blonde. Not too young, but not too old, either."

"We aren't in the habit of tellin' tales about our fares." A tall, balding driver eyed him suspiciously. "Why should we help you just because you're wavin' a bit of coin under our noses?"

"Because this particular lady might have witnessed a crime, and there's a chance she might be in danger."

The balding driver snorted. "What's it to you? You're not a copper."

Smythe fixed him with a hard stare. "Let's just say I'm a concerned citizen and leave it at that." He looked around the group of men, surveying their expressions. This hadn't gone well, but he'd not had time to come up with a decent story. "Still, if no one wants to earn a bit of lolly, that's fine with me."

A thin, ginger-haired young driver asked, "Was this Monday night, then?"

"It was." He wondered whether he should have flashed his money so quickly. This one could be lying through his teeth just to pick up some easy money.

"I had a fare like that. I remember her because you don't often see women like her out on their own at that time of night. She was a lady. You could tell by the way she was dressed. She had on a fur hat. But I didn't pick her up at the Bainbridge— that's where I took her."

"Where did she get in the cab?"

"Just by Queens Road Station. She was standing under a gas lamp and waved me down."

Smythe relaxed a bit as he realized the driver was telling the truth. The train station was close enough to the Wrexley for a woman to walk there quickly, yet crowded enough that she might think she wouldn't be remembered. She'd been wrong about that.

Handlebar mustache poked the lad in the arm. "Here now, you're not supposed to be tellin' tales about your fares." He jerked his head toward Smythe. "We don't know that this fellow is tellin' the truth. Could be he's tryin' to track that lady for other reasons. Maybe he's the one who is dangerous."

"Don't be daft, man. I'm not likely to pose a danger to anyone." Smythe shook his head in disbelief. "I've stood here in full view of half a dozen of ya for a good ten minutes, so you'd know me face if ya saw it again."

"That don't mean you're tellin' the truth," handlebar argued, but he looked a bit sheepish as some of the other drivers started snickering.

"If you think I'm out to 'arm that lady, report me to the

police," Smythe snapped. He turned his attention back to the ginger-haired lad. "What time was it when she flagged you down?"

"It must have been about five minutes to nine," he replied. "I know because I'd just dropped a fare at the station, and they were in a rush to catch the nine o'clock train to Barnsley."

Witherspoon grabbed the handhold as the cab swung around the corner. "I'm not sure Mrs. Pelletier was being entirely honest with us."

"I agree, sir, but she did tell us enough. She must realize that we have to consider her a suspect." Barnes struggled to keep the irritation out of his voice. "She obviously had a motive to want Mundy dead, and her whereabouts at the time of the murder can't be verified by an independent witness."

"Yes, it was a strange combination of evasion and honesty. Her reason for wanting to confront Mundy sounded odd, to say the least. On the one hand, she claimed Mundy 'tricked' her sister out of her money, and considering what we know of Mundy's character, that was probably true. But she was very vague when we asked her what evidence she had as grounds for 'dragging' Mundy through the courts."

Barnes had to bite his tongue. It was the inspector's fault the woman was "vague" with her answers. He didn't doubt that Marianne Pelletier's tears were genuine when she recounted her sister's suicide, but he also thought she was playacting toward the end of the interview. Witherspoon had started pressing her about her sister's financial losses, but instead of answering his questions, she'd started sobbing so loudly and was in such obvious distress that the inspector had ended the interview.

"But she did agree not to leave London," Witherspoon continued. "And if she'd not had hysterics, I'm certain we could have found out more."

"Perhaps she'll be in a calmer state when we speak with her again," Barnes said drily. He knew he shouldn't be so exasperated. The inspector was one of the bravest men he'd ever met. The constable had seen him stand up to all manner of pressure in his pursuit of justice. Arrogant aristocrats, powerful businessmen, or the bureaucratic bunch running Scotland Yard didn't in the least intimidate him. He had faced down armed killers on a number of occasions, but he crumbled like one of Mrs. Goodge's scones at a woman's tears. Barnes shook himself slightly as the cab pulled up at the curb. Everyone, he decided, including the inspector, was entitled to one fault.

They stepped out onto the pavement. Witherspoon stared at the three-story redbrick building while he waited for Barnes to pay the driver.

The establishment had seen better days. The gutters along the roofline sagged, the paint on the window frames was so faded it was impossible to determine its original color, and huge chunks of stone were missing from the concrete path leading to the front door.

"Let's see if Mr. Wright is still in residence," Witherspoon said.

"I think this place is a lodging house," Barnes said as he and Witherspoon started up the short walkway to the door. The constable banged the knocker against the wood.

A few moments later, a dour-faced, gray-haired woman wearing a dirty apron over her dress poked her head out. "What do you want?"

"We'd like to see Mr. Wright," the inspector said.

She stared at them for a moment and then reluctantly stepped back and waved them inside. Witherspoon stepped inside and paused to take a quick look. The foyer was small and dark. The linoleum on the dark green floor was cracked, the coat tree was missing a peg, and the metal umbrella stand was dented and tarnished.

"Come on, then, I've not got all day. I've got mutton boiling on the cooker." She pointed to a narrow staircase. "Wright's the first room at the top of the stairs."

"Thank you, ma'am." Witherspoon nodded politely, and the two men started up.

Barnes reached the room first, waited till Witherspoon had joined him, and then gave a hard knock on the wood.

"I've told you, I'll pay you as soon as I've finished packing," yelled a voice with a distinctly American accent. Suddenly the door flew open, and they found themselves face-to-face with a tall, blond-haired, blue-eyed man. His shirt collar was open, and a tie dangled around his neck.

Through the now-open door, Witherspoon could see an open suitcase on the unmade bed. "Are you Daniel Wright?"

"I am." His gaze flicked to the constable. "And you're obviously the police."

"That's correct. May we come inside?" Witherspoon asked. "We'd like to ask you a few questions."

His mouth flattened into a thin line, and then he shrugged. "I don't think I've much choice in the matter." He stepped back, opening the door wide as he moved.

The room was as miserable as the rest of the house, with faded wallpaper, mismatched furniture, and an open wardrobe next to a window bordered by a pair of lank gray curtains.

Wright closed the door and stepped around them to the far side of the bed. "Have a seat if you want."

Witherspoon took a seat on the rickety-looking straight-back chair next to the door while Barnes went to the corner and sat on what appeared to be an old piano stool.

"You're an American, Mr. Wright, is that correct?" Witherspoon asked.

"Yes. I'm from California. Los Angeles, to be exact."

"Mr. Wright, we have it on good authority that you were acquainted with Thomas Mundy."

"I was." He turned to his wardrobe and pulled out a pair of trousers.

"Mr. Mundy was murdered three nights ago."

"I know, Inspector. It was in the newspapers." He folded the pants and put them carefully into the case. "But what's his murder got to do with me?"

"Can you tell us the nature of your acquaintance with the victim?" Witherspoon shifted his weight to get more comfortable, then went rigid as the wood creaked and he felt it move.

"We had business dealings together in California." He looked up from his packing. "He stole a great deal of money from me, and I came here to get it back."

"He robbed you?"

Wright smiled slightly. "He did more than rob me, Inspector. He stole my life. He ruined me. But unfortunately, before I could squeeze what he owed out of him, someone murdered him."

"How long have you been in England, Mr. Wright?" Barnes asked. Laverne Hamlin's description of one of the people who'd been tracking Mundy came into his mind. *There was a nice-looking, middle-aged blond-haired fellow as well. He had the prettiest blue eyes, but that's of no interest to you.*

"Four weeks. I came over on the *Northern Star*. She's due back into Southampton in three days, and I'm hoping to go home on her"—he gave them another tight smile—"unless I'm under arrest."

"It doesn't take three days to get to Southampton." Barnes nodded at the open suitcase.

"No, but lodging in Southampton is cheaper than London. As I explained, Constable, Mundy took everything from me. I had to sell what little I had left to scrape together the funds to come after him. As it is, I barely have enough left to pay what I owe here and get home."

"When was the last time you saw Thomas Mundy?" Barnes watched him carefully.

"Four days ago. It took time to track the fellow down."

"And you found him at the Wrexley Hotel?" the constable asked.

"That's right."

Barnes nodded in admiration. "You did well to find him at all. There are hundreds of hotels in London."

"I had help, Constable. Someone told me where Mundy was staying."

"And so you went to the Wrexley and confronted him?" Witherspoon asked. He, too, recalled what Mrs. Hamlin had said and how she had remarked on Wright's eyes being a very noticeable shade of light blue.

Wright shook his head. "Oh no, I left that up to Mr. Hart. He was the one who was bound and determined to find and confront Mundy."

"You mean Ronald Hart?" Barnes asked. "He told you where Mundy was?"

Wright looked confused for a moment. "I don't know who that is. It was Oswald Hart who told me."

"Oswald Hart?" Witherspoon repeated the name. It was one they'd not heard.

"He owns an antiques shop in Market Harborough. I went there first, Inspector. Mundy had slipped up once, and over one beer too many at our local saloon had mentioned that was where he was from. That's where I started tracking him." He smiled bitterly. "In my experience, scared rats run for a familiar hole."

Barnes nodded. "Why was Mundy scared? Did he know you were coming after him?"

Wright gave a harsh, short laugh. "I doubt that, Constable. The bastard left me for dead in an alley off Market Street in San Francisco."

Witherspoon frowned. "Are you saying that Mundy tried to kill you?"

"He thought he had killed me, Inspector. He knew I was onto him and that I was on my way to see Crowley to have him arrested, when he attacked me."

"Crowley?" Barnes interjected.

"Patrick Crowley—he is the police chief in San Francisco. I'd found evidence that Mundy had drugged me, stole the combination to my safe, and then arranged for me to be found with a drugged prostitute and almost face a prison sentence myself."

"What kind of evidence?" Witherspoon allowed himself to relax but immediately wished he hadn't when the chair gave another loud creak.

"There was a witness. One of my workers had brought a broken handsaw to my office the night that Mundy stole my money. He saw him leaving, and he was carrying a bulging carpetbag. Once he came forward, the police began to rethink the case. That's the only reason I wasn't thrown in jail. When Mundy found out I was in San Francisco, he knew his days were numbered and that he'd be facing a long prison sentence. That's why he attacked me. He meant for me to die."

"What did Mundy do to you?" The inspector shifted his weight with care. The chair groaned, and he prayed it would continue to hold his weight.

"He didn't do anything. He hired two thugs to do his dirty work. Luckily for me, a police patrol showed up before they could finish the job. That's the only reason I'm not dead."

"And the San Francisco police have a record of this?"

"They do." Wright smiled slightly. "And I'm sure the first thing you'll do when we finish here is send them a telegram verifying my account. They saved my life, but I was in terrible condition. I was so broke, I had to go to a charity hospital for care, and it took months before I was healed enough to start looking for Mundy. But by then, he was long gone. I had a few assets left, so I sold them and went after him. The first place I looked was Market Harborough, and within a few weeks, I found one of Mundy's other victims. Oswald Hart hated him even more than I did, and as I said, he was the one who told me where I could find Mundy."

Barnes looked up from his notebook. "He just gave you that information out of the goodness of his heart?"

Wright hesitated. "Not initially. He was tongue-tied when I first approached him, but after I told him what Mundy had done to me and that I planned on making the bastard pay me every cent he'd stolen and then some, he talked. He said he and several other members of his family had been considering bringing a lawsuit against Mundy when they found out he'd returned to England, but they'd found the statute of limitations had run out on the crime he'd allegedly committed."

"What had Mundy done to him?" Witherspoon's backside was almost asleep. He stood up.

"He didn't say and I didn't ask. By that time, my funds were running dangerously low, so I knew I had to get to London. But I will tell you this—I know that Oswald Hart was in London on the night Mundy was murdered."

"How do you know that?" Barnes stood up as well.

"Because I saw him, Constable. I was standing across the road from the Wrexley Hotel when I saw him get out of a hansom cab. But he didn't go in the front door. He went around the mews to the back door and slipped inside."

"You saw this from across the road?" Witherspoon commented.

"No, I followed him. I was curious to see what he was up to."

"Had you met with Mundy since you'd come to London?" Barnes asked.

"No, but I wasn't in a great hurry, and I wanted to take his measure before I confronted him directly. I'd bribed one of the bellboys for information, so I knew that Mundy was at the hotel and had paid through the end of the month. I also learned he paid all his bills in cash. That was useful information."

"In what way was it useful?" the constable asked. So far, his account matched Laverne Hamlin's statement. She'd seen Wright with the bellboy. "How could you afford to be so patient?"

"Mundy had no idea I was here and that I was watching

him. I never saw him go near a bank. So that meant he had cash. Knowing what I knew of his character, I was certain he kept it close by. A man like him never knows when he's going to have to make a run for it. So, I decided to act."

"What, exactly, had you planned on doing?" Witherspoon asked. "Despite what he'd done to you, I very much doubt the Home Office would agree to sending Mr. Mundy back to California to face trial. He was a British citizen."

"I know that, Inspector, so I resorted to something far more basic."

"And what was that to be?"

"I was going to scare him into giving me my money. I intended to let him see, to let him know I was watching him so that by the time I met him face-to-face, he'd be so relieved I wasn't going to beat him senseless that he'd pay what he owed."

"So you assumed he would be frightened of you?"

"I was counting on it, Inspector. You see, the man's a coward," Wright said. "Why do you think he hired thugs to do me in instead of using that gold-headed walking stick of his? But before I could corner the bastard, someone killed him."

Witherspoon asked, "What time was it when you saw Mr. Hart?"

"Half past six," he replied. "I'd just checked my watch. Dinner is served here at seven o'clock on the dot, and as my funds were low, I didn't want to miss a meal and go hungry."

"So you admit you were at the Wrexley on the night of the murder?" the inspector pressed.

"I admit to standing in front of the Wrexley until half six that evening, but I didn't go inside and I was back here in time for dinner. You can ask the landlady."

"Rest assured we will," Witherspoon said. "Did you stay in all evening?"

"I did."

Wiggins waited until the inspector and Barnes disappeared through the front door of the lodging house before dashing around the corner and after the housemaid. He'd seen her leave from a side door with a shopping basket over her arm almost at the same time Witherspoon and the constable arrived in a hansom. He couldn't follow the girl without being spotted, so he'd ducked behind the trunk of a huge oak and hoped he'd be able to catch up with her.

As he came out onto the road, he couldn't see her, so he broke into a flat-out run. He ran hard, weaving left and right to avoid crashing into shoppers, and then veered almost into the road to miss careening into a man wearing a sandwich board advertising Newsom's Bilious Pills. Determined not to show up at their afternoon meeting with nothing to report, he kept on running. His breath came in short, hard bursts, and his legs were so rubbery, he was certain they'd collapse, when he spotted her going into the greengrocer's.

Wiggins stopped running and sagged against the wall of the London and Merchant's Bank. He kept his gaze on the shop entrance and silently prayed she'd stay in there long enough for him to recover. But he couldn't waste time resting. He shoved away from the wall and started walking slowly. By the time he reached the greengrocer's, his breath was back to normal and he'd come up with a plan.

Two minutes later, the housemaid, a nice-looking young

woman with light reddish hair, blue eyes, and a perfect complexion, emerged from the shop. Wiggins timed it perfectly, smashing into her just as she reached the busy corner.

She yelped as her basket went flying and potatoes, cabbages, and turnips scattered along the pavement.

"Oh my goodness, miss, I'm ever so sorry." Wiggins scrambled after the rolling vegetables, scooping up a cabbage and both the turnips.

"Watch where you're goin'," she cried as she lunged for a potato rolling toward the edge of the pavement. "Oh Lordy, the mistress will have my head if any of these are ruined," she wailed.

Wiggins dumped the vegetables in her basket. "I'm so sorry, miss. I didn't see you. This is all my fault."

"Of course it's your fault," she cried. She rolled the cabbage from side to side, looking for torn leaves and bruises. "If this isn't fit to eat, I'll get the sack," she mumbled before her narrowed eyes flicked over the turnips and potatoes.

"I'll pay for any that are damaged," he apologized again. "Look, let me buy you a cup of tea, and you can have a good look at your shoppin' and make certain everything is fit for the table."

Her head jerked up, and she stared at him skeptically. "You offerin' to buy me a cup of tea? What do ya take me for, some lass straight off the farm? I don't go off with strangers. I've got to get back, and I'll not be botherin' with the likes of you."

This was not going how Wiggins had imagined it would, but he wasn't going to give up. "Please, miss, I'm only tryin' to do right. I know we've not been properly introduced, but I feel so bad. Especially as you said that if anything was damaged"— he pointed to her basket—"you'd get the sack. I know how that feels. My old master used to terrify all of us. He was a right miserable man, and the happiest day of my life was when I left his service."

Her expression softened. "Well, I might have been exaggeratin' a bit. I don't think the mistress would actually sack me. She pays such miserable wages, she'd not get anyone else to work at that place. I was just angry that you slammed into me the way you did."

"That's a relief, miss." He gave her his most winning smile, and to his surprise, she smiled back. "But I would feel better if you'd let me buy you that cup of tea. There's a nice little café just around the corner."

Her smile disappeared, and Wiggins was sure she was going to refuse.

"Alright, then." She cocked her head to one side and looked him up and down. "You look a decent sort. But don't get any ideas in your head. I've got four older brothers, and they taught me how to take care of myself."

Wiggins used the short walk to the café to come up with a story that might get her talking. He wasn't sure his original idea of being a reporter would work. But by the time they reached their destination and he'd seated her at a small table and then gone to the counter to get their tea, he still hadn't come up with a better one. But he needn't have worried about how to get her to chatting; she started speaking as he put her teacup down in front of her.

"Sorry I was so nasty before. You're bein' right nice." She gave him a shy smile. "I do love tea, but we're only allowed a cup with our breakfast, and the tea served at midmorning is so weak, you can barely taste it."

"Your mistress sounds as stingy as my old master used to be."

Emily Brightwell

"She's awful, but it was the only post I could get. Mind you, the one nice thing about working at a lodging house is that the lodgers tend to complain when she gets too stingy with food and drink."

"You work at a lodging house? That sounds interesting." Wiggins took a sip from his cup.

"It's a bit better than being a scullery at a posh house. That was the first position I had, and it was awful. One of the advantages of a lodging house is that she takes in short-term lodgers, mostly from America or Canada, and they're generally very good, not as demanding as some of them Frenchies and Italians."

Wiggins had been waiting for a good opening. "Are there any there now? Americans or Canadians? I'm interested because my cousin lives in New York."

She took a quick sip before she answered. "Well, there's Mr. Gilman. He's from Canada, and he's here to sell wheat. Then there's Mr. Wright. He's from California"—she frowned—"but that's a long way from New York, isn't it?"

He nodded and she kept on talking. "Mind you, he's a bit of a dark one, is Mr. Wright. He's nice enough, but he's right closemouthed about what he's doin' here. I don't think he's got much money, either."

"Why do you say that?"

"Because I heard him askin' Donnie—he's the mistress' nephew, and he works as a general dogsbody around the place—if he knew any reputable pawnshops. Donnie told him to try a place on the Commercial Road over in the East End."

Wiggins thought fast and made certain not to drop his "h's" as he spoke. "Poor fella, must be hard bein' such a long way from home and then havin' to sell your possessions." He hoped that by appearing to be both sympathetic and slightly better

154

educated than she was, he'd get more out of her. "Sounds like he's not here in London to see the sights."

"He's not; I can tell you that." She leaned close. "A couple of nights ago, he made a big show of goin' up to his room right after supper, said he was dead tired and wanted to get some sleep. But he was lyin' through his teeth. He slipped out the side door and was gone until almost midnight."

"Isn't the house locked up good and proper?" Wiggins asked. "How'd he get back in?"

"He slipped in through the window in the dry larder." She looked down as she spoke. "I should have told the mistress, but I was afraid I'd get the sack if I said anything."

Wiggins understood. He gave her a sympathetic smile. "You were in the larder, weren't you."

She opened her mouth and then looked down at the tabletop.

"Don't be embarrassed," Wiggins said quickly. "I've done the same myself more than once when I worked for my old master. He was a right stingy sod with food, and some nights, the evening meal would be so tiny, my belly would be stickin' to my spine."

She smiled timidly. "I'm glad you understand. So you can see why I couldn't say anything to the mistress. I'd crept in to get a slice of bread, when I heard someone outside the window. I didn't know what to do, I was so scared, but I couldn't shout for the mistress because even if someone was breakin' into the house, I knew that after the ruckus died down, she'd want to know why I was down there. I hate the place, but I've nowhere else to go. I'm just workin' there long enough to get a decent reference so I can go elsewhere."

"I did the same," he murmured. "So what happened next?"

"I grabbed my bread and slipped out as fast as I could, but

he was already inside, so I couldn't get up the back stairs before he saw me. I hunkered down under the stairwell. I figured if it was a thief, he'd steal a few things and then be off. But it was Mr. Wright that come out of the larder. I think he must have unlocked the window earlier that evening."

"It must have been very scary."

"It was, but I shouldn't have been so surprised. I already knew there was something odd about Mr. Wright."

"Why do you say that?"

She looked around, making certain the two matrons at the next table were engrossed in their own conversation before she leaned toward him. "He slips in and out of the house at the oddest times, and what I told you about him comin' through the larder window, that weren't the first time he did it. I saw him slipping down the stairs the night before that. I think he went out that time, too. He was moving slowly, like he didn't want anyone to know he was leavin'."

Wiggins wasn't going to embarrass her by asking how she knew. He was fairly certain the night of the murder wasn't the first time she'd gone downstairs to pilfer a bit of food, so he merely nodded.

"But that's not the worst of it," she continued. "That's not what I find so strange about him."

"What is?"

"He's got a gun, and considerin' how much he has the thing out, playin' with it, I think he intends to use it."

"Look who's finally come home," Luty yelled as she swept into the kitchen, followed by a rather embarrassed-looking Hatchet. "I told him if he'd not shown up this afternoon lookin' like something the cat dragged in, I was goin' to send out a search party." She grinned from ear to ear, and it was clear to everyone at the table that she'd missed him terribly.

"Don't be so melodramatic, madam. I kept you informed as to my whereabouts on a daily basis," he said, but his broad smile took the sting out of his words. He nodded at the others as he helped Luty out of her peacock blue cape before pulling out her chair.

"Anyone could claim to be you and send telegrams," Luty argued as she slipped into her seat. "We chase murderers, Hatchet, and you were gone long enough to git me worried."

"He was only gone two days," Mrs. Goodge reminded her. "But we're glad he's safely back." She bounced her knees up and down, sending Amanda, who was sitting on her lap, into fits of giggles.

"I'm delighted to be back." Hatchet took his chair and nodded his thanks as Phyllis passed him a cup of tea. "And I've a lot to report."

"I've a feeling we all do." Mrs. Jeffries glanced at the clock. "So let's get the meeting started. You never know when the inspector might decide to come home early. Hatchet, you go first."

"Thank you. I had some success, but I'm sure there was more I could have found out about Thomas Mundy if I could have stayed a bit longer. Still, I'll tell you what I know." He took a sip of tea. "The first twenty-four hours were spent trying to track down the law firm where Mundy was supposed to have worked. It was difficult because they went out of business twenty years ago. But I finally found a man who'd been employed there. His name was Horace Varlee, and he'd been hired to take Thomas Mundy's place. The name of the firm was Bartleby, Warnock, and Sherwood."

"Mundy left the firm?" Betsy clarified.

"And the country." Hatchet grinned. "He was going to be arrested. Mr. Varlee didn't know all the details of what happened, but from what he was able to piece together, it involved Mundy's pilfering of a client's estate."

"Mundy stole money?" Mrs. Goodge asked.

"No, jewelry. He'd been tasked to go with Edgar Sherwood and record an inventory so the estate could be appraised and sold." Hatchet took another quick sip. "But the day after the inventory, two of the heirs came to the firm's office and insisted that some valuable diamonds and emerald jewelry had been stolen. The firm was outraged and denied that any such thing had happened, but unfortunately for its reputation, a stonemason repairing the bedroom window lintel had seen Thomas Mundy put the jewels in his pocket. The firm's partners went to confront Mundy, who was supposed to be sitting at his desk in the outer office, but he was gone. The firm closed its doors less than three months later. The poor fellow hired to take Mundy's place was unceremoniously sacked, and because the firm's reputation was in tatters, he had to move to Nottingham to find another position."

"One little incident with a dishonest employee was enough to make the firm close its doors?" Betsy asked incredulously.

"It wasn't just that," Hatchet replied. "Let me tell you the rest of it. Thomas Mundy was a hardworking, energetic young clerk who arrived at the office before any of the other clerks and left for the evening after they did. The partners were delighted with their clerk and congratulated themselves on finding such a bright young man. But there was a good reason that Mundy kept those hours, and his employers, all a bit on the elderly side, had no idea as to what he was really up to. Little by little, they began entrusting more and more of their responsibilities to Mundy, till eventually he had access to everything—the keys to the partners' offices, the safe, and, most important, the clients' files."

"Is that unusual?" Phyllis asked. She glanced at Wiggins, who gave her a smug smile, so she quickly looked away. It wasn't fair! She'd done her best today, but she knew, she just knew he was going to go her one better.

"Yup." It was Luty who answered. "My solicitor keeps my client box under lock and key, and the keys to the client boxes are locked in his top drawer."

"Maybe things are a bit less formal outside of London," Mrs. Jeffries suggested. She also didn't need to mention that Luty was a very rich woman and had the best firm of solicitors in London at her beck and call. Ordinary people rarely got the level of service that she did.

Hatchet shook his head. "That's what I thought, but Varlee said the firm was very formal, and over the three months he was employed there, he was given only limited and supervised access to client files."

"Even old dogs can learn new tricks," Smythe muttered. "Sounds to me like they'd learned a lesson. What had Mundy done?"

"They never proved it, but he was accused of altering wills."

"How could he possibly do that?" Betsy protested. "Don't wills have to be witnessed?"

"Of course, but the witnesses sign on the last page of the document, and all it would take is to hang on to the signature page and then change the other pages so that one heir might receive more than his or her fair share."

"And that's what Mundy did?" Phyllis toyed with the handle

of her cup and tried to think of a way to phrase the information she'd learned from the butcher so that it sounded important. "Change the amounts that an heir would receive?"

"That's one of the many things he was suspected of doing," Hatchet replied. "But it was never proven."

Smythe looked doubtful. "I don't see 'ow somethin' like changin' a will would work. The partner who wrote out the terms of the will would know something was wrong when the changed will was read."

"You'd like to think so," Hatchet replied. "But as I said, the three partners were very elderly, and many of the wills had been drawn up years earlier. They couldn't remember most of the details, especially if the changes weren't huge. In other words, let's say there were three heirs to an estate and each of them was supposed to get a thirty percent share."

"That's only ninety percent," Luty said.

"I know that, madam, but many people leave ten percent of their estates to long-serving servants or charities or other organizations, so that would add up to the total one hundred percent," he explained with exaggerated patience. "Let's get back to our example."

"Right, each heir gets thirty percent," she agreed. "Go ahead. Tell us how Mundy did it."

"Say that one of the heirs was a bit greedier than the others and found out there was someone in the firm who, for a modest fee, would change his share to forty percent, which would leave twenty-five percent to the other two heirs. An additional ten percent of a large estate could be a lot of money."

"But what about the heirs who got their inheritances cut? Wouldn't they complain?" Betsy argued.

"Some of them did, but in most cases it couldn't be proven."

He shrugged. "How often does someone tell their heirs how much they might get? It's one thing if it's a single piece of property or something like that, but if it's an estate that's going to be sold and then the money split between a number of heirs, most people wouldn't realize they'd lost part of their inheritance."

"Surely the witnesses would remember," she pointed out.

"Most witnesses aren't privy to the contents of the will," Hatchet explained. "They just witness that it's a specific person's will and sign where they're told."

"Surely he couldn't name himself as an heir, so why would Mundy do it?" Mrs. Jeffries asked.

"Money. He was suspected of contacting one of the heirs and letting that person know that for a fee, his share could be increased."

"How did he know which heir to approach?" Mrs. Jeffries reached for the teapot and poured herself another cup. "Not everyone is susceptible to being a party to cheating their own relations."

"I asked my source the same question, and he said that from what he'd heard of Mundy, the fellow was good at finding out others' weaknesses. Market Harborough isn't a huge metropolis, and if one put his mind to it, one could easily find out who gambled or drank or even used laudanum to excess."

"What a nasty little sod 'e must 'ave been." Wiggins shook his head in disgust.

"Mundy's activities were the reason the firm closed its doors. The jewelry theft was a scandal that couldn't be hushed up or swept under the rug. The rumors were so horrible that Edgar Sherwood suffered a fatal heart attack. The office was closed, and the remaining two partners retired. Mundy went to the United States and disappeared."

"Did you get the names of the people who might have been cheated?" Phyllis asked.

"Only two, I'm afraid. Bernard Hart's was one of the wills that might have been changed. Apparently, instead of the estate being divided up among all his nieces and nephews, most of it went to one person, Ronald Hart. The other heirs were furious, but nothing was ever proven."

"We've 'eard his name before." Smythe helped himself to a slice of Madeira cake.

"And another client, Horace Talbot, his two cousins claim he'd always promised his estate would be equally divided among them as well, but it all went to a third cousin, Henrietta Talbot. Unfortunately, she's dead and she willed her money to a local charity hospital." He sat back in the chair. "That's about all I was able to find out. No, I tell a lie—Mundy was back in the area about eight or nine months ago but not Market Harborough. He was staying at a lodging house further out."

"Thank you, Hatchet," Mrs. Jeffries said as the clock chimed the hour. "Oh dear, we'd best get moving a bit faster. Who wants to go next?"

"I'll have a go," Wiggins offered. "I met a housemaid from Daniel Wright's lodgin' house," he began.

Luty poked Hatchet in the arm. "That's the feller I told ya about. The one who got beat half to death in San Francisco."

"I remember, madam," he replied. "Madam gave me a report on what I'd missed on our way here. Sorry, Wiggins, we didn't mean to interrupt. Please continue."

Wiggins nodded and told them about his meeting with the young lady. "She was a bit embarrassed havin' to admit she was pilferin' food. I felt sorry for her, but I'm sure she was tellin' the truth."

"So Daniel Wright has a gun and wasn't home on the night Mundy was murdered," Mrs. Jeffries murmured. "That's very interesting."

"But Mundy wasn't killed with a gun," Betsy said.

"I've got an idea about that," Wiggins said. "I gave it a good think as I was walkin' home. I think Wright did it and he took the gun with him to Wrexley. But once he got there, he realized that in a posh place like that, a gunshot would be loud enough to wake the dead, and he wanted Mundy to suffer like he did. So he used Mundy's own walking stick."

"That's certainly possible," Mrs. Jeffries said. "But let's not assume anything without evidence, and we've no direct proof that Wright did the killing."

"Wright wasn't the only person who was out and about on the night Mundy was murdered," Smythe said. "That blonde mystery woman who was asking after Mundy the day before he was killed, I found a hansom driver who picked a woman matching that description up near Mundy's hotel and took her to the Bainbridge Hotel."

"What's the Bainbridge got to do with anything?" Wiggins looked confused. "Have I forgotten something?"

Smythe realized they didn't know what he was talking about. "Let me start over. I talked to two drivers today. One of them described a woman he'd taken to the Wrexley from the Bainbridge the day *before* the murder. The description he gave me matched the one the Hamlin woman gave to our inspector. The one who sat in the lobby and waited for him for a long time. So I went to the Bainbridge, and lo and behold, I see the inspector and Constable Barnes goin' inside."

"How'd they find out about her?" Mrs. Goodge demanded.

"I don't know. We'll have to wait until the inspector gets

home and he and Mrs. Jeffries have a chat," he said. "I couldn't 'ang about the place trying to talk to a waiter or a bellboy, but there was a cabman's shelter just off the Uxbridge Road, and I figured one of them drivers might know something. I was right. On the night of the murder, one of the drivers picked this blonde lady up at the Queens Road Station and took her to the Bainbridge Hotel. He remembered her because he said you didn't often see a posh lady like that out on her own at night. It was almost nine o'clock when she waved him down."

"And we know she has some sort of connection to the victim," Mrs. Jeffries murmured. "We just don't know what it might be. Anyone else have something to report?"

"Nothing from me," Mrs. Goodge said. "None of my sources knew anything." She shifted her body and propped Amanda against her right arm. The little one's eyes were closing, and she was falling asleep.

"Phyllis?" Mrs. Jeffries gave the housemaid a bright smile. "Did you have any luck with the local merchants in Hart's neighborhood?"

Phyllis hesitated and almost said she'd not had any luck at all. Compared to Wiggins, what she'd learned about Ronald Hart was dismal. But as Mrs. Jeffries always said, every bit of information could well be important, so she should tell them. But goodness, she was going to look like an incompetent fool. Pride warred with honor. Honor won. She told them what she'd learned from the butcher, taking care to repeat his words correctly. "I know it's not much"—she shrugged self-consciously—"but maybe it'll help."

"I doubt it." Wiggins smirked at her. "The only thing it tells us is that Ronald Hart is a miserable excuse for a human being."

CHAPTER 7

The moment the words were out of his mouth, Wiggins wished he could take them back. Phyllis was staring at him with a stunned, hurt expression he'd never seen before, and he felt lower than a worm.

"Yes, I suppose that's true." She looked down at her lap.

Mrs. Jeffries had had enough. Why the footman was acting this way was a mystery, but as soon as the maid was out of earshot, she intended to give him a piece of her mind. For the moment, she contented herself in giving him a good glare. "Phyllis, we've no idea what your information may or may not mean. I, for one, think it's very valuable. Ronald Hart isn't just a miserable excuse for a human being," she said, deliberately repeating Wiggins' words. "He doesn't pay his bills, which means he's defrauding merchants."

"That means he's no better than a thief." Betsy shot the footman a dirty look before turning to the maid. "Which is important. Lots of thieves commit murder, so maybe we ought to keep our eye on Mr. Hart."

Wiggins realized that every female at the table was staring daggers at him. Phyllis was slumped against her chair, and from the way she was chewing on her lip and blinking, he thought she was trying not to cry. He frantically tried to think of what he could do to make it better. "Cor blimey, I didn't mean to start a ruckus. I just said somethin' stupid off the top of my head. I'm sorry, Phyllis. I didn't mean anything."

"It's alright." She reached for the teapot. "I'll top this up." Her voice shook, and she kept her head down as she got up.

There was a knock on the back door. Mrs. Jeffries looked at the cook. "Are you expecting a source?"

"Not this late in the day."

"I'll see who it is." Phyllis put the pot down and raced off down the back hall. A moment later, they heard her say, "Oh my goodness, you're back. Come in, come in. We're still having our afternoon meeting."

"I was hoping you'd all be here," a familiar voice said.

"Look who it is," Phyllis announced as she led Lady Ruth Cannonberry into the kitchen.

"I do hope I'm not intruding," Ruth apologized as she headed to the table, "but when I realized that Gerald was handling the Mundy murder, I had to come. I had a feeling I might be needed."

"But of course you came," Phyllis exclaimed. "And we always need you."

"You're one of us," Wiggins added. He was glad to have the attention off him and onto her. Once the others were gone, he'd apologize properly to Phyllis. Maybe they could have a bit of a chat as well. Things had gone funny between them, and it was more his fault than hers. But she wasn't without blame, he told himself. She'd been free with her tongue as well.

"We're just glad you're here," Luty said. "You're right, we're spread pretty thin on the ground with this one."

"We can most definitely use more help on this case." Hatchet grinned broadly.

Smythe glanced toward the back door. "Let's hope the inspector doesn't take it into his head to come home before we have a chance to tell Ruth everything."

"You know you're always welcome." Mrs. Jeffries pointed to the spot where Ruth usually sat. "Take your seat and have some tea. Mrs. Goodge and I will tell you everything you've missed once our meeting is finished."

Phyllis grabbed the teapot and hurried to the cooker. A few moments later, she added the boiling water to the pot while Betsy got another teacup and plate from the sideboard.

"You've had that baby long enough," Luty said to the cook. "It's my turn. Hand her over."

"She's not a baby anymore, and she's heavy. Do you think you can manage?"

"Of course she can." Hatchet flattened his hand, palm up, and shoved it a few inches beneath Luty's elbow, all without her being aware of it. He'd make certain Amanda was safe and cozy. Mrs. Goodge glanced at Smythe, who got up, reached for his sleeping daughter, and put her gently into Luty's waiting arms.

The elderly American settled back in her chair, a contented smile on her face.

"Thank you all so much." Ruth laughed as she sat down. "You always make me feel so welcome."

"Phyllis was just telling us about one of our suspects, a man

167

named Ronald Hart, who apparently doesn't pay his bills," Mrs. Jeffries said. "And then threatens the merchants he cheats out of their rightful payment."

"You know the sort," Smythe said. "He's a blowhard and a bully, one of them people born with a silver spoon in their mouths but who convince themselves they've done it all on their own."

"He might be a nasty person, but that doesn't make him a murderer," Mrs. Goodge declared. "We've gone down that path before, so before we're all puttin' a noose around the man's neck, let's make sure we have a good look at the others in this case. Now, if we're all finished, let's end the meeting so Mrs. Jeffries and I will have enough time to tell Ruth what's what before the inspector gets home."

There was a scraping of chairs as the meeting ended. Phyllis started to clear up the tea things but stopped when Mrs. Goodge put her hand on top of the big brown pot. "Leave the table, dear. I'll tend to it after we're finished. You go upstairs and lay the dining table."

"After that, you need to tidy the inspector's study," Mrs. Jeffries added. "But it shouldn't take long. There are only a few newspapers scattered about and bit of dusting."

"What about the drawing room?" Phyllis was already at the bottom of the back stairs.

"You've enough to do. I'll take care of that," Mrs. Jeffries replied.

"I guess you won't let me keep her." Luty reluctantly handed a yawning Amanda to Betsy as Hatchet went to the coat tree to retrieve their outer garments.

"I might as well take Fred for his walk before it gets too late," Wiggins grumbled as he watched the maid disappear up the stairs. He'd hoped to have a quick word with her, to tell her how sorry he was, and now he'd have to wait until after dinner. He grabbed the leash from the top drawer of the pine sideboard as the dog jumped up, dashed across the room, and danced impatiently until they were heading for the back door.

"She's getting heavy." Betsy looked at her husband. "Can you take her?"

Smythe shook his head. "She should walk. Why don't the two of you go outside and let her have a run around in the garden. I'd like a quick word with Mrs. Jeffries. You know, about what we discussed on our way here."

"Oh good, something needs to be said." She put Amanda down and took her hand. "Come along, sweetie, we'll wait for Papa outside."

"Papa . . . Papa outhide . . . Papa . . . ," Amanda repeated as they pushed past Smythe and disappeared.

"Is something wrong?" Mrs. Jeffries asked as she joined him. He pulled her farther down the corridor. "Nothin's wrong, but I can see you're fixin' to box young Wiggins' ears."

"And you object to that?" She crossed her arms over her chest. She wasn't going to have any male sticking together nonsense. She was fed up with the lad's behavior.

Smythe grinned broadly. "'Course not, I've had Betsy chewin' my ear off for the past week about the situation. But there's more to this than meets the eye, and in all fairness, Wiggins isn't the only one with a sharp tongue. Phyllis has done her fair share, too."

"She's defended herself." Mrs. Jeffries jabbed the air with her finger to make her point. "I've watched the situation very carefully, and he's far ruder to her than she is to him. Frankly, I was glad when she started fighting back. When Phyllis first came here, she was as nervous as a whipped pup. It took a long time for her to blossom. Look what happened today. Wiggins made fun of her accomplishment. He belittled her in front of everyone and made her feel as if what she'd contributed was worthless."

"He apologized."

"He said he was sorry after he realized that everyone, including Mrs. Goodge, wanted to box his ruddy ears. If Wiggins keeps picking at her, she'll go right back into being the shy, unattractive chubby girl she used to be."

"And that's the problem in a nutshell," Smythe declared softly. "She's become a right pretty young woman, and Wiggins is havin' a hard time makin' the adjustment. He used to treat her like a little sister, but now, I think he's seein' her differently."

It took a moment before she understood. "Are you saying that Wiggins is . . ."

"Fallin' a bit in love with the lass." Smythe nodded. "And I know how he feels. If you'll remember back to when we first come together here, I treated Betsy the same way Wiggins is treatin' Phyllis."

"But you were never mean to Betsy," she argued. "You didn't make her feel small and worthless. You used to tease her a bit, but that's all."

"Maybe that's 'ow you recall the situation, but I'll bet if you asked Betsy, she'd remember it differently," Smythe said. "Look, all I'm askin' is for you to let me 'ave a word with the lad."

Mrs. Jeffries wasn't sure what she should do. They were a family of sorts here at Upper Edmonton Gardens, and sometimes, unexpected changes could have dire consequences. "But if what you say is true and he's developing feelings for her, what if she doesn't reciprocate those feelings? That could prove very painful for Wiggins and Phyllis, not to mention the situation would be awkward for all of us."

"Do you have any better ideas? I've seen the way he looks at 'er when he thinks nobody is watchin', and tellin' him to behave isn't goin' to change 'ow he's feeling."

"Oh dear, I suppose you're right. I just don't want anyone to be hurt."

"Neither do I, but none of us get through this life without a bit of hurt. Just let me talk to 'im," Smythe urged. "If nothin' else, I'll put a stop to him jabbin' at her all the time."

"And I'll have a word with Phyllis and let her know that she could be a bit kinder as well."

"Lady Cannonberry is back," Mrs. Jeffries announced as she hung up the inspector's hat and coat. Witherspoon had come home earlier than expected.

He broke into a broad smile. "That's wonderful news, Mrs. Jeffries. After her last letter, I was afraid she was going to be away far longer."

"Luckily, her relative improved enough that she could hire a nurse for the lady, so she could come home." She started down the corridor. "She stopped in this afternoon. If you're not too exhausted, she'd like you to have a drink with her after dinner. She's acquired a very nice bottle of Bordeaux she wants you to sample."

He fell into step behind her. "Did she say what time?"

Mrs. Jeffries opened the double door leading to the study. "Unfortunately, there's a meeting she has to attend this evening. She says she'll be home by eight o'clock. But if you're too tired, I can send Wiggins over with a—"

"I won't be tired," he interrupted. "I'm so grateful she was able to come home a bit early." He went to his chair, flopped down, and rubbed his hands together. "You and I can have a lovely glass of sherry before dinner."

Mrs. Jeffries got their drinks and took her seat. "Tell me about your day, sir."

"It started off quite well." He took a sip of sherry. "We went through Thomas Mundy's possessions and actually found something useful." He told her about finding the slip of paper with the three names and addresses. "As you can imagine, we were intrigued to see Ronald Hart's name at the top of the list. His name has come up previously in this investigation, so we spoke with him first."

"Gracious, sir, that is interesting. What did he say?"

"Quite a bit," he replied. He told her about his meeting with Hart.

"Let me see if I understand. Hart claimed he'd not seen nor heard from Thomas Mundy in twenty years, yet he initially denied even being at the Wrexley Hotel on the morning of the murder?" Mrs. Jeffries repeated. "And he only changed his story when you caught him out? Don't you think that was rather suspicious behavior?"

"Of course, but once he explained his reasons for wanting to keep his presence there confidential, it was understandable. No one wants to admit they've met with someone for the sole purpose of gaining political support to take a dying man's spot on the county council."

"But Ronald Hart is known to have political ambitions," Mrs. Jeffries argued. "He's always giving speeches to one group or another. I don't see how admitting he was meeting with a political supporter could have any negative consequences."

"Politicians tend to be very careful, Mrs. Jeffries," Witherspoon explained. "So his actions were self-serving and, to my way of thinking, foolish. But that doesn't make him a murderer."

"Does he have an alibi?"

"He has one, but I'm not satisfied with his explanation of his movements. He claims to have gone to his club after his mysterious meeting at the Wrexley and talked about the political situation here in London with, as he put it, 'other like-minded men.' He stayed till five o'clock. Then he came home and changed into some warm clothes." Witherspoon's spectacles slipped down his nose, but he didn't seem to notice. "After that, he says he went for a long walk and didn't get home until almost ten o'clock. He said that he was trying to prepare for his place on the council by seeing firsthand how the poor and 'less fortunate' had to live. Then he claimed that he often walked when he had thinking to do. His butler verified that he was wearing a heavy greatcoat when he got home that night."

"Did anyone see him when he was on this walk?" Mrs. Jeffries asked.

"Not that he could recall. But as he was in impoverished areas, none of his friends or acquaintances could possibly have seen him." Witherspoon smiled skeptically. "He said he went along the Uxbridge Road toward Shepherds Bush and from there to Hammersmith. I reminded him that there are a number of fixed point constables along those roads and that as he was a well-known local politician, I was sure one of them would recall seeing him. That was when he asked us to leave."

"And did you?" It wasn't like Witherspoon to let someone bully him.

He nodded. "It was obvious we weren't going to get any

more information out of the fellow, and as the day was getting on, we wanted to get to the Bainbridge Hotel to interview Marianne Pelletier. But we've sent constables both to the club to verify that part of his story and to speak to the fixed point lads who were on duty." He continued with his recital.

Mrs. Jeffries listened closely. Once again, the inspector had found out so much that between his information and everything they'd learned at the afternoon meeting, it would be prudent to write it down. It wasn't that she didn't trust her memory, though she was the first to admit it wasn't as good as it used to be; it was simply that making notes helped her to see connections. "So let me see if I understand," she said when he paused to take another drink. "Marianne Pelletier never met Mundy, but she holds him responsible for her sister's suicide?"

"That's right, and to some extent, she's right. His behavior was abominable."

"Did she strike you as a stupid woman, sir?" She took a sip from her own glass.

He smiled knowingly. "Not at all, and I'm quite sure she realized her statement meant that we had to consider her a suspect."

"Does she have an alibi?" Mrs. Jeffries knew that if Marianne Pelletier was the mysterious blonde who had flagged down a hansom near the Wrexley the night of the murder and been dropped at the Bainbridge Hotel, she most definitely didn't.

Witherspoon shrugged. "She claims to have had an early dinner and then gone for a walk before retiring for the evening."

"Goodness, sir, half of London seems to have been out walking," she muttered. "Odd, really, as it was quite a chilly evening."

He laughed. "But like Mr. Hart, no one else can verify this

information. So, lacking any evidence to the contrary, we'll have to take her word for it. After we spoke with her, we interviewed Daniel Wright. He was the last of the names on the list."

"How is he connected with the victim?" Mrs. Jeffries asked. Thanks to Luty's source, they not only knew how Wright and Mundy were connected, but Wiggins had also been able to find out some very pertinent information about him.

"Mundy worked for Wright in California." He told her about the interview with the American. "I wasn't sure what to make of his statement. On the one hand, he accused Mundy of both theft and attempted murder, but on the other, he claimed his reason for being here was to get his money back."

"If he was telling the truth, sir."

"We've sent a telegram to the San Francisco Police Department. They should be able to verify Mr. Wright's claim that Mundy hired men to kill him. At least we'd know whether that part of his statement is factual."

"But even if he was telling the truth, that doesn't mean he didn't come to kill," she pointed out. "It could well be he planned on murdering Mundy and then stealing the money he was owed."

"True, but we know his whereabouts at the time of the murder. His landlady confirmed he was back at the lodging house and that he stayed in for the rest of the evening."

She wished she could think of a way to let the inspector know that Wright hadn't stayed inside and that he'd not only gone out and slipped back inside but that he also had a gun.

"However, I'm not sure she'd know what the man might or might not have done. The lodging house is a dreadful, almost derelict place," he continued. "The landlady doesn't appear to have spent any money on keeping the property in decent repair. The front door lock is flimsy and cheap, and I imagine the locks on the windows are even worse. Additionally, Wright's occupation means that he has the skills to get in and out quite easily."

"What do you mean, sir?"

"Wright is a builder, so even if every window in the place had good, sturdy locks, which I doubt, he'd know how to ensure that they were easily circumvented."

"Are you saying that you think he went out and came back in a window?"

"It's certainly possible." He took another sip of sherry. "As long as the rent is paid, it's not the sort of household where the landlady is overly concerned with her guests' activities."

"Did you speak with the servants?" Mrs. Jeffries asked. "Did you ask if any of them had noticed anything?"

"No, but I will. I'm going to reinterview everyone again tomorrow," Witherspoon said. "It was getting late, Mrs. Jeffries, and I wanted Constable Barnes to get home at a decent hour. I've kept him working very long hours the last two nights. He'd never complain, but I thought he looked tired. Mr. Wright also agreed not to leave town, but just to be sure, I've asked the local lads to keep an eye on him."

"What about this Mr. Oswald Hart?" Mrs. Jeffries toyed with the stem of her glass. "Mr. Wright claimed he saw him at the Wrexley on the night of the murder. Are you going to try to find him?"

"We've already sent a telegram to the Leicestershire Constabulary asking for help as to his whereabouts. He owns a business on the local High Street in Market Harborough, so someone should know where he is."

Mrs. Jeffries had no idea what to make of any of this. There was now so much information buzzing about in her head, she wasn't even sure what questions she ought to be asking.

"Then again, we may be looking at this murder from the wrong angle."

"Why do you say that, sir? Thomas Mundy appears to have an inordinate number of enemies. From what you've learned so far, any one of them could have killed him."

"Because, as Constable Barnes pointed out, Mundy lived well while he was in London, and he wasn't living on credit. Yet there was no cash, no record of an English current account, nor any letters of credit among his possessions. So what was the man using for money?"

"Perhaps he had some funds hidden, sir?"

Witherspoon nodded in agreement. "He must have. Which means we might have been wrong all along about the motive for the murder. Indeed, there are at least three and possibly more people who hated him and might have wanted him dead. But it could just as easily be someone who realized he constantly used cash, never went to a bank, and therefore concluded that he kept a great deal of money in his hotel room."

"So he could have been killed by someone who simply noticed his habits but wasn't necessarily connected to him?"

"It's certainly possible."

"But if he was a thief, why not take the victim's watch and ring?"

"Perhaps the killer heard someone coming, or perhaps he or she knew that the ring and the watch could be traced back to him or her if they tried to sell them." He shrugged. "But money leaves no trail. I was foolish to dismiss the notion of theft as a motive. I should have considered it and acted accordingly from the very start."

"But you did, sir. That first evening, when we talked about it, you mentioned robbery as a possible motive."

"Yes, but I'm wondering if I should have pursued that line of inquiry more forcefully."

"What would you have done differently, sir?" She could see he was starting to doubt himself, and in truth, now that he'd laid out the case for good old-fashioned theft as the motive, it made sense. But there was something about the case, something about the way the man had been murdered that led her to believe there was more than money at stake here. "You've conducted a thorough investigation, and you've discovered that Mundy was an unsavory character who had many, many enemies. It's true that the killer may have taken whatever cash he or she could lay hands on when they killed Mundy, but as you yourself pointed out"—she stopped and desperately searched her mind for something he'd said that would build his confidence in himself—"if it were a case of theft, the killer would have taken everything of value, including the murder weapon, Mundy's gold-headed walking stick."

Witherspoon stared at her. "I said that?"

She wasn't sure if he had or hadn't, but she couldn't take the words back now. "You did, sir. You probably don't remember. It was at the beginning of the investigation, and you were more or less thinking aloud. You said, 'But if it was a case of a robbery, why didn't the killer take the walking stick as well as the watch and the ring?'" She watched him carefully, all the while holding her breath and hoping he'd believe her.

Finally, he smiled faintly and nodded. "Yes, I do recall something like that. It's as you always say, Mrs. Jeffries, sometimes I lose faith in my 'inner voice.'" He got to his feet. "Do you think dinner is ready? I'd like a chance to freshen up afterward before I go see Lady Cannonberry."

Mrs. Jeffries walked to the back door and checked that it was locked. It was very late, but she knew she wouldn't be able to sleep. The inspector had come home half an hour earlier with a spring in his step and a smile on his face. The rest of the household was now in their beds, and she was wandering the halls like a frustrated spirit. She came out into the kitchen, put her lantern on the table, and pulled the bottle of brandy she kept for emergencies from the bottom cupboard of the pine sideboard. She was exhausted but knew that in her current state of mind, she'd not sleep.

Her notes were neatly written up and tucked in her desk, but even after reading through them twice, she was no closer to unmasking Mundy's killer. There were now four, or possibly five if one included Oswald Hart, suspects with a strong reason for hating the victim enough to kill him.

Opening the top cupboard, she grabbed a glass and poured herself a small shot of brandy before sitting down. Mrs. Jeffries took a sip and closed her eyes as the liquid warmed the back of her throat. Mentally, she started going over the facts they had thus far.

First, there was Jennifer Payton. She claimed that all she wanted out of Mundy was the fifty pounds she'd lent him. It was by no means a fortune, but murder had been done for far less. Could she have been driven to kill him because she knew he'd renege on paying back what he owed? Or was it possible that she had murdered him and stolen whatever money she could find in his room? But if that was true, why go through the motion of showing up at the Wrexley the day after he'd died and creating a scene? No sane person would deliberately bring himself to the notice of the police. Yet that was exactly what Jennifer Payton had done.

Then there was Marianne Pelletier. She held Mundy responsible for her sister's suicide. She'd been in London for a month and, according to her statement, had hired a private detective to find Mundy. But did it really take that long for a professional to track someone down? Mrs. Jeffries didn't think so, but she wasn't sure. She wished the inspector had asked Mrs. Pelletier exactly when the detective had located Mundy. Perhaps she'd mention this to Barnes tomorrow.

Third, there was Ronald Hart. He had political ambitions and went to great lengths to ensure that the general populace had no idea that he was a thoroughly unpleasant person. What was more, there was no evidence he had had contact with Mundy in twenty years. But if Hatchet's information was correct, it was possible that Mundy altered a will that made Hart the heir at the expense of his relatives. But was an alleged crime from twenty years ago a motive for murder?

She took another sip of brandy. Then there was Daniel Wright. To her mind, he was the person most directly affected by Mundy. He'd lost everything and almost been killed. Yet he claimed he was only interested in getting his money back. She sighed and closed her eyes for a moment.

Last, there was Oswald Hart. According to Wright's statement, he loathed Thomas Mundy. But he'd not given a sufficient reason why Oswald Hart should hate Mundy enough to murder him. What was more, Wright had a very good reason for wanting to cast the shadow of suspicion onto someone else, so until she had more facts, Oswald Hart was the least likely of the bunch to have done the deed.

She sat in the semidarkness, staring across the long kitchen toward the window, and let her mind wander. Snippets and snatches from their meetings popped in and then out of her head. *"Someone in Hinckley died, and Thomas Mundy's name was bandied about by the gossips."* Could the dead person be Marianne Pelletier's sister? Mrs. Jeffries asked herself. It was certainly possible, but she wasn't going to assume it as fact just because it seemed to fit nicely. But she'd add it to her notes when she went up to her room and see if it could be verified.

"In the last day or so, one of the maids found a gold button on the back staircase and a bellboy found a lace handkerchief in the hallway and another maid found a pearl hatpin. All of them kept what they'd found." Now, why did that spring to mind? she wondered. But over the years, she'd learned to trust the bits and pieces that came and went, so she let her thoughts wander where they would. Was it possible to determine which of the motives was the strongest? But she immediately discarded that notion. Hatred and vengeance were deeply personal to the individual, so figuring out which one of the four wanted him dead the most was impossible.

She got up, put the brandy back in the sideboard, and took her glass to the sink. As she rinsed it under the pump, she realized that despite all she'd learned today, she was still a long way from figuring this one out.

Constable Barnes frowned ominously. "This is a lot of information the household has discovered, and it won't be easy getting it to the inspector."

"I know." Mrs. Jeffries smiled sympathetically. "But much of it dovetails nicely with what you already know."

"Pull the other one, Mrs. Jeffries," he shot back. "You've found out that Daniel Wright had a gun and was goin' in and out by the larder window. Plus, Marianne Pelletier was probably within a hundred yards of the Wrexley when Mundy was killed . . ."

"But disproving her alibi should be simple," Mrs. Jeffries interrupted. "All you need do is find the hansom driver who picked her up by the station. It should be easy. He uses the cabman's shelter off the Uxbridge Road and has ginger-colored hair." She'd spent a good part of the early morning coming up with ways the constable could confirm their information. It was important that it be presented to the inspector as just another facet of the investigation. "Smythe will point him out."

"Right, then, that's one bit taken care of, but what about Daniel Wright? Unless that maid is willing to tell me what she told young Wiggins, we've no way of disproving his statement." Still frowning, he took a swig of his tea.

"Perhaps she will talk to you," Mrs. Jeffries insisted. "Well, maybe not to you, but she seems susceptible to young men. Why don't you send Constable Evans or Constable Griffiths along to have a word with her? She's not interested in hiding what she knows from the police; she just doesn't want her mistress to know she was pilfering food. Tell them to make sure they take her statement out of earshot of the landlady."

Barnes considered the idea. "That might work. We have to go to the station this morning anyway to see if we've had replies from the Leicestershire Constabulary and the San Francisco Police Department. I suppose I could send one of the lads to the lodging house. But what about the rumors that Mundy was fiddlin' with wills from twenty years ago?"

"You don't need to do that one," Mrs. Goodge interrupted. "I can."

Both of them looked at the cook.

"I've an old colleague who used to work in Leicestershire," she explained. "Howard Burrell."

"The man who came by the other evening?" Mrs. Jeffries asked.

"That's right. I can always go to the inspector and tell him that I'd heard this rumor from Howard."

"Hold off on that," Barnes said. "There's a chance the Leicestershire police will know Oswald Hart's whereabouts, and if he's still in London, he might be able to speak to that matter. If he's already gone back to the Midlands, then you can use your friend as a source and mention it to the inspector." He put his mug down and rose to his feet. "I'll do my best with the rest of what you've told me." He headed for the back stairs.

"I'm sure you'll do an excellent job," Mrs. Jeffries called after him. "You always do." As soon as he'd gone, she turned to Mrs. Goodge. "Before everyone arrives for our meeting, I wanted to let you know that Smythe is going to have a chat with Wiggins."

"About Phyllis?"

"Yes, he thinks he knows what the problem might be between the two of them."

The cook snorted faintly. "The problem is they're both acting like children. It's not just our lad bein' rude, you know. Phyllis has given him the sharp side of her tongue as well."

"But he's been far worse."

"I don't think so." The cook put her hands on her hips. "You've

183

always been willing to look the other way because you felt sorry for the girl, as do I, but she stirs it up when she gets the chance."

"And you've always been willing to take his part," Mrs. Jeffries charged. "You're so close to him, you think he can do no wrong."

"That's not true."

Mrs. Jeffries opened her mouth to retort and then clamped it shut and shook her head. "Look at us . . ." She trailed off as they heard footsteps on the stairs. "Oh drat, someone's coming. We'll discuss this later."

"Well, if Smythe knows what he's about," the cook whispered, "maybe we won't need to. If he talks to Wiggins and brings him to his senses, maybe she'll come to hers as well and this house can get back to normal."

Mrs. Jeffries nodded as if in agreement, but she had a feeling that getting back to "normal" wasn't going to be easy.

The Durwood Hotel was a narrow redbrick building near the Hammersmith Bridge. The small lobby was clean, and the desk clerk had been most helpful when the inspector requested Oswald Hart's room number.

After leaving Upper Edmonton Gardens, the two policemen had stopped in at the Ladbroke Road Police Station to see if either of the two telegrams Barnes had sent the previous day had received a reply. There was nothing from San Francisco, but the Leicestershire Constabulary had obtained Oswald Hart's London address. Barnes had also used the time to have a quick word with Constable Evans, and Barnes hoped the lad would be able to get a statement from the maid at Wright's lodging house.

"Let's cross our fingers that Mr. Oswald Hart hasn't decided to go back to the Midlands," Barnes muttered. He stopped at the top of the fourth-floor landing to catch his breath.

"His key is still at reception, and the clerk said he'd not seen him leave the premises, so let's assume he's still here. I'd hate to think we climbed all these stairs in vain." Witherspoon sucked in a lungful of air before starting down the dimly lighted corridor. The hotel hadn't been fitted with electric lights, and the gas lamps were turned off for the day.

Barnes stopped in front of room 410. "This is it, sir." He banged his knuckles against the wood.

There was a rustling sound from inside, and then the door cracked open an inch. "I told you I didn't wish to be disturbed . . ." The voice trailed off and the door swung open. "Good Lord, you're not the chambermaid."

"No, we're the police," Witherspoon replied. "Are you Oswald Hart?"

"I am." He was a short, stout man with thinning hair the color of dirty sand, hazel eyes framed by bushy eyebrows, and a florid complexion. "What do you want? Why have you come to my room?"

"We'd like to ask you some questions," Barnes said.

"Why?" He leaned against the door frame with one hand on the knob.

"I'm Inspector Gerald Witherspoon, and this is Constable Barnes. May we come in, Mr. Hart? It's very important we speak with you."

He nodded curtly and waved them inside. The walls were covered with dark red and green patterned paper, green muslin curtains hung from the one window, and the iron bed was covered with a maroon bedcover badly frayed along the bottom.

Hart gestured toward the wardrobe and the one chair that stood beside it. "I hope this won't take too long—there's just the one place to sit." He gave them a sour smile.

"I can stand." Barnes propped himself against the door frame and pulled out his pencil and notebook.

"I can stand as well," Witherspoon said. "Mr. Hart, we'll be as quick as possible, but it's going to take more than a moment or two. I suggest, Mr. Hart, that you'd be more comfortable sitting."

Hart stared at him for a moment and then crossed the room and flopped down on the chair. "What's this about, Inspector?"

"Are you acquainted with a man named Thomas Mundy?"

"I am." Hart crossed his arms and legs. "I suppose this is about his murder."

"That's correct."

"I read about it in the papers, and I can't say I'm surprised." He gave them another sour smile. "Thomas Mundy had a lot of enemies."

"When was the last time you saw him?" Barnes asked.

"About seven months ago."

"Where did you see him?" Witherspoon asked.

"He was coming out of a cottage in Hinckley. That's in Leicestershire. I own an antiques shop in Market Harborough. I'd gone to Hinckley to evaluate the estate of an elderly woman who'd passed away."

"You go that far to do estate evaluations?" Barnes stared at him skeptically. "That's almost twenty-five miles."

"It was worth my while, Constable. The estate in question had some very valuable silver pieces as well as some early-Regency furniture, and I'd done valuations for the family on previous occasions. They specifically wanted my services," he said. "But that's neither here nor there. You asked when I last saw Thomas Mundy, and I've told you."

"Did you speak to him when you saw him?" the inspector asked.

"Why would I? I'd not seen him in twenty years." Hart unfolded his arms and placed his hands flat against his thighs.

"How were you and Thomas Mundy acquainted?" Barnes asked. If he was very lucky, he might lead Hart down the path he needed him to walk.

"He was a clerk at a law firm my family once used."

"Were you acquainted with all the clerks at the firm?" Barnes kept his attention on Hart, but he could feel the inspector's curious gaze in his direction.

"No, just Mundy."

"Are you acquainted with a man named Daniel Wright?" Witherspoon asked. "He's an American. We understand he came into your shop."

Barnes sagged in relief. The inspector had realized it was important to keep pressing Hart about his prior relationship with Mundy.

Hart sucked in air. "We've met. He came into my shop, asking questions about Thomas Mundy."

"Mr. Wright claims you told him where Mundy was staying in London." Witherspoon smiled slightly.

"That's absurd. I've no idea what this Wright person is talking about. I told him no such thing."

"Why would he lie? He insists you gave him the name of Mundy's hotel." The constable shifted his weight to take some of the pressure off his aching knee.

"He's lying. How could I tell him where Mundy was staying when I didn't even know he was at the Wrexley?" Hart clamped his mouth shut as he realized he'd given himself away.

Witherspoon was surprised. This was twice now someone had revealed they were lying by knowing Mundy's hotel. Ronald Hart had done the same thing. "Mr. Hart, neither the constable nor I mentioned the name of the hotel, yet you knew it."

Hart sighed heavily and closed his eyes. "This is getting tiresome, Inspector. It's obvious you've heard the rumors about Thomas Mundy from all those years ago."

"We'd like to hear what you have to say about them," Barnes said quickly.

"Mundy was a clerk at Bartleby, Warnock, and Sherwood. They were a firm of solicitors that did legal work for a number of respectable people in Market Harborough, including my family. As you can imagine, the firm dealt mainly in property conveyances, leases, and wills, that sort of thing. But they were respectable. They're gone now—they went out of business twenty years ago. But even then, the three partners were old, and if the rumors were accurate, they were half-senile. Mundy was their bright young man, the one who kept everything up and running properly. Mind you, most of their clients were as old and doddery as the partners." He paused and took a breath. "But there were occasions when a will would be read and the heirs would be quite surprised by the contents. Once or twice, matters were taken a step further, but when the documents were examined, everything looked properly done. But on several occasions, especially when the partners had been indulging in a bit too much port after their evening meals, they'd all admit even they were surprised when the will was actually read. Old Bartleby was once overheard to say that he was beginning to suspect that someone was making unauthorized changes."

"Are you suggesting that Thomas Mundy altered wills without the partners' knowledge?" Barnes wanted to get the charge out into the open.

"I'm not suggesting it, Constable. I'm saying I know he did it," he cried. "It happened to my family."

"Thomas Mundy changed the terms of a will in your family?" Witherspoon clarified.

"That's right. I know my uncle Bernard's will was tampered with, and I suspect I know who in the family paid Mundy to do it."

"That's a very serious charge, Mr. Hart. Are you sure of your facts?"

"What do facts matter now, Inspector?" Hart leapt up and began to pace. "Ronald Hart conspired with Thomas Mundy to cheat me and my cousins out of our fair share of Uncle Bernard's estate. Bernard told me specifically that the only thing he was leaving Cousin Ronald was his collection of walking sticks. Bernard loathed Ronald. But when the will was actually read, Ronald ended up with most everything. Needless to say, the rest of us who had been told we were heirs were rather put out. Lawsuits were threatened, but before anything could be done, Mundy mysteriously packed up and disappeared, and Horace Bartleby, the solicitor who had been given instructions on the original will, was so far gaga that no one dared pursue the case, so Ronald got it all."

"In other words, there was nothing you could do," Barnes murmured.

"That's right, so even though Thomas Mundy did something reprehensible, why would I kill him? If I was going to murder someone, it would be Ronald, my despicable cousin."

"You're sure that Mr. Ronald Hart paid Thomas Mundy to alter the will?" Witherspoon looked thoughtful.

"Of course he did. But none of us could ever prove it." He smiled again. "But now that Ronald has decided he wants a career in Parliament, he may need the goodwill of his family. Now, if that is all . . ." He started to get up, but the inspector held up a hand.

"Your relationship with your cousin is your affair, providing it has nothing to do with Thomas Mundy's murder."

"As I said, Inspector, if I were a murderer, I'd have killed Ronald years ago. He's a loathsome specimen and always has been."

There were moments when Witherspoon was glad he didn't have many blood relatives. "But we've still more questions to ask. Regardless of what one may think of Mundy's character, no one had the right to take his life, and it is our duty to find his murderer."

"Don't expect me to waste any tears on Mundy's death. He was rotten through and through. I've heard that when he came back to Leicestershire, he left some poor woman from Hinckley at the altar and that she later killed herself."

Witherspoon wasn't going to debate the fellow. "Where were you on Monday night?"

"The night that Mundy was killed?" Hart shrugged. "I went to the West End to see a play, but it was fully booked, so I stopped in at a pub on Oxford Street and then came back here."

"We have a witness who said that you were seen sneaking into the back of the Wrexley Hotel that night," Witherspoon said.

"Who's the witness? Daniel Wright?" He laughed. "Wright has his own reasons for saying he saw me. Take my word for it, Inspector. Mr. Wright had more reason to want Mundy dead than I did, so of course he'd lie and say he saw me."

"Why did you come to London, sir?" Barnes asked.

"Why else? To buy and sell antiques."

CHAPTER 8

Smythe banged on the back door of the Dirty Duck Pub. It wasn't open, but he needed to speak with Blimpey and didn't want to wait around twiddling his thumbs before getting out on the hunt. The morning meeting had been very short. There hadn't been any specific instructions from Mrs. Jeffries, so they'd all more or less said they'd get out and about to see what they could find.

He'd tried to have a quick word with Wiggins, but the lad had said he was going to Bayswater to have a go at finding one of Hart's servants. Luty and Hatchet had immediately said they'd drop him off on their way back to Knightsbridge. Neither of them were meeting with their own sources until later in the day. Smythe frowned and knocked again. Where was everyone?

The door opened, and Eldon, Blimpey's man-of-all-work, as he called himself, stuck his nose out. "Guv said you might be comin' today." He waved Smythe inside, closed the door, and led the way down the darkened corridor. "He don't have a lot of time today. He's taking Nell and the baby out somewhere," he said. "You want somethin'?"

"No." Smythe shook his head. "I'm in a 'urry myself."

"Give us a shout if ya change yer mind." Eldon veered off and ducked into the storage room behind the bar. Smythe continued on into the pub proper. Blimpey was seated at his usual spot. He was reading a newspaper and holding a mug of tea.

"I hear you're in a hurry." Smythe sat down on the stool.

"You heard right. Nell wants us to take the baby so her old aunt in Colchester can have a look at the lad. I've put her off as long as I can, but she's insistin'. Claims that between the two of us, we've so little family that the boy needs to meet the few that are left." He shrugged. "She's got a point."

Smythe grinned. He knew that half of Blimpey's complaints about his wife's demands were just for show. He'd do anything for his Nell and his baby son. "Women are like that, Blimpey. They want ya to do right. I told ya that when ya married your lady. But as you're in a rush, what've ya found out?"

"For starters, Mundy is a full-on confidence trickster. He's wanted in New York, Chicago, Denver, and San Francisco. His specialty is preying on lonely spinsters or elderly women. He's got two main tricks. One, he finds an older spinster, hopefully someone with little or no family. Then he courts her, plans an opulent, expensive honeymoon, and at the last moment, he'll come up with some tall tale about his money being temporarily tied up and would the lady mind waiting for a while to have a proper honeymoon."

Smythe looked disgusted. "Let me guess—the lady agrees they'll use her money to buy the tickets. She hands over the cash and he disappears, right?"

"Right you are. He's pulled that one on at least three women in the States and one woman here, a lady named Phoebe Cullen. She committed suicide." He drew back. "'Ave you heard this before? You don't look surprised."

"We knew about the one here, but we didn't know her name," Smythe said. "And I'm pretty sure I know what his other trick is as well—he cons elderly ladies out of their money by claiming to represent a rich group of investors."

Blimpey nodded. "Guess I've not found out much you don't already know. But you'll 'ave to pay anyway."

"I intend to," Smythe retorted. "Go on, tell me the rest. I can tell by your face there's more."

"Well, Mundy has been in England more than a year, and as soon as he got back, he went up to the Midlands, close to where he used to live." He took another sip. "He took rooms at a decent lodging house and presented himself as a grieving widower. He met Phoebe Cullen at church, and within five months, he was engaged to the lady. When she died, there were rumors some very nice pieces of jewelry were missing from her cottage."

"He's been here almost a year," Smythe repeated. That was something they'd not heard before, but it made sense. Mundy had to have had some time to "court" his victim. "What kind of jewelry was taken?"

He gave a negative shake of his head. "I couldn't find out, and it'd not do ya much good anyway. He'd have sold it to a fence within a day or two. Confidence men rely on cash."

Smythe nodded in agreement. "Yeah, and what could a fence tell us that we don't already know. Thomas Mundy was a miserable little sod and a thief."

"Why is your lot workin' so 'ard to find his killer?" Blimpey stared at him curiously. "Seems to me the world's a bit better off without the likes of him in it."

"Sometimes we wonder that ourselves." Smythe got up. "But once you start pickin' and choosin' who you think deserves justice, then the whole idea of justice goes right out the window."

"Please make yourself comfortable, Lady Cannonberry," the butler said as he led her through the double oak doors into Octavia Wells' drawing room. "Mrs. Wells will be down shortly. Would you care for tea?"

"No, thank you." Ruth sat down on one of the twin wing-back chairs facing the matching sofa and looked around the huge room. It was both calming and elegant. The furniture was upholstered in navy and cream fabric, and the walls were painted a pale sky blue. A crystal chandelier was suspended from the cream-colored ceiling, and blue velvet drapes topped with balloon valances hung at the windows facing the garden. Colorful blue, gold, and green Oriental rugs were strewn across the oak parquet floor.

"Oh, my dear, what a delightful surprise. I do hope I haven't kept you waiting too long." Octavia Wells burst into the room like a force of nature. She was petite in stature, plump as a pigeon, and dressed by the best seamstress in London. Her eyes were brown and her hair a flaming red. She was rich, eccentric, and smart enough to let the world at large think of her as an empty-headed socialite interested in nothing but parties, clothes, and gossip. In reality, she used her social connections and the information she picked up in the ballrooms and salons of the wealthy and powerful to raise funds for the London Women's Suffrage Society. She was also their treasurer.

Ruth adored her. "Not at all. I'm grateful you've time to see me. I apologize for barging in like this, but it's rather important."

"No apology is necessary. We're old friends, Ruth, and you're always welcome here. Now, let's get right to it. Unfortunately, I don't have much time." She sat down in the other wing chair. "I'm having morning coffee with Margaret Loomis Jones. Apparently, that philandering husband of hers has finally gone to meet his Maker, and Margaret now has her hands on his very fat purse strings."

"Is she sympathetic to our cause?"

"Not particularly, but as her late spouse loathed our movement, she'll make a rather hefty donation if for no other reason than to spite him and his relatives. They are a reactionary bunch. But do tell me why you've come. Do you need some information to pass along to that nice inspector of yours?"

Ruth started to protest and then thought better of it. She'd used Octavia as a "source" on previous occasions and knew she could trust her. "I do. It's about his latest case."

"Wonderful. I was hoping you'd come see me. This is just like being in one of Mr. Arthur Conan Doyle's stories." She laughed in delight and clapped her chubby hands together. "I do have some information that might prove useful, but as you were out of town, I wasn't sure it would be prudent to pass it along to anyone else."

"What is it?"

"I take it you're referring to the Mundy murder? The man who was bludgeoned to death in his hotel room? Right? I just want to ensure your inspector hasn't already solved that one and moved to another, because if that's the situation, then I'm afraid you've wasted your time."

"Visiting with you is never a waste of time, but he's still on the Mundy case," Ruth assured her. She'd forgotten that Octavia was the sort of person who verified every little detail, which, of course, made her an excellent treasurer for their group.

"Good. I found out that a man named Mundy was courting Gemma Ridley. She has a big house on Hanover Square. Her aunt left it to her. Gemma is a spinster. She's forty, plain as a pikestaff, and from what I've heard, socially awkward. She's from a religious family, and I don't mean Church of England. Her father was purported to be an Anabaptist of some sort and didn't approve of playing cards or dancing or anything else that could give a young woman either social confidence or the ability to spot an absolute cad. She was raised in Plymouth and moved to London when she inherited the house and a bit of money from her mother's sister."

"Her parents didn't come with her?" Ruth asked.

"Her mother lives in Plymouth with another daughter, and the father is dead." Octavia glanced at the clock on the mantelpiece. "Oh dear, time is getting short. Let me get all this out, and you can make of it what you will."

Ruth nodded.

"The gossip I heard is that Thomas Mundy was asking questions about Gemma Ridley before he met her."

"What kind of questions?" Ruth suspected she could guess.

Octavia smiled knowingly. "What do you think? He wanted to know how much money she had, who had control over it, and if she'd ever been married. It didn't take him long to find out she was naive, lonely, and rich. Supposedly, that's when he contrived to meet her."

"Do you know who introduced them?"

"No one did." Octavia glanced at the clock on the mantelpiece. "Miss Ridley had money, but she didn't have access to London society. Mundy met her at a political speech given by that dreadful man, oh dear, what's his name? Oh yes, it's Hart. Ronald Hart. He's awful. He's always haranguing about the evils of giving women the vote or letting them handle money or buy property. You know what I mean. He's just another disgusting old reactionary terrified that the world is changing. But I digress."

"Where and when was this?" Ruth knew exactly what she meant.

"A fortnight ago at the Portman Institute. The local Conservatives put on a program, and Hart was one of the speakers. Dulcie Makepeace was there . . ."

"Mrs. Makepeace is a Conservative?" Ruth couldn't believe it. "But she's one of our staunchest supporters, and the Conservatives hate our cause."

Octavia waved a hand. "Dulcie's no Conservative. She only went so she could report back to our executive committee what they were up to these days. But you see, she knows Gemma Ridley, not well, but they are acquainted. She's been hoping to interest Miss Ridley into joining our cause. She was trying to catch up with her, when she noticed a very attractive man who deliberately bumped into Gemma as they were all leaving. A few days later, she spotted Gemma with this man."

"Where?" Ruth wanted as many facts as possible, and Octavia was the kind of woman who understood the importance of details.

"At the restaurant in the Wrexley Hotel." Octavia smiled knowingly. "Interesting, isn't it. That's where Mundy was murdered, but again, I digress and we've no time for that. One of Dulcie's lunch companions identified the man with Gemma as

Thomas Mundy. He supposedly worked as an agent for an American investment consortium."

"He's a confidence trickster," Ruth replied. "So perhaps Miss Ridley had a lucky escape. He might have tricked her out of all her money."

"Even worse, he might have married her."

"What do you think of Oswald Hart's statement, sir?" Barnes asked as they came down the staircase and into the quiet lobby.

Witherspoon sighed. "He was forthright enough about Thomas Mundy's past transgressions, but I noticed he took care to make it seem as if he blamed his cousin and not the victim for the loss of his inheritance."

Barnes nodded politely to the young man at reception as they crossed the small space to the door. "True, sir." He pulled open the front door and came face-to-face with Constable Evans.

"Thank goodness you're still here. I was afraid I'd missed you." Evans sucked in a lungful of air as he stumbled backward to avoid colliding with Barnes. The two policemen stopped for a split second before continuing outside.

"Is everything alright?" the inspector asked.

Evans bobbed his head up and down as he tried to catch his breath. "Yes, sir," he finally gasped. "I've just been walking fast. I wanted to make sure I caught you before you left here."

"What is it?" Barnes asked.

"As you instructed, sir, I had a chat with the housemaid at Wright's lodging house," he replied. "She told me that Wright wasn't home the night Mundy was killed. She didn't know exactly what time he went out that evening, but she says it was past eleven when he came back inside. He climbed in through a larder window."

"Was the lock broken?" Witherspoon knew he'd been right about that place.

"No, sir. The girl says it's always locked up properly. She thinks that Wright slipped in and unlocked it himself. She said it wasn't the first time she'd seen him come and go that way."

"Why didn't she tell us that when we spoke with her?" Witherspoon muttered.

"She was probably pilfering food, sir," Barnes suggested. "You said the landlady didn't look like someone who spent a penny unless she was forced. The poor girl was probably hungry. Houses like that don't feed the servants decently. We're the police, sir. She was scared if she said anything to us, we'd tell on her."

"But I'd never do such a thing," Witherspoon exclaimed.

"She didn't know that, sir, and there're plenty on the force that wouldn't have any pity for the poor lass and would have said something about it," Evans blurted. "Sorry, sir, I didn't mean to speak out of turn."

"You're not. Your insights are valuable, Constable." Witherspoon grinned. "And I think I know why she spoke with you and not us."

Evan blushed all the way to the roots of his black hair. He knew he was attractive to women. The lads at the station were always teasing him about his looks, calling him "Handsome Harry" and silly things like that. "Well, sir, I think maybe she felt a younger person might be more sympathetic."

Witherspoon laughed. "I daresay you're right. Thank you, Constable, excellent job."

"Have you spoken to any of the fixed point constables on Ronald Hart's route?" Barnes asked.

"The route is spread over three divisions, sir. Constable Griffiths is talking to the lads at B and T Division, and I'll take F Division, sir. But I've not had a chance to speak to anyone yet. I'll get it done today, sir, and leave a report with the duty sergeant. Constable Griffiths is doin' the same, sir."

"Good idea." Witherspoon nodded approvingly. "That way we'll have the information regardless of what time we get back to the station."

"I'll be on my way, sir." Evans nodded respectfully and disappeared down the quiet street.

"I thought we were going to speak to Hart right away." Barnes surveyed the road, looking for a hansom. He didn't fancy walking all the way to Bayswater. "But would it be better to wait until we get the reports from the fixed point lads?"

"Let's not wait. I want to hear what Mr. Ronald Hart has to say about his cousin's assertion that he stole his inheritance."

Wiggins' mood didn't improve as the day clouded over. He turned the corner onto Florian Street and kept his eyes peeled for number 12. Ronald Hart's neighborhood was posh, so he couldn't keep walking up and down the street without someone noticing. But maybe his day would get better and a servant would stick their nose out of the back of number 12. Cor blimey, the day couldn't get much worse. He'd not slept much last night, and at the morning meeting, Phyllis hadn't even glanced in his direction.

He'd wanted to have a word with her, to apologize, but trying to get some time alone with her was like trying to see the ruddy Queen. Twice he'd started to ask her if they could slip out to the garden to talk, and both times he'd been interrupted, once by Mrs. Goodge, who was looking for Samson, her mean old cat, and once by the inspector, who took it into his head to come down to the kitchen to see Fred.

He pulled his coat tighter against the sudden chill and wished he'd worn his scarf. Not only would it have kept him warm, but if someone noticed him loitering about, it would have prevented his face from being recognized. He passed number 8, then 10, and he slowed his footsteps. He moved as slowly as he dared but saw no one. He got to the end of the street, crossed, and retraced his steps.

Just as he reached the Hart house, the side door opened, and a skinny, dark-haired boy raced out from around the house, shoved the gate open, and continued running down the street. Wiggins went after him. He considered himself a decent runner, but by the time he reached the corner, the boy was halfway down the long block. Wiggins ran after him, pushing himself hard to catch up.

The boy didn't realize he was being chased, so when Wiggins caught him by grabbing his shoulder, he yelped like a hurt puppy. "Oy . . . what you doin'?" He lunged to one side, trying to dislodge Wiggins' hand. "Leave off, let me be."

"Hold on, now." Wiggins released him and stepped back, both his hands raised in the air. "Sorry, I'm tryin' to do you a good turn. I didn't mean to scare you."

"I'm not scared." The boy stared at him suspiciously. "What do you mean? Do me a good turn how?"

Wiggins pulled a shilling out of his pocket and saw the lad's eyes widen. "I wanted to give this to you, that's all."

"What for?"

"I need some information about the man who owns the house you just come out of," Wiggins said. "If you'll answer me questions, I'll give you this and another one when we've finished chatting."

He studied Wiggins with an uncertain, speculative expression on his young face. "You don't look like you're a friend of his, so who are ya?"

"I work for a newspaper, and your guv is startin' to make a name for himself in some political circles. I just want a quick word."

The boy hesitated for a split second and then stuck out his hand. "Give it here, then. But you've got to walk with me to the omnibus stop. His nibs is sendin' me on one of his ruddy errands, and I've got to be back in time to get his evening clothes laid out proper."

Wiggins handed him the money and fell into step beside him as the boy started walking. "What's your name? I'm Albert Jones," he said, using his most common alias.

"I'm Nicholas Foley. What is it you're wantin' to ask? I don't know anythin' about the master's politics."

"I want to know where he was last Monday." Wiggins thought it best not to mention the murder. "My paper had a report that he was in the East End meetin' with one of them radical foreign groups."

Nicholas laughed. "Don't be daft. He was at his ruddy tailor's for half the day. I know because I had to go with him to carry his clothes." He stopped. "And they're bloomin' heavy— I can tell you that."

"You sure this was Monday?"

"Do I look stupid? 'Course I'm sure. My arms ached all day Tuesday because he stood about chattin' with the old fool he'd met inside the tailor's. Then, he made me run and fetch a hansom for the old man, and when I come back, loaded down with a huge bundle of his clothes, he stood there, showin' off to one of his mates. But he made a right mess of it, and I had to duck my head so he'd not see me tryin' not to laugh."

Wiggins realized this was a waste of his time, but he couldn't stop now. "Made a mess of what?"

Nicholas started walking again. "He does this trick with a coin, a Queen Victoria Jubilee half crown. So he's standin' there, lookin' all pleased with himself, and he takes out the coin and uses his fingers to walk it across the back of his hand. He does it all the time 'cause he loves showin' off how ruddy clever he is, but this time, something caught his eye, because all of a sudden he dropped it. I couldn't believe it—he never messes that trick up. But he did, and then his friend asked if he was alright, so I looked at him and he was staring down the road, watchin' a man and woman. I think they'd just got out of a hansom cab. I've never seen Mr. Hart look the way he did."

Wiggins was getting interested. "And how was that?"

"He'd gone right pale, and his mouth was gapin' open like he'd just had a shock. Then all of a sudden, he said he had to go. He yelled at me to find his ruddy coin and to go home, and he took off like the hound of hell was chasin' him. His friend just shrugged and walked away."

"Can you describe the man and woman?"

Nicholas shook his head. "No, I didn't get a good look at them, but I think Mr. Hart must've known one of 'em, because he followed them into Hanover Square."

"Followed them? Are you sure?"

"I know what I saw."

"Was he out all day?"

They'd reached the omnibus stop. Nicholas craned his neck, trying to see over the heads of the others standing on the pavement. "He come home about four that afternoon and shut himself up in his study. But he went out again that evening. I know because the housekeeper told the kitchen they all had to stay up till he come home. He wanted a hot dinner."

"If we have time, Constable, we'll interview Jennifer Payton again," Witherspoon murmured to Barnes as they stood in Ronald Hart's drawing room. "As you rightly pointed out, she followed Mundy to the Wrexley, and thus far, most of the others we know who had reason to want him dead do not have a sufficient explanation for their whereabouts at the time of the murder. I agree with your idea that she may have seen one of them."

Barnes heaved a silent sigh of relief. He'd been dropping hints that they needed to interview her again. "I think that would be wise, sir. I know there were guests coming and going, but if she had her eye on Mundy, she might have noticed more than she realizes."

"I want to ask her again about her relationship with Mundy." He frowned in confusion. "I simply don't understand why she lent him all that money."

Barnes hadn't found a way to let the inspector know it was pure greed. "Perhaps she wasn't candid with us about the rate of interest he'd agreed to repay. Mundy was such a cad, he might have lied to the lady and told her he'd pay her back double what she lent him." That was as close as he could come without flat out telling him.

The door flew open and Ronald Hart stepped inside. "For God's sake, this is getting tiresome. You do realize your mere presence here is fodder for the gutter press? I shall hold you responsible if any of this business is printed in the newspaper, do you understand?"

"I understand perfectly, Mr. Hart, but we've more questions to ask you, and solving a man's murder is more important than your political ambitions," Witherspoon said calmly.

"That's easy for you to say now," Hart sneered, "but you'll be singing a different tune soon enough."

"That's as it may be, sir, but for now, you'll need to answer our questions."

"I don't appreciate your coming to my home." He flopped down on the sofa. "I've already spoken to your superiors about you and your disrespectful manner."

"That is your right, sir. Nonetheless, we must do our duty." Witherspoon stifled a sigh. "If you don't like us coming to your home, we're quite willing to escort you to the station."

Hart's hands clenched into fists and his face turned red. "I don't have time for nonsense like that. I've a meeting with the local committee soon, so just get on with it."

"Thank you, Mr. Hart," Witherspoon said politely. "We spoke with one of your cousins, a Mr. Oswald Hart."

He snorted in derision. "Oswald. I can imagine what he had to say."

"Mr. Hart, according to your cousin, you inherited the majority of the estate of your uncle, Mr. Bernard Hart. Is that correct?"

"Yes, what of it?"

"Was Thomas Mundy the clerk for the law firm that handled your uncle's estate?" Barnes asked.

"Yes, but that was twenty years ago."

"We understand the rest of the Hart family was quite surprised when your uncle left most of his estate to you," Witherspoon said.

"You understand wrong," Hart retorted. "Uncle Bernard couldn't stand Oswald or any of the others in the family. He left the estate to me because he knew I'd do something useful with my life and wouldn't waste his money. As I've already told you, I'm being groomed for Parliament. I'm a personal friend of the prime minister. Lord Salisbury himself is supporting my candidacy, and the Conservatives are going to select me to stand in this constituency in the next election."

The inspector studied him for a long moment. "Mr. Oswald Hart claims the only thing your uncle was going to leave you was his cane collection."

"Oswald always was a liar. He's the one who got the cottage in Earl Shilton," Hart retorted. "Which he then sold. That's where he got the funds to open that pathetic little shop of his. The man has failed at everything he's done."

"Your cousin believes that you paid a clerk at Bartleby, Warnock, and Sherwood to alter Bernard Hart's will," Witherspoon charged.

Surprise flicked across his features before he caught himself. "Of course he'd say that. As I said, he's a liar and a coward. When he accused Thomas Mundy of altering the will, Mundy laughed in his face and threatened him with legal action if he repeated his ridiculous ideas publicly. That shut him up fast enough."

"But he wasn't the only one who had suspicions about Thomas Mundy," Barnes interjected. "Apparently, there were a number of rumors about the man's ethics."

Hart got to his feet. "Yes, I'll admit there were rumors about him. I believe there was even a time or two when relatives who thought they'd been cheated out of an inheritance insisted the will be examined by their own solicitors. But no one ever found anything wrong. Nothing was ever proven against the firm or Mundy."

"So why would your cousin insist that you and Thomas Mundy conspired to deprive him and other members of your family out of their rightful share of Bernard Hart's estate?" Witherspoon asked.

"Spite, Inspector, pure spite. Oswald and the rest of the family have hated me all my life. None of them has come near having the success that I've achieved. Now, unless you've more questions, I'd like you to go. I've important people coming, and I won't have my reputation damaged by the police hanging about the place."

Betsy kept her head lowered as she wheeled the pram through the lobby of the Wrexley Hotel. Mrs. Jeffries had assured her that she was in no danger of running into any police who might know her as they'd finished searching the premises, but she wasn't taking any chances.

She smiled at the residents, most of them elderly women, as she made her way to the entrance of the dining room. Amanda did her part as well, grinning and giggling at everyone they passed. Betsy hoped the little one's good mood would last through lunch. If not, this was a wasted trip.

She'd dressed in an elegant maroon and gray striped day dress with a fitted jacket and matching hat. She'd worn the outfit deliberately as she wanted to give the impression she was a young matron of means. Which, of course, she was, but she generally had to hide that fact.

As she reached the entrance to the restaurant, the maître d' saw her and hurried over.

"Madam is here for lunch?"

"Yes. It'll be just the two of us." Betsy gave him a dazzling smile as she surveyed the room, looking for the most likely spot. The restaurant was half-full. Three men in business suits occupied a table near the entrance, so she dismissed that as a likely prospect and focused on the four tables along the window. Women were chatting and laughing together at three of them, so Betsy decided that she wanted the only empty table in the row. "May we sit by the window?"

"Of course, madam. Right this way." He led her across the room and pulled out a chair so she could angle the pram away from the aisle. "Will this do for you?"

"Of course, thank you." She let him pull out her chair and sat down. As he hurried off to get her a menu, she studied the occupants at the table to her left. Both the women had their heads together; one was quite young, very pretty, and the other middle aged. Probably mother and daughter, Betsy thought, and it looked like the mother was doing all the talking. She dismissed them as likely sources and glanced to her right. There were women there as well, but they were laughing among themselves, and from the snippets of conversation she caught, they had come into town for a nice luncheon.

The maître d' returned with her menu. "Your waiter will be here in a moment, madam."

"What time do you serve dinner?" She wanted to get him talking.

"We start at five, madam." He turned as an elderly woman using a cane appeared at the entrance. "Excuse me, madam."

Betsy nodded and noticed that Amanda's smile had disappeared. She grimaced, hoping Amanda wasn't going to be difficult. She was generally such a sweet-natured, curious child that it was a pleasure taking her to new places. She'd been fine earlier, giggling and wanting to pet the horse that pulled the four-wheeler carriage Betsy had hired to get them here. She'd enjoyed sitting in her pram and grinned from ear to ear when they'd entered the lobby, but now she was staring solemnly at the floor. Betsy scanned the menu, made her selections, and was all smiles when the waiter came to take the order. Amanda, though not her usual self, at least hadn't been fussy.

But nothing went as she'd hoped; no matter how much she smiled and tried to engage him in conversation, the waiter wasn't chatty. He answered her overtures about the "murder" with barely concealed irritation. The ladies on her left barely glanced in their direction when they finished their lunch and rose to leave, and she was too far away from the table on her right to hear anything but the occasional word or phrase. To top it off, Amanda's mood had definitely gone from solemn to stormy.

"Your lunch, madam." The waiter put the food in front of her as well as the empty plate she'd requested so she could mash up Amanda's. She'd ordered a lamb chop with boiled potatoes and carrots.

"Thank you." Betsy picked up her fork and scooped some of the boiled potatoes and carrots onto the empty plate. She smashed them up and glanced at the chop. Poking it with her fork, she realized it was tough, and that irritated her further. Amanda loved meat, but it would take a mallet to make this cut tender enough for her baby.

She picked up the knife and sliced through the chop, took a quick bite, and wished she'd ordered coddled eggs for both of them; the meat was not only tough, it was tasteless.

Amanda's face crinkled as she saw her mother eat. "Mama . . . I 'ungry."

"I know, sweetie, but I wanted to see if the food was soft enough for you. You've only a few teeth, and Mummy doesn't want you to choke. Here, have a bite of this." Betsy quickly put a tiny mound of the mashed vegetables onto a spoon and reached it toward her daughter's open mouth. Amanda ate like she was half-starved, chewing and swallowing and then opening her mouth for more. Betsy fed her one spoonful after another in a steady stream; if she tried to slow down, Amanda waved her fists and whimpered. "Slow down, darling. We're in no hurry. Here, let's have some bread."

Betsy grabbed a slice of bread, cut off the crust, and tore off a small bit. She handed it to Amanda, who stuffed it in her mouth, made a face, and spit it back out.

"Don't you like it? You usually love bread."

"Mummy, I 'ungry, 'ungry . . ." She pointed at the chop. "'Ungry, Mummy, 'ungry."

"I know, sweetie, but this chop is too greasy for you." She looked around for the waiter, intending to order the eggs, but like an omnibus when you needed one, he was nowhere to be seen.

"I 'ungry, 'ungry," Amanda screamed.

Betsy put more vegetables on the spoon, added a bit of the lamb juices, and shoved them into Amanda's open mouth. That was a mistake, because all of a sudden Amanda spit out the food, spraying it far enough to land on both the fronds of a potted fern and the back of a chair at the next table.

"Sweetie, what's wrong?" Alarmed, Betsy dropped the spoon as her daughter's face turned red and her eyes filled with tears. Her breath came in jagged gasps as her little chest and stomach pumped up and down. Betsy leapt out of the chair and grabbed the toddler under her arms just as a stream of vegetables erupted out of her mouth. A few moments later, it was over, but Betsy was covered with foul-smelling scraps of food and bile. Amanda was grinning like a drunken sailor.

The maître d' must have sent for help when the episode began, because a chambermaid suddenly appeared out of nowhere. She was a dark-haired young woman with brown eyes. "Would you like to go downstairs, ma'am?" She pointed toward the back corridor. "You can tidy up if you like."

"Thank you, that's very kind. I'll leave the pram here for a moment if you don't mind." She picked up Amanda and followed the maid.

She took them down a short corridor to a set of stairs that led to a room near the kitchen. Inside were a long table with mismatched chairs and a glass-fronted cupboard filled with plates, glasses, and soup bowls. "We take our meal and tea breaks here. Please sit down and I'll be right back, ma'am."

Betsy pulled out a chair and sat down, turning her daughter so they were face-to-face. Amanda giggled. "You little minx, it's impossible to stay angry." She dropped a kiss on her daughter's head. "I'm glad you're feeling better. So that was the problem, a rummy tummy. Well, it happens to all of us at one time or another."

"Rummy tummy," Amanda repeated.

Betsy spent the next few minutes playing the rhyming game with her daughter until the chambermaid returned carrying a tray with clean tea towels and a bowl of water.

"The water's warm, ma'am." She put the tray down.

Betsy stood up and put Amanda in the chair she'd just vacated. "I'm so sorry to put you to such trouble," she said as she grabbed a towel, dipped it in the dish, and began wiping the mess off her outfit.

Amanda giggled. "Mummy . . . Mummy."

"Your little one seems fine now." The girl chucked Amanda under the chin.

Betsy smiled gratefully at the young woman. "My daughter usually is so good-natured. I should have known she wasn't feeling well and not brought her here."

"No damage done, ma'am." The girl grabbed the toddler's waving hands and jiggled them in a baby game. Amanda squealed in delight. "And it was funny watching Boris—he's the maître d'—have a fit about a little one taking ill."

Betsy decided to try one last time to find out something useful. "You're being very understanding, and I do appreciate it." She gave a theatrical sigh. "I had so hoped this outing would be a success, but I expected too much."

"How's that, ma'am? It's no bother your little one taking ill. We've seen much worse than that here."

"I'm not too upset about that," Betsy said, "but I came because I wanted to try the food in the restaurant and see if it will be to my aunt Clara's liking. She's elderly and very particular."

"You mustn't judge the food by today's luncheon menu, ma'am." She glanced over her shoulder at the open door to make sure no one from the kitchen was loitering nearby, and then lowered her voice. "Our regular chef has the day off. He's really very good. I'm afraid his assistant isn't up to the task, if you get my meaning."

"That's good to know. Perhaps I'll come again tomorrow. But that's not the only reason I came. You see, one hates to admit such things, but I was curious about the murder you've had here."

"The murder?" The maid's eyes widened, and she glanced over her shoulder again. The corridor was still empty. "It was awful, ma'am. Elsie is the one who found Mr. Mundy's body. It put her in such a state."

"Poor girl, I'm sure it must have been dreadful for her." Betsy let out the breath she'd been holding. "Did she have to talk to the police?"

"Of course, ma'am, all of us did. Mind you, there wasn't much I could tell them. I wasn't working the evening he was killed."

"Still, I'll bet someone as capable as you probably noticed something odd going on here." She wasn't above using a bit of flattery to keep the conversation moving in the direction she needed it to go. "From what the papers said, it looks like the killer might have been here more than once before the actual murder." The papers had said no such thing, but Betsy was hoping the maid hadn't read all the newspapers.

"I don't know about that, ma'am, but I know Elsie is still upset."

"About the murder?"

The girl shook her head. "No, about the police. You see, she forgot to tell them something, and she thinks it might be important. I told her she had to speak up, that the police need to know everything."

Betsy threw caution to the wind. "What did she see?"

"It was the carpetbag, ma'am. She forgot to tell them about the carpetbag."

Jennifer Payton answered the door before Barnes had even knocked. "What are you doing here? I've told you everything I know," she murmured. "I told you if you needed to speak to me, that I'd come to you."

A voice from inside the house shouted, "Who is there? Is it Mrs. Blodgett with my medicine?"

"No, Cousin, it's not Mrs. Blodgett. She can't come until after supper." She raised a finger to her lips, indicating they should be quiet. "You go on upstairs and take a rest. I'll deal with this."

"But who is it?"

"It's a salesman. Go on upstairs. I'll bring you some cocoa in a bit."

Witherspoon wasn't sure he liked being referred to as a salesman. He looked at the constable, who shrugged. From within, they heard the creaking of floorboards and the shuffling of feet. Jennifer held up her hand and eased the door shut.

"This is very odd, Constable," Witherspoon whispered.

"Miss Payton obviously wants to keep our presence a secret from her family." Barnes tried to recall what she'd said in her formal statement and what she'd told Phyllis. He didn't want to muddle them up. "I believe she told us she lives with an elderly relative."

"That's right, she did."

"Let's give it a moment, sir. I think she wants us to wait."

They didn't need to wait long before the door opened and she motioned them inside. Holding her finger to her lips, she led them down the corridor to the kitchen.

She closed the door behind them and pointed at the table opposite the cooker. There were only two chairs.

"Please sit down." She spoke softly, her voice barely above a whisper. "I'm sorry about this, but my cousin doesn't know anything about this matter, and I'd like to keep it that way. I'll bring another chair in from the dining room. It'll only take a moment."

She was as good as her word. "You've more questions for me, but I've told you everything I know." She sat down.

"We do." Witherspoon kept his voice low. "In your statement, you said you followed Mr. Mundy to his hotel because you didn't trust him."

"That's correct."

"And you followed him all the way to the Wrexley, also correct?"

"I've already said that I did." She brushed a strand of hair off her cheek. "I don't see why you're making me repeat myself."

But Barnes knew she did have more information; she'd given a far more detailed account to Phyllis. "Miss Payton, you said the two of you dined at Babcock's on Oxford Street. When you came out of the restaurant, did you see anyone taking notice of the victim?"

She cocked her head to one side. "How'd you know about that?"

"We don't know anything in particular, miss," Witherspoon interjected. "It's merely a question we need to ask. You seem to be a very observant person, and we're hoping that either at the restaurant or when you arrived at the hotel, you might have seen someone who displayed an inordinate amount of interest in Thomas Mundy."

"I see what you mean." She took a breath. "Actually, I should have said something earlier, but I was so rattled, I forgot."

"Forgot what?" Barnes asked quickly.

"There was someone watching Thomas. It was at the restaurant. I remember now, because I'd ducked around the corner to fool him. When I came back, I saw Thomas staring across the road, not Oxford Street, that little road next to Babcock's. There was a man there, staring at him, and Thomas had spotted him. They looked at each other for a few seconds, and then Thomas turned and took off like he was being chased by the devil himself."

"What did the man look like?" Witherspoon asked.

"He was nice-looking. He had blond hair." She smiled.

"Are you sure it was blond?" Barnes pressed. "Could it have been reddish or sandy colored?"

"He was standing right under the light, Constable. It was blond, and before you ask, I'd recognize him again if I saw him."

CHAPTER 9

Ruth was the first to arrive at their afternoon meeting. Except for Betsy, the others arrived soon after and took their places around the table. Mrs. Jeffries looked at the clock. "Oh dear, I hate starting without everyone. But time is moving along, and from the expressions on your faces, most of you have something to report."

"Don't worry about Betsy," Smythe said. "She and Amanda went to the Wrexley for lunch today. I'm sure she took the little one 'ome for a nap. She'll be here soon, and if she isn't, I can always catch her up on what she's missed."

"Let me go first," Mrs. Goodge declared. "I'll be getting up and down. I need to keep the roast chicken basted properly."

"We're 'aving roast chicken." Wiggins grinned broadly. "That's my favorite."

"I know, Wiggins." The cook had made it especially because

she knew he loved it and, unlike Mrs. Jeffries, she was of the opinion that the lad was being treated a bit unfairly. To her way of thinking, Phyllis' behavior could use some improvement. However, she was going to hold her tongue and see what happened. "By the way, the bricks to mend the wet larder were delivered today. I had Mr. Beals stack them on the terrace, so please bring inside after our meeting. He said not to let them get wet, and it might rain tonight. There's not many." He nodded and she continued. "I've not got much today, but I did have a note from one of my old associates, Howard Burrell."

"The man who was here the other night." Mrs. Jeffries reached for a slice of brown bread and put it on her plate.

"That's right." Mrs. Goodge paused. She didn't want to explain too much. "Howard and his wife, Maisie, live in Fulham now, but before he retired, he and Maisie lived in Leicestershire, on an estate close to Market Harborough. Now, when Howard came to see me, he'd not heard of Thomas Mundy before he read about the murder, so there wasn't anything he could tell me. So he did me a great favor and wrote his old employer to see if he might know something useful. The gentleman was very helpful. He knew all about Thomas Mundy." She stopped talking, trying to find just the right words. She didn't want the household to think badly of her former colleague on account of her telling them he'd spent a number of years working for a retired crook. Perhaps it would be best just to blurt it out and say as little as possible. "In his letter to Howard, he said that the gold-headed walking stick, the one used to kill Mundy, originally belonged to old Bernard Hart. Hart had a whole collection of walking sticks and canes."

"How did Mundy end up with it?" Luty took a quick sip of tea.

"I don't know." Mrs. Goodge got up and went to the cooker.

"I'll wager 'e stole it and then put the weights in it," Smythe said.

"But he didn't." Mrs. Goodge grabbed a pot holder and opened the oven door. "He might have stolen it, but he didn't put the weights in it. Bernard Hart did. Apparently, he was a peculiar person, one of those people scared of their own shadow. He had weights put in all his walking sticks and canes." She pulled the chicken out, put it on the top of the cooker, and basted the bird.

"Was your source sure of his facts?" Mrs. Jeffries asked. "This is very surprising. Knowing what we do of Mundy's character, it seemed only logical that he would have added the weights."

"But he didn't." She put the chicken back and closed the oven door. "My source says it was no secret. Everyone in the neighborhood knew to give old Bernard Hart a wide berth when they saw him coming. He always carried a stick, and apparently if someone annoyed him, he used it." She returned and sat down. "That's all from me."

Mrs. Jeffries wanted to think through the implications of what they'd just heard, but unfortunately, she needed to focus her attention on the meeting. "Who would like to go next? Phyllis?"

"The only thing I heard was something we already knew." She smiled self-consciously. "The only person I could get to talk to me today was a bellboy at the Wrexley, and all he had to say was what Wiggins already found out, that the staff sometimes keep the bits and pieces they find. The lad just repeated what we know, that Elsie Scott found an expensive gold button on the third floor and another maid found a lace handkerchief and kept it."

"Don't feel bad—you got more details than I did." Wiggins gave her a quick, genuine smile. He started to continue speaking, when they heard the back door open and footsteps rush up the corridor.

Betsy hurried into the room. "Sorry I'm late, but I had to get Amanda home. She needed a nap. The neighbor girl is watching her for me." She'd also taken the time to change into a less-expensive day dress, one the household had seen on previous occasions. "What have I missed?" She slipped into the chair next to Smythe and grabbed his hand under the table.

"I'll tell ya when we get home, love."

"Wiggins, finish what you were going to say," Mrs. Jeffries instructed.

"I met a lad who works for Ronald Hart." Wiggins told them about his meeting with young Nicholas. "I felt sorry for the lad. He hates workin' for Hart. He claims the man keeps the staff up late so he can 'ave a hot dinner when he gets home. He did that the night of the murder, didn't get home till after ten and had all of 'em waiting on him. Nicholas said he came home in a foul mood, that when he tried to take Hart's coat, he cuffed him on the side of the head and told him to scarper off. It confused Nicholas—Hart never hangs up his own things."

"How old is he?" Phyllis asked.

"When we was waitin' for the omnibus, he said he was fourteen, but he looks younger. I know I shouldn't have spent so much time with the boy, but he seemed lonely, like he just needed someone to listen to 'im."

"We all need that." Phyllis gave him a shy smile.

"Well, I knew I'd not got much from him, so after I saw him onto the omnibus, I went to the Bainbridge Hotel. Seems to me we don't know enough about Marianne Pelletier, and she had a real, personal reason to hate Mundy. But I didn't 'ave any luck at all."

Luty smiled sympathetically. "It happens that way sometimes. I didn't find out anything, either."

Hatchet looked at Wiggins. "But I had a bit of luck with Marianne Pelletier. My source confirmed she was indeed at the Wrexley on the night Mundy was killed. But we already suspected that was the case."

"She was in the hotel?" Mrs. Jeffries asked.

"That's difficult to say." He smiled apologetically. "My source saw her on the back steps. It appeared to him that she'd just come out the rear door, but he didn't actually see it."

"What was your source doing at the back of the Wrexley?" Luty demanded. She hated it when he found out more than she did.

"He was taking a shortcut through the mews to the station."

"What time was it?" Mrs. Jeffries was trying to keep it straight in her mind.

"Half past eight."

"So let me see if I understand," Betsy said. "Mrs. Pelletier was at the Wrexley at the time of the murder, Oswald Hart was seen going to the back door of the Wrexley at half past six that night, and Daniel Wright slipped out of his room sometime after dinner and didn't return till late that night."

"Which means any of them could have killed Mundy." Mrs. Goodge got up again to check on her chicken.

"Don't forget Ronald Hart and Jennifer Payton," Phyllis said quickly. "Both of them had reason to hate the victim. She admitted to following Mundy to the Wrexley, and we just have her word for it that she only did it because she wanted to know where he was living. Hart was seen there earlier that day, and he doesn't have an alibi for that night. He could have gone back and murdered Mundy."

"But he's the one with the least motive to do the killin'," Mrs. Goodge pointed out. "If what we've learned so far is true, Mundy did him a favor twenty years ago when he fiddled with old Bernard's will. Why would he kill him now?"

Phyllis sagged back against her chair. "I suppose you're right."

"I'm not so sure." Wiggins gave Phyllis a quick smile. "Ronald Hart 'as political ambitions, and havin' someone like Mundy hangin' about could do him a lot of harm."

"All of you are making very valid points," Mrs. Jeffries said. "But until we've more facts, we mustn't speculate. Ruth, did you find out anything?"

She nodded. "I'm afraid it wasn't much, but I did learn an interesting tidbit about Mundy. To begin with, several weeks ago he was at a political function where Ronald Hart was giving a speech." Ruth told them about her meeting with Octavia Wells, without, of course, mentioning Octavia's name.

"Gemma Ridley's one lucky woman that he died before he could do whatever it was he was plannin'," Luty quipped. "Oh Lord, that doesn't sound right. No one should be murdered, but you know what I mean."

"Of course we do, and you're right." Hatchet patted her hand. "He was a cad."

"I'm glad I've written much of this down." Mrs. Jeffries sighed and looked at Betsy and Smythe. "You're the only two left. Who wants to go next?"

"You go ahead, Smythe," Betsy said. In truth, she was saving her information for last.

"Thanks, love. Like the rest of ya, it wasn't my best day, but I did find out that Mundy's been in England longer than we thought. He's been here more than a year." He told them the rest of what he'd learned from Blimpey and then looked at his wife. "Your turn."

Betsy sat up straighter. "As Mrs. Jeffries suggested, I took Amanda, and we went to the Wrexley for lunch. But it didn't turn out quite as I expected." She told them how the two of them ended up in the staff room off the kitchen. "The chambermaid told me that Elsie Scott is upset because there is something important that she forgot to tell the police. Mundy had a carpetbag in the wardrobe of his room. But when she found his body, the carpetbag was gone. She was so rattled, she didn't mention this to the police, and now she thinks it might be important."

"Maybe the police have it," Wiggins suggested.

"No, she saw them taking his possessions out of the hotel, and the carpetbag wasn't there; she was sure of it. She'd have noticed, because the reason it stayed in her mind so much was that it was a woman's carpetbag. It was small, cream colored with pink roses on the sides and a nice brass handle."

"What was Thomas Mundy doin' with a woman's carpetbag?" Wiggins mused.

Mrs. Jeffries' brows drew together in a puzzled frown. "More important, where is it now?"

The meeting broke up shortly after. Smythe whispered something in Betsy's ear, and she nodded and left with Ruth. Luty and Hatchet had already departed. Mrs. Goodge was at the cooker, basting again, while Phyllis and Mrs. Jeffries had gone upstairs to take care of a few chores before the inspector came home.

Wiggins started for the back door. "I'd better get those bricks moved. It looks like it's goin' to pour any minute now."

"I'll give ya a hand." Smythe followed him. He waited till they were outside and the back door firmly closed before he spoke. Wiggins had gone to the edge of the terrace and squatted down next to the bricks. "Put those down. I've got somethin' to say."

Puzzled, Wiggins stood up and brushed off his hands. "What is it? Is somethin' wrong?"

"Not with me, but the ladies of the 'ouse have been jawin' my ear off about the way you're treatin' Phyllis."

Wiggins' mouth flattened into a thin line. "I was nice to her today."

"Yeah, today, but what about the past few weeks? You've been snarlin' at the lass like she's stolen your dinner."

"She gives as good as she gets," he insisted. "I've felt the sharp edge of her tongue plenty."

Smythe studied him for a moment. His cheeks were flushed, and his shoulders hunched defensively. "True, but you don't take it to heart the way she does. Your life 'asn't been easy, I'll give ya that, but hers has been a sight more miserable. When she first come 'ere, she wouldn't say boo to a goose in a barn-yard. It's taken a long time for her to come out of herself the way she has, and when you make her feel small . . ."

"I'm not tryin' to make her feel small," Wiggins interrupted. "I . . . I . . . oh, cor blimey, I don't know why I'm acting this way, but she's different now. When she first come here, she was like a plump little pigeon, quiet and shy, timid like and, well, we all were right protective of her."

"She's not timid anymore, and she don't need our 'elp to get out and about. She's sure of 'erself these days because of all the care she's had from us. I'd think you'd be happy for her, knowing that she's not so scared of life that she wants to curl into a little ball and roll into a corner where no one can see her. What's got into you, lad? You've a heart as big as a hunter's moon. It's not like you to begrudge someone betterin' themselves and losin' their fear."

"I don't," he protested. "I'm glad she 'olds her head up high now and that she isn't scared, but she doesn't need to always be tryin' to outdo me. Just look at how she's behaved with this case, and it 'appened on our last case, too, but I held my tongue. She used to respect my opinion, but now she flounces out on 'er own without so much as a by-your-leave, and when she's talkin' to the local merchants about one of our suspects, if it's a man behind the counter, you should see the way she smiles and bats her eyes. But she don't smile at me like that. She treats me like a horrible little brother who put bugs in her shoes."

"And actin' like a 'orrible little brother isn't going to 'elp you win the lady's affections, either," Smythe retorted.

Wiggins' jaw dropped. "Don't be daft. I'm not tryin' to win anything from her. 'Ow could you say somethin' like that?"

Smythe crossed his arms over his chest. "Because it's true, and you're a man now. There's no shame in wanting to court a lovely young woman. I've 'ad the same ailment you do, and I know the symptoms. But back when I was trying to woo my Betsy, it was worse for me. I'm a lot older than my lady. At least you and Phyllis are the same age."

Wiggins stuck out his chin. "I don't know what you're on about. I'm not courtin' Phyllis."

"That's obvious. If ya were, you're makin' a right old mess of it. I've said my piece because we're friends and I can tell you're hurtin' inside."

225

Wiggins snorted and made a face. Smythe ignored it and kept on speaking. "Listen, I'm not goin' to waste my time or yours arguin' about whether you've feelings for the girl. All I'm sayin' is if you do, if you really care for her, you might try talkin' to her with a bit of sugar on your tongue. Works a lot better than all that sour sarcasm."

Witherspoon looked tired when he arrived home but was not so exhausted that he didn't want a drink with Mrs. Jeffries. She handed him his glass. "Here you are, sir. How was your day? Productive?"

He took a sip and then thought for a moment. "It was, I think. Sometimes it's difficult to tell. Let me see, oh yes, we started off at the station. The Leicestershire lads had done a fine job and supplied us with Oswald Hart's London address. He's at the Durwood Hotel. He was going to leave tomorrow, but I persuaded him to stay on for a few more days. Just to be on the safe side, though, I did post a constable to keep an eye out."

Mrs. Jeffries listened closely as he repeated everything Oswald Hart had told him. She silently sighed in relief when it became apparent that he was certain Oswald Hart's cousin, Ronald, had paid Mundy to change Bernard Hart's will.

"He loathes his cousin, but he did make an interesting admission." Witherspoon took another sip. "He said something to the effect that 'now that Ronald wanted a political career, he'd need his family's goodwill.' I'm not certain what he meant."

Mrs. Jeffries had an idea. But it wasn't one she was ready to share as yet. "And do you think Oswald Hart really went to the West End to see a play on the night of the murder?"

"It's impossible to prove or disprove. Unlike his cousin, he's not a well-known figure, so even if he walked past a fixed point constable, I doubt the officer or anyone else would remember him." He put his glass on the table next to him. "When I pressed him as to the name of the pub he was supposed to have stopped in for a drink, he couldn't remember."

"And there are dozens of pubs on Oxford Street. What did you do next, sir?"

"We had a word with Ronald Hart." He stopped. "Oh wait, before I tell you about it, there's something else. Constable Evans arrived as we were leaving the Durwood. He'd had a chat with the housemaid at Wright's lodgings, and the girl admitted that she'd seen Wright come in late the night Mundy was murdered."

"So he was lying about being in all evening."

"It appears that way. We're going to see him again tomorrow. I've put a constable on watch at the lodging house, and if Wright attempts to leave, he'll let us know. After we left Hart, we had a quick word with his cousin." Witherspoon frowned heavily and downed half his drink before continuing. He told her everything that had transpired at the Hart house. "He insisted that his cousins hate him because he's so successful. Actually, I suspect they dislike him because he's a tiresome, arrogant man who loves the sound of his own voice. But that doesn't make him a killer."

"Did you get a report back from the fixed point constables?" She wasn't ready to eliminate Ronald as a suspect. Not yet. "Had anyone seen him walking that night?"

"No, and that is a problem. Both Constable Griffiths and Constable Evans asked all the men they spoke with if they knew Hart by sight. All but one of them did."

"Did you ask him about that?"

"Not yet. We only got the reports when we got back to the station at the end of the day, but I shall bring it up with him again."

She was somewhat relieved. At this point, she didn't think it wise to eliminate anyone. "You still consider him a suspect?"

"I do, but he has less of a motive than any of the others. After we left him, we went to have another word with Jennifer Payton."

She got up and reached for his glass. "Another, sir?"

"Only if you have one. It's been a very long, tiring day."

She poured their drinks. "What did Miss Payton have to say?"

"It was a bit awkward." He described how Jennifer Payton had kept them on her doorstep until her elderly cousin had gone upstairs. "I'd forgotten that she'd told us if we needed to ask more questions, she'd come to us. Nonetheless, she was able to answer our questions, and she did recall seeing someone that night."

Mrs. Jeffries sipped her sherry as she listened to him repeat what they'd already learned from Jennifer Payton. There were so many questions she wanted to ask, so many details she needed to know. But there was so much buzzing around in her mind, she simply blurted out the first thing that popped into her head. "Are you sure that Jennifer Payton was telling the truth about seeing that man? Or is it possible she just told you Mundy seemed frightened of him so you'd not look at her so closely?"

"It's possible, but I don't think she was lying," he replied. "As I told Constable Barnes when we first encountered Miss Payton, Mundy owed her money. Even if she hated him, as long as she had a hope of collecting, she wouldn't want him dead."

Unless, of course, she killed him and stole what she found in his room, Mrs. Jeffries thought, but she said nothing. Tomorrow morning, she'd tell Constable Barnes about the missing carpetbag.

Witherspoon continued. "When she told me she'd seen this man watching Mundy, I was going to ask her to take a look at all the male suspects, but then she said the man was a good-looking blond. I think that eliminates both Ronald and Oswald Hart. Nonetheless, I'm going to have her take a look at both of them as well as Daniel Wright."

"You're leaning toward Wright as the killer, aren't you?"

"Yes, and for a very specific reason."

"What is the reason, sir?"

His expression was thoughtful. "Daniel Wright was beaten half to death by ruffians Mundy had hired, and he only escaped death by the arrival of the local police. He convalesced in a charity hospital and then had to sell what few assets he had left to track Mundy. A lot of people would have just given up and tried to go on with their lives. But he didn't. He came after Mundy. His motive seems far more—I'm not sure how to put it—personal."

"But couldn't you also say that Marianne Pelletier has a very personal motive? She held Mundy responsible for the death of her sister. She claims to have gone for a walk on the night of the murder, but she could have gone to the Wrexley and killed him."

"True, but how could she have known that Mundy's walking stick would make a convenient weapon?" he countered. "She wouldn't have known the head and part of the shaft were filled with lead weights."

Mrs. Jeffries nodded as if she agreed, but she wasn't convinced. "I suppose that's true, unless, of course, her sister mentioned it in her correspondence to her." She thought it unlikely. It wasn't the sort of information genteel ladies wrote about, but nonetheless, it needed to be said. "But if Mrs. Pelletier didn't know about the lead weights, how would Daniel Wright?"

"Mundy worked for him in California."

"Yes, but as a clerk in his office. A gold-headed walking stick doesn't strike me as the kind of thing one would take along to work, especially in a city like Los Angeles. Luty says it's quite a lawless place and that most of the men there carry guns." Luty had said no such thing, of course, but she was desperate to make her point. Witherspoon quite enjoyed a penny dreadful, and Mrs. Jeffries was counting on his belief that any city west of New York or Boston was filled with cowboys, gunslingers, and outlaws. "If Luty is right, sir, do you really think Mundy would have risked getting something that valuable taken from him at gunpoint?"

Witherspoon stared at her with a bemused, speculative expression. "I hadn't thought of it in quite those terms, but you make an interesting point. Though I must say, I'm not sure California is as uncivilized as Luty claims. The police in San Francisco sent us quite a detailed confirmation of Wright's statement. There were no misspelled words, and even the grammar was correct. But I understand your concern, and I'll make it a point to ask Mr. Wright about it tomorrow."

Mrs. Jeffries stared out the window at the gas lamp across the road. She'd gone through her notes twice, and the more she thought about everything they knew thus far, the more it was obvious that this case wasn't going to be easy to solve. It might even be impossible. Thomas Mundy was a terrible human being, loved by none and hated by many; so many in fact that it was becoming increasingly difficult to determine which of his enemies might have actually murdered him.

She pulled her robe tighter against the frigid fall air and tried to bring some discipline to her thoughts. To begin with, there was the murder weapon. Was it possible that whoever killed Mundy didn't know the walking stick had been altered? But that alteration hadn't been made by Mundy but by Bernard Hart, and according to Mrs. Goodge's source, it was common knowledge in Leicestershire that old Bernard swung a very mean stick. So what did it actually mean? Neither Daniel Wright nor Marianne Pelletier was from the Midlands, so how would they know the stick would be useful as a murder weapon? In all fairness, it was possible that both of them might have stumbled upon the information, but to her mind, it was highly unlikely.

Yet Mrs. Pelletier and Wright were the two with the most "personal" of motives. On the other hand, both Ronald Hart and Oswald, his cousin, would have known that the walking stick could be a lethal weapon. But did either of them have reason to want Mundy dead? That was the real question. Oswald claimed that if he was the murderer, he'd have killed his cousin rather than one of Ronald's hirelings, and Ronald Hart was equally adamant that he'd never hired or conspired with Mundy to cheat his relatives out of their fair share of Bernard's estate. Which of them was telling the truth? That was the question.

Then there was Jennifer Payton. Could she have followed Mundy up to his room that night? Did she know or suspect that he had money hidden somewhere close, and if so, would it be enough to turn her into a killer? Mrs. Jeffries shivered and realized the room was getting colder. She went to her bed, slipped off her dressing gown, and climbed beneath the covers. She lay there a long time, staring at the ceiling as she thought about the case. What was the significance of the missing carpetbag, and more important, where had Mundy obtained it?

She tossed and turned, trying to make sense of everything; then she finally gave up and just let her mind wander free. Two minutes later, she was sound asleep.

"You two are killing me." Barnes closed his eyes and shook his head. "That's even more information than yesterday. How am I goin' to get all of it to the inspector?"

"You'll find a way." Mrs. Goodge bent down to stroke Samson, her mean old yellow tabby, across his big head. The cat purred and butted against her shin. "You always do."

"You've got to go back to the Wrexley in any case," Mrs. Jeffries pointed out. "You must have a word with Elsie Scott about the carpetbag, and if I were you, I'd speak with the waiters in the restaurant."

"We've already done that," Barnes reminded her. "Hart didn't eat there. He met with a party boss to discuss snatching a dead man's job. He won't tell us who this man is, either. He's adamant about that, and frankly, if we press him too hard, he could bring a world of trouble down on the inspector, especially as he's not the likeliest suspect in this case."

"I understand that," Mrs. Jeffries said. "But I wanted you to have another word with the maître d' and confirm that he mentioned Mundy's room number to the waiter he sent upstairs. The man that Mrs. Hamlin mentioned she'd seen."

Barnes thought for a moment. "That's right, Mrs. Hamlin claimed a man fitting Wright's description told the maître d' he was dining with Mundy. But then he scarpered off before the waiter came back."

"Yes, I think that Daniel Wright used that method to learn what room Thomas Mundy occupied."

"He could have found that out at the reception desk," Mrs. Goodge grunted as she bent down again to stroke her cat.

"But he didn't. I specifically asked both the reception clerks if anyone had asked for Mundy's room number. No one had, not even Mrs. Pelletier. She waited for him in the lobby, then left," Barnes said. "Right, I'll add that to my list. I still don't see how I can let the inspector know about the walking stick or the fact that Marianne Pelletier lied to us." He got up. "But I'll think of something."

The reception clerk at the Bainbridge Hotel turned and looked at the row of keys. "Mrs. Pelletier is in her suite. Would you like me to send a bellboy?"

"We know where she is," Barnes said. "We'll go up to her." He'd done some very fast talking to get Witherspoon to see the wisdom of having another chat with Marianne Pelletier, and now that they were here, he didn't want any delays.

"I don't think the hotel staff likes our being here," Witherspoon complained as he and Barnes climbed the wide staircase. "Everyone wants a decent society with a proper code of justice, until it's embarrassing or inconvenient for their business."

"That's true, sir." The constable was thinking furiously about the questions he had to ask. They had to be worded just right; if he was wrong about it, the inspector would begin to wonder why he was privy to facts they'd not learned from their investigation. It was a risk, but it was worth taking.

Barnes knocked softly when they reached her door. The chambermaid who answered was so surprised to see them that it took a moment for her to speak. Finally, she said, "Goodness, you're policemen. What do you want here?"

"We'd like to speak to Mrs. Pelletier." Witherspoon smiled politely. "Tell her Inspector Witherspoon and Constable Barnes are here."

"Let them in," Marianne Pelletier called from inside the room. "Then you can go. I can serve myself."

"Yes, ma'am." The girl opened the door wider and bobbed a curtsy before disappearing down the corridor.

Marianne Pelletier sat in one of the wing chairs. A serving tray with a silver pot, a plate of croissants, and jam and butter sat on the low table in front of her. She held a delicate pink cup and saucer on her lap. "You'll join me, won't you? The hotel kitchen makes delicious hot chocolate."

"Thank you, Mrs. Pelletier, but we don't have much time today." Witherspoon smiled apologetically. "We've more questions."

"Go on, ask them."

"The night that Mundy was killed, you stated you went for a walk."

"I did." She took a sip and stared at him over the rim of her cup. "What of it?"

"Exactly where did you walk, ma'am?" Barnes asked.

She put her cup down on the tray. "I walked on the Uxbridge Road. It was dark, so I wanted to stay where it was light and there were people. There was a policeman on the corner."

"The fixed point constable is always on that corner." Barnes smiled slightly and silently prayed his bluff would work. "Are you sure it was the Uxbridge Road?"

"I am. I've been in this neighborhood for a month. I know the area well."

"That's odd, ma'am. We had a word with the fixed point constable, and he doesn't remember seeing you that night."

"Why would he?"

"Because he always takes a close look at unaccompanied ladies who are out at night. It was past the dinner hour, ma'am, and few women are out at that time." The implication was obvious; the police assumed that any unaccompanied woman out after dark was likely to be a prostitute. "We described you to the constable, and he saw no one matching your description between half past six and eight o'clock." He heard the inspector's sharp intake of breath and knew his questions had surprised him. Barnes hoped he'd not gone too far. Witherspoon was an excellent policeman, but he was also a gentleman.

She tilted her head slightly, her expression amused. Finally, she laughed. "Really, Constable, I'm a bit too long in the tooth for that particular activity."

"Where did you go, ma'am?" Witherspoon hoped he wasn't blushing.

"I don't remember."

"We have a witness who saw a woman matching your description at the Wrexley Hotel," Barnes continued. "She was wearing a fur hat. Do you have a fur hat, Mrs. Pelletier?"

For a moment, she said nothing. "Alright, I suppose you were bound to find out. I went to the Wrexley to see Mundy. Obviously, someone saw me, or at least, they saw my hat."

"I understand it was quite distinctive, ma'am." Barnes whipped out his notebook. "What time was this?"

"I'm not sure—between half seven and eight o'clock. I went into the lobby, but then I saw him. He was going upstairs."

"Did you follow him?"

She shook her head. "No, I went back outside and tried to think of what to do. I wanted to speak to him in private. I knew his room number."

"How did you know that?" the inspector asked.

"The first time I went to the Wrexley, I bribed a bellboy. A few coins will buy a lot of information in this town, Inspector. May I continue?" She waited a fraction of a second for him to nod. "I decided to try the back—some hotels have more than one door. But when I got there, it was locked. I hoped that someone would come out, so I waited."

"How long?" Barnes looked up from his notebook.

"It seemed hours, but it wasn't more than ten, possibly fifteen, minutes. Just as I was getting ready to leave, the door flew open and a man rushed out. He moved so fast, he almost knocked me over."

"What did this man look like?" Witherspoon demanded.

"I don't know. He was there one second and then he was gone, running down the steps and into the mews. There was something tucked under his arm. I noticed that because he was dressed completely in dark clothing. I think it was a large overcoat of some sort, but whatever he carried was light in color."

"Is there nothing about him you can tell us?"

"His hair, it wasn't dark."

Witherspoon glanced at Barnes. "Blond?"

She let out a sigh. "I can't be sure, Inspector. He had a hat on, and his collar was turned up. I only had a glimpse of the back of his head."

"What did you do then?"

"I came back here. I went to the station and found a hansom cab. I'm so ashamed of myself, Inspector. I lost my nerve." She smiled bitterly. "I'd gone to the Wrexley in hopes of finding justice for Phoebe, but instead, I was frightened. One stupid little shove in a darkened mews sent me running like a coward." Her eyes filled with tears. "Phoebe deserved better."

"You're not a coward, Mrs. Pelletier." Witherspoon got up. "And I'm sure your sister knows you've done your best for her."

"You're very kind, Inspector." She gave him a weak, watery smile. "Do you have any more questions for me?"

"No."

"Will you be here much longer, Mrs. Pelletier?" Barnes rose to his feet and tucked his little brown notebook into his pocket.

"I want to stay until you make an arrest." She picked up her hot chocolate. "I suppose I need to know who killed him. I'm not sure why."

"We'll be going now, Mrs. Pelletier. If you think of anything else that might help, you can contact us at the Ladbroke Road Police Station."

Neither man said anything until they were on the pavement outside the lobby.

"What do you think, sir?" Barnes waved at a hansom that had just dropped a guest.

"I don't know, Constable. I must say, I was quite surprised when you told her the fixed point lads didn't recall seeing her. Wrexley Hotel, please," he called to the driver as he climbed into the cab. "That was an excellent strategy to get her to tell the truth. What made you think of it?"

"You did, sir. The report from the fixed point constables

about Ronald Hart's supposed walk got me to thinking—and it is true, sir, the lads do keep an eye on unaccompanied women after dark." Barnes got in and banged on the ceiling.

Witherspoon's eyes twinkled. "Luckily, Mrs. Pelletier didn't take offense at that remark. As to whether I think she's telling the truth, I'm inclined to believe her."

"You are, sir?"

"Yes. She wouldn't know that the main suspects in this case are men with light hair, yet that's what she reported seeing."

"That mews isn't well lighted, sir. If she saw light hair, it's most likely it was Daniel Wright rather than either of the Harts. What little Oswald has is more of a dirty sand color, and Ronald Hart's is the same as his cousin's."

"Yes, we'll go have a word with Mr. Wright after we make a quick stop at the hotel." Witherspoon grabbed the handhold as the hansom swung around the corner. "Now, what was it you wanted to ask the maître d'?"

The closest cabman's shelter to Hanover Square was on Carlton Lane, a good quarter of a mile away. Smythe had already spoken to half a dozen drivers, but none of them remembered taking a couple to Hanover Square. He made a face as another cab pulled around the corner and into the lay-by reserved for hansoms. This was a fool's errand, but at their morning meeting, Mrs. Jeffries had thought it important that they try to find the cab that had dropped off Mundy and Gemma Ridley.

He waited till the driver had got a cup of tea before he approached. "Can I 'ave a word, please."

The driver was a young, dark-haired man with long sideburns and deep-set blue eyes. "Yes, as long as I can drink my tea. I'm not for hire now."

"I just have a couple of questions. My guv sent me 'ere to find a hansom that dropped off a man and woman Monday afternoon."

"Why are you asking?"

"My guv accidentally got the man's overcoat, and he'd like to return it to him," Smythe explained. The driver stared at him skeptically. He gave a weary, theatrical sigh. "Look, I've been to half a dozen cabman's shelters and my feet 'urt. They were both at Babcock's restaurant, and my guv got this man's coat instead of his own."

"How does he know this fellow was going to Hanover Square?"

"They was both after a cab and this man got his first. My guv heard him tell the cab driver to take him to Hanover Square. We're hoping the man picked up my guv's coat by accident as well. Now, I can give ya all the borin' details, but take my word for it, we're just trying to get the coats sorted properly. My guv's coat was brand-new, and the one he got stuck with isn't near as good."

"Sorry, I can't help. I didn't take anyone to Hanover Square on Monday." The driver shrugged.

"Do you know anyone who did?" Smythe knew it was a stupid question.

The driver laughed. "You havin' me on? Drivers don't talk about where they take a fare unless it's something excitin' or different. Nothing different about the toffs at Hanover Square."

"Or excitin', either." Smythe nodded. He'd thought this might be a waste of time; it turned out that he had been right. "Did any of the drivers you know hear of anything excitin' happenin' early Monday afternoon?" He was grasping at straws and he knew it.

"Not that I've heard."

"Well, thanks anyway." Smythe turned to leave.

"Wait a minute, there was one funny incident. One of my mates told a strange story. Someone jumped in his rig and told him to follow the cab in front of 'em."

"Where was this at?"

"I'm not sure exactly." The driver took a quick sip from his mug. "But if you'll go to the shelter near Marble Arch, you can find the driver. His name is Harry Dickson."

"Yes, of course, I told the waiter Mr. Mundy's room number. The waiters wouldn't know, and after putting me to the trouble of sending Tommy Lutz upstairs to the third floor, the man disappeared." The maître d' frowned irritably. "Now, if you'll excuse me, I'd like to get back to the dining room."

"Just one more question," Witherspoon said quickly. They were in a quiet spot in the corridor off the lobby. "Would you be able to identify the man? The one who claimed he was dining with Mr. Mundy?"

"Of course." Panic swept across his features. "You're not going to bring him into the restaurant, are you? Please, you mustn't. We can't have more trouble here. The Wrexleys are terribly upset. There's been a telegram every day since Mundy's murder. They're considering coming to London, and we don't want that, do we. If you want me to have a look at the fellow for you, I'll come to your police station. Gracious me, if Mrs. Wrexley goes into the kitchen and starts poking about, Chef will have a fit, and we don't want to lose Chef, do we."

"Certainly not," Witherspoon muttered. The maître d' turned on his heel and marched back to the dining room.

"The Wrexleys aren't very popular with the staff, are they." Barnes chuckled. "Where to now, sir?"

"Let's go have a word with Daniel Wright." The two policemen headed for the front door.

"You there, policeman people, can you stop, please." The voice was loud and female.

Witherspoon turned to see a small, gray-haired woman getting up from one of the overstuffed chairs. She raised a hand and waved them over.

"She wants to speak to us, sir." Barnes moved toward her. "May we help you, ma'am?"

"More like I'll be the one to help you." She sat back down. "Why haven't you spoken to me? I've been waiting for one of you policemen to take my statement. But no one has bothered to speak with me. Honestly, if that's the way the police conduct themselves, it's a wonder we're not all murdered in our beds."

"I'm sorry, ma'am, we've been very busy, but you're right, we should have spoken to you immediately." Witherspoon smiled apologetically. "May I have your name?" He glanced at Barnes, who was taking his notebook and pencil out of his pocket.

"I am Mrs. Harold Ottley." She pointed at two straight-back chairs at the card table. "Bring those over. This is going to take a few minutes, and you might as well be comfortable."

It took a few moments to get settled. Barnes crossed his legs and balanced his notebook on his knee. Witherspoon said, "Now, Mrs. Ottley, what do you want to tell us?"

"It's about the day Mr. Mundy was murdered."

"The day, not the evening," the inspector clarified.

"That's correct. Something very, very suspicious went on that day, and I think you need to know about it. It was earlier in the afternoon. I'm not certain of the exact time, but it was after luncheon. I'd gone upstairs to my room to take a headache powder."

"What floor is your room on?" Barnes asked.

"The first. My room is halfway down the corridor, and that is pertinent information, so please listen carefully," she instructed. "I'd taken the medicine, and I was going to come back downstairs. I like to have a chat with Mrs. Hamlin or one of the twins in the afternoon. I came out of my room and started to close the door, when I noticed a man standing at the top of the stairs. He didn't see me at first. He was standing there, staring into the lobby, as if he were watching someone."

"What did this man look like?" Witherspoon asked.

"At that moment, all I noticed was that he had light-colored hair. I didn't notice his clothes until I came out the second time. You see, I realized I'd forgotten my shawl, so I went back into my room to get it. The lobby gets chilly in the afternoons. I've spoken to Mr. Cutler and Mr. Stargill about it, but to date, they've done nothing to increase the heat in the lobby. Still, this is a decent enough place."

"Yes, ma'am, please go on," Witherspoon pressed.

"Well, when I came outside the second time, the man was still there. He was dressed in a dark green jacket with very gaudy, bright buttons on the sleeves, dark trousers, and a green and gold cravat. But I didn't see the cravat until he turned in my direction—he was still staring into the lobby at this point. What bothered me about this person was that when he looked around and saw me coming down the corridor, he deliberately dropped his glove onto the floor."

"How do you know it was deliberate, ma'am?" Barnes asked.

"He was furtive, Constable, very furtive."

"And why do you think he did such a thing?" Witherspoon asked quickly.

"I know why he did it, Inspector. He timed it so I couldn't see his face as I passed by him."

CHAPTER 10

"Mrs. Jeffries, I have an idea." Phyllis tucked the feather duster under her arm as the housekeeper came into the drawing room. "It may be silly, but—"

"Of course it's not silly," Mrs. Jeffries interrupted. "You're a smart young woman, and your ideas are rarely if ever silly. Now, what is it?"

Both women had taken a whirlwind run through the upper floors, dusting, polishing, and tidying up so that Phyllis could get out on the hunt and Mrs. Jeffries could have a good think about the case.

Phyllis gave her a wide, grateful smile. "Well, I was thinking about the carpetbag and the fact that from the description, it definitely belonged to a woman."

"I agree." Mrs. Jeffries opened the heavy velvet curtains to let some sun into the drawing room. "Go on."

"But if you look at the carpetbags ladies have in this country, they're all very practical. You know, dark reds and greens with Oriental patterns, material that doesn't show the dirt."

"What are you getting at?"

"This bag wasn't like our English ones. It was delicate, cream-colored with pink roses and a brass handle. I've never seen a bag like that in England."

"But that doesn't mean it doesn't exist."

"I know, but I think that bag was made in Paris and that Marianne Pelletier bought it and sent it to her half sister, Phoebe Cullen. Maybe Thomas Mundy took it when he stole Miss Cullen's jewelry, and after he sold that, used it to carry the cash. It would be handy for carrying cash."

"Even if that is true, how do you think it would help us find Mundy's killer?" Mrs. Jeffries wanted to hear her thoughts on the matter. She, too, had been thinking about the carpetbag.

"I think the killer took it," Phyllis said. "I think there was money in it. We know that Mundy paid for everything with cash, and from what the chambermaid told Betsy, Elsie Scott claimed he had that bag in his room. If we find the carpetbag, I think we find the killer."

Mrs. Jeffries said nothing for a long moment. "I think you're right, Phyllis. Unfortunately, I've given this a great deal of thought, and I don't see how anyone in the household would be able to do such a thing. We'll have to leave that to the police."

"I guess you're right." She laughed. "It was a daft thought. It's just that part of me feels that since I got into the Wrexley without being caught, I've had a bit of practice for slipping in and out of hotels and lodging houses."

• • •

"I know I should have mentioned this before," Elsie Scott said, looking as if she were going to burst into tears, "but the truth is, I forgot. I'm so glad you've come back."

"These things happen, miss. That's why we often have a second interview with the person who found the body." Witherspoon smiled in an effort to put her at ease.

"An experience like that can be very troubling, and sometimes it's easy to forget details that later become important." Barnes had been relieved when the inspector had accepted his suggestion they speak with her again.

"So please, go ahead. Tell us what you forgot." They were in the staff room near the kitchen, and the inspector had made certain the door was firmly closed. He wanted the maid to feel free to speak.

She nodded and straightened her spine. "Mr. Mundy was always very careful about people, even us, going into his room. But the truth is, we have to go in every day to change the towels and do a proper tidy up. You can't have people staying for days on end without the room being turned out properly."

"We understand," Barnes prompted.

"So even though he was fussy, I went in anyway, even if he wasn't there."

"And the carpetbag was always in plain sight?" Witherspoon asked.

"Oh no." She shook her head. "Not at all. He had it tucked in the bottom of the wardrobe."

"Then how do you know it was always there?" Barnes asked.

"The wardrobe had two doors, one over the side where Mr.

247

Mundy hung his clothes and one on the side of the shelves. The door on that side didn't close properly, and every time I went to make that side of the bed, if I so much as bumped the door, it would open. It was irritating. I'd told the housekeeper that it needed fixing, and twice she mentioned it to Mr. Mundy, but he kept putting her off."

"And every time you bumped the door, you saw the carpet-bag?" Witherspoon wanted to make certain of that fact.

"I did. I noticed it because it didn't look like the sort of thing a man would carry. You know, it was a light cream color and had those lovely roses on the side."

"Is there anything else you've forgotten to mention?" Barnes watched her carefully. The household had found out that the staff frequently kept the small items they found in both the guest rooms and the common rooms.

Elsie drew back slightly. "No, I don't think so. Just the carpetbag—that's all."

"No one on the staff reported finding anything in the corridors or in the common rooms on the day that Mr. Mundy was killed?"

She swallowed and licked her lips. "Not that I've heard, sir."

"Are you sure?" He smiled as he spoke.

"Oh, alright, I suppose someone must have told you already, but please, don't tell Mr. Cutler. He'll sack me for sure. It was just a small thing. I didn't think it was valuable. It wasn't like Jenny finding that pearl hatpin last week or the bellman keeping that fancy lace handkerchief. This was just a shiny brass button that would look pretty on my Sunday dress."

"I assure you, we won't say a word to Mr. Cutler," Witherspoon said quickly. "Where did you find this button?"

"On the third floor. It was on the stairs that lead up to the storage rooms."

"What time did you find it?" the constable asked.

"And you're sure it was the day that Mr. Mundy was killed," the inspector added.

"I'm positive, but I found it in the early afternoon. I don't remember the exact time, but I know it was hours before Mr. Mundy was murdered."

"Ta, Mrs. Goodge, those scones was fit for a king." Jerry Blackburn, a tall, gangly youth with brown curly hair and the beginnings of a beard across his pale cheeks, nodded to the cook as he got up from the table. "I'll just drag the laundry basket in so you'll not have so far to walk."

"Thank you, Jerry. I'd appreciate that." Mrs. Goodge glanced at Mrs. Jeffries and shrugged, indicating that her scones hadn't resulted in learning anything useful from the laundry boy.

Mrs. Jeffries poured herself another cup of tea. From the corridor, she could hear the scraping as Jerry pushed the huge wicker basket up to the archway. She tried to concentrate on the matter at hand, mainly Mundy's murder, but she kept thinking back to something Phyllis had said. She tried to recall every word, but it was far more difficult than one would imagine. The maid had said something important, something that triggered a notion in the back of her mind, but the idea was gone as quickly as it had come.

"Here ya are, ladies. I'll be back next Tuesday." Jerry popped his flat gray cap on his head. "Thanks again for the scones. They was great."

Mrs. Goodge waited till she heard the back door close before she spoke. "Well, feedin' him was a waste of time." She pulled out her chair and sat down. "Poor Jerry hadn't even heard of the murder or Thomas Mundy, and his laundry don't deliver to the Wrexley Hotel. But then, I didn't know that, did I? So I had to try. But I do wish some of my sources would read a newspaper."

Mrs. Jeffries gazed at her friend in amusement. "You talk so tough, but you feed that boy every week whether we've a case or not. You're just an old softie."

She was glad the cook had sat down with her. There had been a bit of tension between the two of them over the situation between Wiggins and Phyllis. She knew the cook thought she was unfairly favoring the maid, and if she was honest with herself, she was convinced the cook was overly partial to the footman.

"I am, aren't I." The cook laughed. "But you're no better. I've seen the way you slip the street lads coins when they show up at our back door, and half the time, they've not even got much to report."

"True, but we want to keep them at the ready so that they're available when we need them. Those youngsters have been very useful in many of our cases." There was a small army of poor street boys who made their money running errands, carrying packages, and delivering messages. Mrs. Jeffries had two of them who came by regularly.

"It's too bad those boys have to earn a living instead of going to school. Doesn't seem fair, does it. Some were born with so much and don't appreciate it while others have to struggle every single moment just to earn enough to fill their bellies." She sighed. "We've been lucky, Hepzibah. A twist of fate has given us so much. We've found a place that gave us both a real home and family. Speaking of which, Wiggins has been behaving a bit better. He was nice to Phyllis at our meeting this morning."

"And she was nice to him as well," Mrs. Jeffries agreed. "Smythe spoke to him yesterday, and perhaps it did some good. We can always hope. Mind you, Phyllis and I had a chat this morning before she left." Her brows puckered. "She seemed in a better frame of mind."

"That's good, then. Why are you frowning?"

"I'm annoyed with myself," she admitted. "Phyllis shared her ideas with me, and she said something that prompted an idea about the case, but the moment it popped into my head, the notion popped right out again."

"It was important, too." The cook nodded wisely. "It's generally those impressions and thoughts of yours that lead to the killer. No wonder you're upset with yourself. Let's hope you get it back."

"There was definitely no carpetbag when we searched Mundy's room," Barnes said. They were in a hansom driving toward Hammersmith and Daniel Wright's lodging house.

"I think the killer took it." Witherspoon frowned as he pulled on his gloves. "And I'm not sure if that is good news or bad."

Barnes braced himself as the cab swung around a sharp corner. "You mean, if the killer took it, it might mean that none of our suspects are guilty."

"That's what worries me—the crime might simply have been one of opportunity." Witherspoon glanced out the window and then back at the constable. "We know that Mundy paid cash for everything and that he frequented the local pub and a number of local restaurants. He could easily have been spotted by

251

a thief who then followed him, killed him, and found his money."

"I don't think so, sir," Barnes replied. "You said it yourself when we discussed this possibility earlier. A casual thief wouldn't know that the walking stick was loaded with weights. The reception clerks were both adamant that no one had inquired at the desk about Mundy's room number, which means the only way he could have known that Mundy was on the third floor was by following him. That's highly unlikely. They'd have been seen going in and out of the hotel. All our real suspects were seen at one time or another."

"Perhaps you're right. Mundy stopped on his way through the lobby to have a word with Mrs. Blanding and Mrs. Denton. The killer wouldn't have hovered near the front door waiting for him to go upstairs. By the way, were we able to locate the mysterious comte de Valois? Supposedly, Mundy was meeting him the night he was killed."

"We didn't spend too many man hours looking for him," Barnes admitted with a smile. "As you pointed out, if the fellow existed and Mundy had missed an appointment, he'd have come to the hotel. He didn't. But the lads made some inquiries and found no one of that name in any of the major hotels or inns."

"I didn't think we would, but we did our duty. How did you know to ask Elsie Scott about finding 'things' around the time of the murder?" Witherspoon stared at him curiously.

"I had help, sir." Barnes contrived to look amused but knew that he had to be careful. "One of the other maids hinted that the girl had found something. She hadn't wanted to come right out and tell tales about her friend, but she wanted me to know that on the day Mundy was killed, the chambermaid had found a button and kept it instead of turning it in to the housekeeper.

But as it had been found *before* the murder, I didn't pursue it as vigorously as I should have."

"But confirming the time Elsie Scott found it was important." Witherspoon glanced out the window. "We're here. Good, I've a number of questions for Mr. Wright."

They climbed out and had a quick word with the constable they'd assigned to watch the lodging house. Daniel Wright was still in residence.

The landlady wasn't surprised to see them. "He's in the parlor, reading the paper." She jerked her chin toward a closed door farther down the dark hall. "Go on in."

Barnes grabbed the handle and shoved into the room. It was in as sad a shape as the rest of the house. There were dull green curtains at the two narrow windows, a three-piece horsehair suite so old it was impossible to determine the original color, and two mismatched side tables.

Daniel Wright looked up from the overstuffed chair closer to the window. He stared at them for a moment, then folded the *Times* and put it down on the arm of his chair. "I can't say that I'm surprised to see you. But I've told you everything I know."

"I'm sure you think so, but we do have more questions." Witherspoon sat down on the sofa. Barnes took the other overstuffed chair and pulled out his notebook and pencil.

Wright shrugged. "Go ahead. But before you begin, I think it only fair to tell you that I've been in touch with the U.S. Embassy. If you arrest me, they'll come to my aid."

"That is your right, sir," Witherspoon replied. "And as of this moment, you're not under arrest. However, it would be in your best interest to answer my questions honestly."

"I have been honest, Inspector, and I'll continue to be."

"You said you were here all evening the night Mr. Mundy was murdered, is that correct?"

Something flickered briefly across his face, but he quickly masked it. "It is."

"You're not being honest now, Mr. Wright." Barnes fixed him with a hard stare. "We've a witness who saw you coming through the larder window late that night. How do you explain that?"

"Your witness is lying."

"They have no reason to lie," Witherspoon replied. "But you have every reason to prevaricate. Now, please tell us the truth."

Wright stared at him for a long moment, his expression unreadable. "Alright, I wasn't here. As soon as dinner was over, I slipped out."

"Through the larder window?" Barnes wanted to establish that Wright had gone to some lengths to keep his activities a secret.

"That's right. I didn't want people sticking their noses into my business." He glanced at the closed door. "I'll wager that right now, the landlady has her ear to the wood."

They heard a muffled thump, as if someone had moved quickly. The inspector tried hard not to smile. "Yes, I see your point, Mr. Wright. But where you were that night is our business."

"I went to the Wrexley Hotel. I figured that I'd tortured Mundy enough, and I was going to go ahead with the next step."

"Could you please explain?" Barnes wanted as many facts and details as possible. "What do you mean, you'd tortured him enough?"

"I told you already that my plan was to scare Thomas Mundy. It was working, too." He smiled. "You see, I'd made sure that he knew I was in town. I wanted him to see me. I wanted him to know that I was after him, because the man was a yellow-bellied little coward. Seeing me would put the fear of God into him. I'd tried it earlier that day."

"What day? The day he was killed?"

"That's right. I'd been on his trail for some time. I'd seen him coming and going from the Wrexley, and I'd been following him for more than two weeks. He really was a disgusting man. He'd connived to meet a lady with little family and plenty of money. She lives in Hanover Square. I don't know her name, but I followed him there that day. I stood across from his hansom cab and hoped he'd see me, but Mundy's attention was completely on the lady. He didn't see me. So I waited till that night, and I stood outside a restaurant and waited for him. This time he saw me, and it scared the hell out of him. He took off like he was being chased by Lucifer himself."

"And you went after him?" Witherspoon asked.

Wright gave a negative shake of his head. "I didn't have to—I knew where he was staying. So I went to his hotel. I didn't go in, though. I stood across the road and watched. Before long, he pulled up in a hansom and hurried inside. I walked by the window and saw him chatting with two elderly women. Then I went around the corner."

"What time did you arrive there?" Barnes asked.

"About seven thirty or seven forty-five. I didn't check the time, so I don't know exactly. My plan was very simple. I was going to go to the back door, wait for someone to come out, and then go inside and confront him."

Witherspoon shifted his weight, trying to find a spot that wasn't lumpy. "You knew the back door would be locked?"

"Of course, I'd been there before." He smiled slightly. "Do listen, Inspector. I've told you, I'd been tracking the man for two weeks."

"So you knew that a lot of people came in and out the back door," Barnes clarified. "It was a shortcut to the station."

"That's right, but apparently, someone else was waiting for the door to open as well, because just as I started across the road, a woman came hurrying around from the front of the hotel and into the mews. I couldn't believe my eyes. She stopped on the back stairs and planted herself like an oak tree. It was bizarre, unbelievable that at the very moment I needed that back door, she stood in my way."

Witherspoon glanced at Barnes. Thus far, he seemed to confirm Marianne Pelletier's account. "What did this woman look like?"

"The mews are poorly lighted, so I couldn't see her face. When she came around the corner, the only thing I noticed was her hat. It was fur. She seemed nicely dressed, or perhaps I just assumed that from the hat. But whatever the case, the woman stood there for a long time. Probably ten or even fifteen minutes."

"Then what happened?" the inspector asked.

"The door flew open and a man rushed out. He almost knocked the woman over," Wright replied.

"I know the mews is dark, but could you see what the man looked like, how he was dressed, anything about his appearance?"

Wright stroked his chin. "Not much, Constable. He was dressed from head to toe in dark clothing, and he had something light colored under his arm. But I couldn't see his hair color. I think his coat collar was turned up. He was on the tall side— that's really all I can tell you."

"Did the lady go inside, then?" Witherspoon watched him carefully. He wasn't one to believe in conspiracies, but they were known to happen. Daniel Wright was either telling the truth, or he'd met and conspired with Marianne Pelletier.

"No, she left. She went to the station and got a hansom cab."

"How do you know?" Barnes stared at him suspiciously.

"Because I followed her."

"You followed her—why?" Witherspoon could tell from the expression on the constable's face that he was thinking conspiracy as well.

"Curiosity. I wondered who she was and why fate had placed her in my way at precisely that moment. I'm a builder by trade, Inspector, but before that, I studied philosophy at the University of California, and though I've fought hard against my leanings, there is still a part of me that believes that sometimes fate or God intervenes in a human life. That's what happened to me that night. She was there, and that kept me from doing something dreadful."

"What were you planning? You said earlier you were going to scare him into giving you your money back," Witherspoon reminded him.

"That's what I told myself, but I'm not sure it was true." Wright looked pensive. "Who knows what I would have done if I'd actually confronted him. I certainly don't know." He glanced from Witherspoon to Barnes. "I can see by your faces that you don't believe a word I've said. But that doesn't matter to me. You see, Inspector, I'm going home. I'm taking a train to Liverpool tomorrow and getting on a ship that leaves on the morning tide the day after. So you can either arrest me or leave me alone."

Witherspoon signaled to Barnes, and both men got up. "We'll be in touch, Mr. Wright. What time tomorrow is your train?"

"Noon. I'm leaving from Liverpool Street Station." He got up as well. "Inspector, Constable, I hated Thomas Mundy, but I didn't kill him."

"Someone did, sir." Witherspoon started for the door and then stopped. "Mr. Wright, when Mundy worked for you, did he ever carry a gold-headed walking stick?"

Wright looked confused by the question. "No, he was my clerk, Inspector, and being a consummate actor, he played the part very well. He was always timid, shy, and badly dressed."

They remained silent until they were outside and away from prying ears. Barnes pointed in the direction of Shepherds Bush. "We should be able to get a hansom up there, sir. What did you think of his statement, sir?"

"I think he was either telling the truth, or he and Marianne Pelletier conspired together to murder Thomas Mundy."

Barnes fell into step next to Witherspoon. "I agree, sir, but we've no evidence they knew each other."

"But both of them have admitted they've been in London for at least a month, and both of them hated Thomas Mundy."

"It'll be difficult to prove, and Wright is leaving tomorrow."

"Not if we arrest him," Witherspoon said grimly.

Wiggins kept his eye on the back door of the Wrexley in the hopes someone, preferably a chambermaid or a bellboy, would slip out to the back steps for a breath of fresh air. But it was cold, and no one had so much as poked a nose outside.

He'd come to the Wrexley because he couldn't think of anything else to do. Smythe was going to speak to more hansom drivers, Ruth had mumbled something about trying to find out more about Gemma Ridley's relationship with the dead man, and Luty and Hatchet were going to see what they could learn from their sources about Oswald and Ronald Hart. There was no point in going to the Bainbridge Hotel; he'd overheard Phyllis say she might go there, and he'd not wanted to trespass on her patch.

Not now, because he'd made up his mind that he was going to have a chat with her and try to put things right between them. Smythe was correct about one thing: He didn't want Phyllis feeling bad about herself. He pulled his jacket tighter and wished he'd worn a scarf; for October, it was getting blooming cold. But Smythe had missed the mark on the other matter. He certainly wasn't trying to court Phyllis. Where on earth had Smythe got that crazy notion?

He scanned the area, hoping that someone, anyone, from the hotel would magically appear, when he saw a lad walking up the mews from the station end. The boy was moving fast. As he got closer, Wiggins realized it was Nicholas.

"Hey, you, Nicholas, what are you doin' 'ere?" he called as he crossed the road.

"What do you think? His nibs has me running another errand." He jerked his thumb toward the hotel. "He wants me to go in there and see if anyone's found one of his stupid buttons. He claims he lost it 'ere on Monday. I think the silly old sod doesn't know where it fell off."

Wiggins grinned. "He sent you all the way 'ere for a ruddy button?"

"It's a fancy one off his green coat, and he claims that it can't be matched." Nicholas stopped. "Mind you, it gets me out of the house and gave me a chance to nip over to my auntie's with my mum's present. Mum's not feelin' well."

"I'm sorry to hear that." Wiggins stared at him curiously. "Do you live with your mum?"

Nicholas' face fell, and he looked at the ground. "Nah, I wish I did. But Mum lives with my aunt Harriet, and, well, they don't have much, so they don't need another mouth to feed. Mum can't work, you see, so I give my auntie my wages for her keep."

Wiggins understood exactly what the boy meant. He'd been sent into service at the Hart house to keep a roof over his head and food in his belly. "You're a good lad. Look, I know this is goin' to sound odd, but if you ever want a better position, I think I know someone who can help ya find one." If Luty didn't need the lad, she'd know a decent house that did.

Nicholas' eyes widened. "You're not foolin' with me? You can really help me get a better place?"

"I can't say for certain, but I'll do my best. When is your afternoon out?"

"Today." He grinned broadly. "As soon as I finish here, I'm off. I just have to go back and get Mum's present. It's her birthday, and this is the first time I've been able to give her a present. It's a nice one, too."

"What did you get her?"

"A carpetbag, a really pretty one with pink roses on the side and a shiny brass handle."

Wiggins couldn't believe his ears.

"What's wrong?" Nicholas' smile vanished. "Why are you lookin' at me like that?"

He caught himself; he didn't want to scare the lad into telling tales. He plastered a cheerful grin on his face. "Sorry, I was thinkin' of something else. Where'd ya buy this carpetbag? I'll bet your mum will be ever so pleased when she sees it."

"I didn't have to buy it. I saw his nibs puttin' it out in the rubbish bin behind the house. Mr. Hart never tosses his own rubbish out, so I got curious, and when he went back inside, I went and had a look. Lucky I did, otherwise I couldn't give Mum anything for her birthday."

Wiggins was the last to arrive for their afternoon meeting. "Where have you been?" Mrs. Goodge demanded as he raced into the kitchen. "It's gone half four already."

"I'm sorry, but I've learned something important, and I had to take care of something before I left to come home." He pulled out his chair and sat down. "I just hope I did the right thing."

"What happened?" Mrs. Jeffries asked.

"I've found the carpetbag, the one that was in Thomas Mundy's room," he explained. "At least, I hope it's the right one."

Mrs. Goodge handed him a mug of hot tea. "Here, have a quick sip before you continue."

"Ta." He took a drink. "I was at the Wrexley. I was goin' to see if I could have a word with someone who might know something useful. I was outside, watching the back door, when I spotted the lad who works for Ronald Hart walkin' up the mews."

"What was he doing there?" Betsy shifted Amanda slightly.

"That's what I asked him." Wiggins took another fast drink and then told them every detail of his encounter with Hart's young footman. When he was finished, he let out a deep breath and sat back in his chair. "I wasn't sure what to do, so I gave Nicholas all the money I had on me and told him to buy his mum a nice present, that I wanted the carpetbag."

"Didn't he ask why?" Ruth asked.

"He thinks I work for a newspaper," Wiggins said. "So I

told him more or less the truth, that the carpetbag he saw Ronald Hart tossing in the dustbin might be connected to a murder."

Mrs. Jeffries was thinking furiously. "You can't let him give it to you," she said. "He has to take it to the police. Now we'll have to come up with a way for the young man to know the police are looking for it."

"That's goin' to be hard," Wiggins warned. "He's a bright young man, and once I mentioned murder, he understood that his employer might be a suspect. I could see it on his face. He'll not want Hart arrested if he thinks he's going to be out in the street. I did my best. I told him I'd make certain he could get another position, but I'm not sure he believed me."

"Tell him to come see me," Luty said. "That big old house of mine needs lots of help."

Wiggins was relieved. He'd been exaggerating just a bit to see if Luty or Ruth would volunteer to take the lad. But he'd not been flat out lying. Once Nicholas understood what was happening, he had been frightened and needed reassurance that when this was over, he'd have a roof over his head. "You won't be sorry, Luty. He's a good lad."

"Where is the carpetbag now?" Mrs. Jeffries asked.

"At the Hart house, in the box room where Nicholas sleeps. It's wrapped in paper and under his bed."

"That's not good. If Hart gets wind that the lad knows something, it could get ugly."

"I told him to take it with him when he went to his aunt's house."

"Will he have any trouble getting it out of the Hart house?" Ruth looked worried. "It would be awful if one of the other servants or even Hart caught him leaving with it."

"He said that Hart is out all day today and that the other

servants mind their own business. He wasn't worried about that."

"What about when he gets to his aunt's house?" Phyllis scooped a spoonful of jam onto her plate.

"I asked him that, too, and he said there was a place he could hide it. There's an old trunk in his aunt's shed. He can nip in there before he goes into her house," Wiggins explained. "I was goin' to have him bring it here, but that didn't feel right."

"And it wouldn't be," Mrs. Jeffries declared. "We'll have to find a way to have Nicholas take the bag to the police. What's more, we'll have to come up with more evidence against Ronald Hart. The bag alone won't be enough."

"What will be enough?" Hatchet asked.

Mrs. Jeffries was worried about that as well. "I'm not sure. But if he had the bag, he must be the killer."

"You don't think there could be another explanation?" Phyllis asked.

"It's possible, I suppose, but frankly, it's all so muddled, I'm not sure what to think."

"I don't understand it." Ruth reached for a scone. "Hart was at the hotel hours before Mundy was murdered."

"And he refuses to give the name of the person he was supposedly meeting with," Hatchet added. "Which I find odd indeed."

"How so?" Mrs. Jeffries asked.

"He could provide the police with the name of the man he was meeting without necessarily making the police privy to the purpose of the meeting. But he didn't do that, and I find that very strange."

"So do I," Luty agreed. "Sounds to me like he didn't meet anyone at all."

"Then why was he there?" Phyllis murmured. "There must have been a reason."

Mrs. Jeffries looked at Wiggins. "Will the lad be at the Hart house tomorrow morning?"

"He said the housekeeper told him he could stay at his aunt's tonight." Wiggins smiled sadly. "His mum is doin' poorly, and I think the housekeeper was tryin' to be kind."

"So once he's at his aunt's, he is safe." Mrs. Jeffries nodded. "Good, then let's put this matter to one side for now and move on. Who'd like to go next?"

"My information won't take long." Ruth glanced at the clock. "I know we're short on time here. All I learned was something we already knew, that Oswald Hart and the rest of the Hart family loathe Ronald Hart and that none of them plan to help further his political career."

"We didn't know that bit. Can't say that I blame 'em, either. Why should they 'elp him get elected to anything?" Smythe said. "If no one objects, I'll say my bit now. I found a hansom driver who had quite a story to tell. It seems that a well-dressed man with sandy-colored hair jumped into his hansom cab and pointed to the cab just in front of it. He told the driver to follow it. The driver thought it unusual, but he did as he was told. He followed the cab to the Wrexley Hotel, and when he started to pull over in front, the passenger shouted for him to go around to the mews, to let him off there."

"Good gracious, can the driver identify this person?" Mrs. Jeffries asked. A glimmer of an idea was forming in her mind, and she was determined to hang on to it.

"Not only that person, but the driver was so curious, he deliberately took stock of the fellow who got out of the cab he'd been following. The description he gave matched Thomas Mundy."

"That means he can identify the man in his cab," Hatchet declared.

"He can and he will." Smythe didn't add that tracking this driver down had cost him a lot of coins and he'd had to promise the driver that he would be fully compensated if he had to take time off to help the police. Smythe didn't mind the cost of it, but his throat hurt from all the hard talking he'd done.

"So someone followed Thomas Mundy on the day he was killed, but he wasn't murdered until that night?" Phyllis cocked her head to one side as she tried to make sense of it.

"Yes, that's what appears to have happened," Mrs. Jeffries said.

"Nell's bells, seems like half of London was following Thomas Mundy the last few days of his life." Luty shook her head in disbelief. "What I can't figure is that he knew he was bein' trailed. You'd think that someone who was constantly lookin' over his shoulder would have had more sense than to open his door to a killer."

"Lady Cannonberry called around this afternoon," Mrs. Jeffries told the inspector as she handed him a glass of sherry. "She's invited you to drop by after dinner and have a glass of port with her."

"That sounds lovely. I think next week I'll invite her to dinner. Perhaps Mrs. Goodge can make something very special."

"She'll find something wonderful in her recipe books." Mrs. Jeffries took her seat. "You seem in a good mood, sir. Was your day productive?"

"Indeed it was. We went back to the Wrexley for what I thought might be a quick stop, but it turned out we learned quite a bit." He told her about the chat with the maître d'. "Which means that if the man who claimed to be waiting for Mundy was indeed Daniel Wright, he found out Mundy's room number without having to ask at reception. After that, we were accosted by a Mrs. Harold Ottley who insisted she had something important to say."

"And did she, sir?"

"I'm not certain." He repeated what they'd heard from the woman. "It may or may not turn out to be useful. Then, Constable Barnes suggested we have a word with one of the chambermaids, the one who found Mundy's body. He said the poor girl was terribly rattled by the experience, but now that a few days had passed, she might recall something useful, and she did." He told her about their brief but enlightening interview with Elsie Scott. "So our short stop at the Wrexley took up a good part of our day."

"I'm sure it did, sir. What did you do after that?" Mrs. Jeffries was trying to keep it all straight in her mind. But the information was coming so fast and from so many directions, she was going to be up half the night writing it all down.

"We went to see Daniel Wright." His expression got a bit grim as he told her about that interview.

"You don't sound as if you believe him, sir," she finally said.

"It's highly possible that he and Marianne Pelletier conspired to murder Mundy," he replied. "Their stories matched too perfectly, and both of them have been in London long enough to have made contact with each other."

"But how would they even know about each other?" Mrs. Jeffries was sure he was on the wrong path, but she couldn't think of a way to get him to step off it.

"Easily." He took a sip of sherry. "She hired a detective to track down Mundy. The detective could have found out that Daniel Wright was looking for him as well and told her. It wouldn't have taken long for them to realize they had a mutual hatred of the man."

"But Jennifer Payton and both the Harts had reason to want him dead as well," she pointed out.

"Not as much reason as Mrs. Pelletier and Wright." He stared off into space. "Both of them have very personal motives; Mrs. Pelletier blamed Mundy for the death of the half sister she helped raise, and Wright lost everything because of him."

"Did you ask Mrs. Pelletier for the name of the detective she used?" Mrs. Jeffries toyed with the stem of her glass.

"I don't think she'll tell me, but I've another plan in motion. I've sent several constables out to make inquiries as to whether Daniel Wright has ever been to Mrs. Pelletier's hotel. Once I can find a witness who puts the two of them together, it will make it easier to prove they conspired to commit murder."

"What if you can't find a witness?"

"Then I'll need to act swiftly." Witherspoon put his empty glass on the side of the table.

"What do you mean, sir?"

"Daniel Wright informed us he is leaving town tomorrow. I've doubled the number of constables watching the lodging house, just in case he was trying to trick me on some level. But unless something happens between now and tomorrow at noon to prove that he's innocent, I'm going to arrest him for murder."

CHAPTER 11

It was half past two in the morning and Mrs. Jeffries had been asleep for less than an hour when she suddenly sat bolt upright. She was wide-awake. Phyllis' words from earlier that day passed through her mind. *"It was a daft thought. It's just that part of me feels that since I got into the Wrexley without being caught, I've had a bit of practice for slipping in and out of hotels and lodging houses."*

Of course, she'd been so blind; now she knew. She knew exactly why he'd been there earlier that day. It had been right under her nose all along. It was the one factor that had nagged at her, that had led her to think that perhaps he wasn't guilty. Sometimes the simplest answer was the correct answer.

By seven o'clock, when Mrs. Goodge and a hungry Samson walked into the kitchen, Mrs. Jeffries greeted them with a smile and a freshly made pot of tea. She put it on the table next to the scones, butter pot, and jam. A stack of plates, four serviettes, and cutlery for four were laid out as well. "Good morning. I've put last night's dinner scraps in Samson's bowl. Come sit down and have your tea."

"You're up bright and early." The cook yawned and then looked at her old friend a bit more closely. "You've sussed it out, haven't you." It was a statement, not a question.

Mrs. Jeffries laughed. "We sussed it out. At yesterday's meeting, the identity of the killer became obvious. The difficult part will be finding enough evidence to actually prove it. But I think I've found a way." She started for the staircase. "I'm going up to wake Wiggins and Phyllis. We're going to need their help."

Ten minutes later, all four of them were assembled at the table. Wiggins kept sneaking glances at Phyllis, who'd been in such a rush, she'd left her hair unbound. It framed her face prettily and hung halfway to her waist.

"You need me to get to the Wrexley and talk Elsie Scott into taking that button she found to the head of housekeeping, is that correct?" Phyllis added another dollop of butter to her scone.

"That's right, Mrs. Ottley stated—"

"Who is that?" Phyllis interrupted. "I'm sorry, but have I missed something? Who is Mrs. Ottley?"

Mrs. Jeffries realized that no one else knew what the inspector had told her when he got home last night. "Don't be sorry, it's my fault. I should have explained it properly." She repeated what Witherspoon had told her about the elderly woman and her insistence the man she saw on the stairs was acting furtive. "And he had gaudy buttons on his sleeve."

"That's why Hart sent Nicholas over to the Wrexley. He wanted him to find that button." Wiggins nodded vigorously and then stuffed another bite into his mouth.

"But Nicholas didn't get the button. Elsie Scott never turned it in to the housekeeper," Mrs. Jeffries said. "Now, we need Elsie to turn that button in, and she needs to do it this morning."

"What if I can't convince her?" Phyllis bit her lip.

"But you can." Mrs. Jeffries smiled. "Tell her that you work for a detective agency, and your agency's investigation has revealed that the button she found is evidence in the Mundy murder. Tell her that you understand why she kept it, but that it's her duty to turn it in, as she should have done when she found it. I want you to wear your best dress and hat and look as commanding as possible."

Phyllis took a deep breath and rose to her feet. "I'll do my best. Fingers crossed that she doesn't just tell me to go jump in the Thames."

As soon as the maid had gone, Mrs. Jeffries looked at Wiggins. "You know what you need to do, don't you?"

"You want me to convince the lad to go the station with the carpetbag and tell them what he knows."

"But before he goes to the police station, you've got to help him get his story straight. The inspector will want to know why Nicholas has brought them the bag, and this is where we must be careful."

"What should I tell 'im to say?"

"That he was eavesdropping, that he overheard Ronald Hart talking to Inspector Witherspoon and Constable Barnes, and that he knew Hart was lying about not knowing Thomas Mundy was in London. He'll have to tell the inspector that he knew Hart recognized Mundy when he was outside the tailor shop. It's just off Hanover Square. He'll say that when Hart came in that night, he saw blood on his hands, and the next morning, when he saw Hart putting the carpetbag in the dustbin, he was afraid that something terrible had happened and—and this is the hard part—his mum is very ill and he's afraid that God will punish him if he doesn't tell the truth."

Wiggins' mouth dropped open. "Cor blimey, Mrs. Jeffries, does he have to do that? His mum is in a bad way."

"I know, I know. I've wrestled with my conscience about this, but all we have against Ronald Hart is circumstantial evidence." She paused. "I know it sounds dreadful and it is, but if he can do this, if he can be convincing, he'll keep an innocent man from the gallows. I should think that would make his mother proud."

Wiggins looked doubtful, but he got up. "I'll see to it, then. Let's hope that young Nicholas is a good actor."

"I don't think this will work, Mrs. Jeffries." Constable Barnes stared at her with a look of disbelief. "First of all, I'm not even sure I can keep the inspector at the station long enough for all these people to show up with 'evidence,' and second, even if they do, it might not be enough to convince him to arrest the man."

"He is going to arrest Daniel Wright on far less evidence."

"No, not really. We've witnesses who put Wright at the hotel when the victim was murdered. Your theory is interesting, but not proven."

"I think it's close enough. You'll have the hansom driver who followed Mundy; you'll have the button Hart lost when he was hiding on the third floor, waiting to see which room his victim went into; but most of all, you'll have the carpetbag. Once Elsie Scott identifies that, you'll have a strong case."

He said nothing for a moment, and then he shrugged. "If

you're wrong about any one of these bits and pieces you've assembled, then Ronald Hart isn't the killer. A man with the kind of powerful friends he has will make it his business to ruin the inspector's career. I've asked around, and Hart has a reputation for being vindictive."

"I know. But I'd rather take the risk on the inspector's being ruined professionally than let him commit a terrible wrong that will haunt him for the rest of his days."

"You're positive that you're right?"

"I am." She folded her hands in her lap and met his gaze.

"Alright, then, I'll trust you on this one." Barnes got up. "Keep your fingers crossed, ladies. We're going to need a bit of luck on this one."

"There's a boy here to see you, sir." Constable Evans stuck his head into the duty room. "He claims he's got something to say about the Mundy murder. He says he works for Ronald Hart."

"Let him come in, then." Witherspoon looked up from the open file on his desk as a lad carrying a parcel wrapped in brown paper was ushered into the room.

"Hello, I'm Inspector Witherspoon, and this is Constable Barnes. What is your name?"

"Nicholas Foley and I'm fourteen years old. I work at Mr. Ronald Hart's house as a footman."

"I understand you've something to tell us."

Nicholas put the parcel on the desk. "I do, sir. I found this in Mr. Hart's dustbin on Tuesday morning. I saw him puttin' it in myself, and after what I heard at the hotel, I think maybe you need to see it. I heard one of the chambermaids say it was evidence."

Witherspoon stared at the parcel, then pulled the string off. He unwrapped the paper and drew in a breath. "Good gracious, take a look at this, Constable. It's the carpetbag. The one from Thomas Mundy's room."

"And it looks just the way Elsie Scott described it." Barnes looked at Nicholas. "Young man, are you sure you saw your master putting this in the dustbin?"

Nicholas crossed his arms over his thin chest. "You think I'd make up this sort of tale? If Mr. Hart finds out I brung it here, he'll sack me for sure."

"Then why did you take such a risk? You know we'll have to speak with Mr. Hart, and we may even have to tell him how we acquired it," Witherspoon warned.

"I don't care. I'm more scared of the God Almighty than I am of Mr. Hart. My mum's real sick, and I don't want the God Almighty angry at me just now. Murder is a great sin, that's what Mr. Vogel who teaches Sunday school down at the chapel says, and if you hide someone's sin, it's just like you did it yourself." He paused for a moment. "And if the God Almighty thinks I'm a killer, he'll not listen to my prayers and Mum might die. That's the only reason I'm here. If I lose my position, I might find another one, but I've only got one mum and I aim to keep her."

Witherspoon stared at him sympathetically. "I'm sorry to hear your mother is ill, but I must ask you, how did you know we were looking for this item?"

"I didn't at first, but then when you and the constable come to the house, I was listening to you when you were talking to the master. He was lyin' his head off. He knew that Thomas Mundy fellow was in town. We saw him on Monday in Hanover Square. Mr. Hart's tailor is there, and when he spotted Mundy and a lady gettin' out of a hansom cab, I heard him say the name. He said it under his breath, but I've got good ears. I didn't understand until later that this Mundy person had been murdered. Then I realized what I saw."

"What did you see?" Witherspoon asked. He wasn't sure he understood everything, but he knew this was important. "Exactly."

"On Monday night, I saw blood on Mr. Hart's hands. He came in late and I was tired. But every time he goes out, he makes us all stay up until he gets home. He likes to be waited on hand and foot, but when I tried to take that big black overcoat from him so I could hang it up, he cuffed me on the side of the head and told me to scarper off. That's when I saw the blood. It scared me, but I didn't tell anyone. When you work for Mr. Hart, you learn to keep your mouth closed. Everyone at that place is scared of him. But when he sent me to the Wrexley Hotel yesterday, I overheard the chambermaids talkin' about a missin' carpetbag from the dead man's room. That's when I knew I had to bring it here."

Constable Evans stuck his head in again. "Sorry to interrupt, sir, but there's a hansom cab driver out here who says he may have some information pertinent to your inquiry."

Witherspoon looked surprised. "Have him wait, Constable. We'll see him in a few minutes." He looked at Nicholas. "Why did Mr. Hart send you to the Wrexley?"

"He wanted to know if anyone there found a button missing from his fancy green jacket," Nicholas sneered. "He lost it there, and it's a big fancy gold one."

Barnes silently sent up a prayer to heaven. But the God Almighty or fate or perhaps just blind luck was on his side, because by the time young Nicholas had finished saying his piece, the driver had made his statement and they'd received a note from the housekeeper at the Wrexley telling them she thought they had a gold button belonging to Ronald Hart. The inspector decided it was time to pay a visit to Ronald Hart.

Witherspoon was silent and his expression thoughtful on the hansom ride to Bayswater. But as they rounded the corner to the Hart house, he said, "Everything is happening at once. Isn't that odd?"

"That's the way you usually solve your cases, sir," Barnes said. He had a reply at the ready, and he hoped it would work. "Events come to a head, and you finish putting the pieces together so that it all makes sense."

"That's good of you to say, Constable." Witherspoon's brows drew together. "But we had three different types of evidence in one short morning. That is very unusual."

"Not really, sir. Like the young lad said, Hart *sent* him to the Wrexley yesterday to see if his missing button had been found, and while Nicholas was there, he overheard the chambermaids talking about Mundy's missing carpetbag. That's the only reason the boy understood he had evidence about Mundy's murder in his possession, and he brought us that evidence for his own reasons."

"I can understand that, but why did the hansom driver wait so long before he came to see us?" Witherspoon frowned in confusion.

"He said that he'd not put two and two together until he went into the pub and told the story about having to follow a cab to the Wrexley." Barnes watched Witherspoon's face. From his expression, he wasn't convinced. "Frankly, I doubt the driver did put two and two together," Barnes continued. "More like someone at the pub pointed out that there had been a murder at that hotel and shamed him into coming to tell us."

"But what about the note from the Wrexley housekeeper?" The inspector pushed his spectacles up his nose. "Yesterday Elsie Scott admitted she'd taken the button. She knew we weren't going to tell the hotel management. So why did she turn it in at this late date?"

The hansom pulled to the pavement and stopped. Witherspoon stepped out and waited while Barnes paid the driver.

"Perhaps her conscience bothered her," the constable suggested as they went to the door. "More like she didn't trust us to keep our word." They'd reached the door. "Sir, maybe I should nip around the corner. There's a fixed point constable there, and if we make an arrest, we might need some extra men."

"I doubt it. Ronald Hart won't do anything as foolish as trying to bolt. He's the sort that will bring in an army of solicitors."

Barnes nodded and banged the oversized door knocker against the wood. The butler answered. He stared at them curiously. "Mr. Hart is unavailable. You'll need to come back at a more convenient time."

"We'll wait." Barnes shoved past the servant and into the foyer. Witherspoon was right behind him.

"Please, you can't come in here." The butler stumbled after them. "Mr. Hart is indisposed at the moment, and he gave me strict instructions not to let anyone interrupt."

Witherspoon turned to look at him. "Tell Mr. Hart we're here and that we must speak to him as soon as possible."

The drawing room doors flew open, and an elderly, white-haired man dressed in an old-fashioned frock coat stood in the doorway. "Ye gods, the police are here again," he exclaimed. "How many times have they been here?" He spoke to Ronald Hart, who'd just walked up to stand beside him, but he didn't wait for Hart to reply.

"Well, answer me." He directed the question to Witherspoon. "How many times has it been now?"

"This is our third time here, sir," Witherspoon answered politely. "I hate to interrupt, but it's imperative we speak with Mr. Hart immediately. It concerns the murder of Thomas Mundy."

"I'm Josiah Thornquist, and I demand to know if you're going to arrest him."

"Don't be absurd." Hart shoved past him and stopped in front of the two policemen. His face was red with anger and his stance belligerent. "No one is arresting me. I've done nothing wrong."

"If the police come once, you're a witness," Thornquist declared. "If they come twice, they suspect you, and if they come a third time, you're under arrest." He looked at Hart and gave a disgusted shake of his head, then started for the front door. "I should have listened when they warned me about you. Everyone said you were a nasty, unsavory character. What were we thinking when we considered letting you take Reed's place?"

"But I've done nothing wrong." Hart grabbed at Thornquist's sleeve. "I'm innocent. You can't condemn me simply because the police have arrived. They only want to ask me more questions. Please wait. I've done nothing wrong, I tell you."

Thornquist shook him off. "They're not just here to talk to you; they're going to arrest you for that murder at the Wrexley. I should have realized you were guilty when you asked me to lie and say that I'd seen you walking in Shepherds Bush on

Monday night. If I'd done as you asked, it would have proven you couldn't have killed that poor man. How dare you try to use me; how dare you?"

"He wanted you to lie for him, sir?" Witherspoon asked.

"He asked me less than ten minutes ago." Thornquist gave Hart a shove. "Get out of my way, you jackanapes. I'm not interested in helping a murderer go free, even if he is a Conservative."

"You're a lying old fool." Hart moved so that he was nose to nose with Thornquist. "I said nothing of the kind, you senile jackass. Tell them, tell them I never asked you to say such a thing."

Witherspoon and Barnes moved simultaneously to get between the men, but Hart was too fast for them. He gave Thornquist a hard push, which sent him tumbling to the ground. Barnes lunged at Hart, but he leapt over Thornquist and raced for the front door. The butler stuck his foot out. Hart tripped and went sprawling, screaming in rage as he crashed against the floor.

"Mr. Hart, sir." The butler smiled bitterly. "I've wanted to do that for years." He moved to the fallen Thornquist and helped him up while the two policemen pulled Hart to his feet.

Hart, his sandy hair disheveled and his face red with anger, turned slowly. He glared at the crowd of servants now standing in the corridor and staring at their master with undisguised contempt and horror; then he turned back to Witherspoon. "You're going to regret this," he vowed. "You don't have enough evidence to convict me, and by the time we go to trial, this old fool might be dead." He jerked his thumb toward Thornquist. "Listen well, Inspector. If it takes the rest of my life, I'll make sure you pay for doing this to me."

Witherspoon ignored him. "Ronald Hart, you're under arrest for the murder of Thomas Mundy."

"What's taking those men so long?" Luty muttered. "They've been gone for hours now."

After everyone had done the tasks they'd been assigned, the men had gone off to see if they could determine what might be happening and the women had gathered around the table.

Betsy put Amanda down on the floor. "It's not been hours, Luty. It just feels that way. Be careful, sweetie. Leave Samson alone. He doesn't like little ones." Amanda's face fell as the big old tomcat ran off toward the cook's quarters.

"He doesn't like anyone but Mrs. Goodge," Phyllis added. She glanced at Mrs. Jeffries. "Are you going to make us wait until the men get back before you tell us how you knew it was Ronald Hart?"

"If it turns out to be Hart." Luty made a face. "We're all in trouble if it ain't."

"Believe me, I know that." Mrs. Jeffries hoped her powers of deduction hadn't led her up the garden path. If they had, Luty was right and they were in trouble. "It doesn't seem fair to explain without everyone here."

"I agree." Ruth took a sip of tea. "We should wait. I do hope Gerald is alright. If they were going to arrest Hart, they'd have taken more constables, right?"

"Of course they would," Betsy said. "They always take additional men when they . . ." Her voice trailed off as the back door opened. "They're back. Thank goodness. I was getting a bit worried."

"Nothin' to worry about, love." Smythe paused long enough to scoop up his daughter and give her a kiss.

"We're just fine." Hatchet was grinning from ear to ear. "But I don't think Ronald Hart is having a very good day."

"They arrested him," Wiggins added. "The constable and our inspector. They brought him out and sent one of the Hart servants for more constables to cart him off to the station."

"We had a front-row view of the whole proceedings." Hatchet slipped into the chair next to Luty. "Lord Devere's carriage was perfect. We pulled up just across the road from the house, and the Devere coat of arms on the door kept the neighbors from bothering us. We must thank him for lending it to us."

"The inspector knows what my carriage looks like." Luty laughed. "And Devere owes me a favor or two. Now, come on, Hepzibah, tell us how you sussed it out."

"Actually, it was something Phyllis said." She smiled at the maid. "You commented that slipping in and out of the Wrexley without being caught was good practice, or words to that effect. You see, what threw me off was I couldn't understand why Hart was there earlier that day. But your words made it crystal clear. He'd gone for two reasons: one, to practice getting in and out without being seen, and two and more important, he needed to find out Mundy's room number."

"But he could have just bribed a bellboy for it," Betsy said. "That's what Marianne Pelletier did."

Mrs. Jeffries shook her head. "But he couldn't. He planned to murder Mundy, whereas she planned to confront the man. I think it happened like this: Hart came out of his tailor's and was chatting when he spotted Thomas Mundy getting out of a hansom. Mundy was with Gemma Ridley."

"The woman he'd deliberately met because she was a rich spinster and he wanted to trick her out of her money." Mrs. Goodge snorted in disgust. "Disgraceful."

"That's right, but Nicholas was there, and he saw the impact that spotting Mundy had on his master."

"That's right." Wiggins nodded. "Hart was doin' his trick, walking that coin on the back of his hand, but he dropped it. Nicholas said he never messed it up."

"Seeing Mundy must have shocked him to his core," she continued. "He sent the lad home and then followed Mundy. He had one goal in mind: He needed to know where Mundy was staying, and he needed to know it quickly."

"Why was he in such a hurry?" Ruth asked. "Why not wait and put out a few inconspicuous inquiries? He certainly had the resources to do it discreetly."

"Politics," Mrs. Jeffries explained. "He wanted a political career, and the first step was the seat that might become vacant on the county council. He couldn't risk Mr. Reed dying before he got rid of Mundy."

"You think he planned on killing him from the start?" Hatchet poured himself a cup of tea.

"Absolutely. Mundy was the one person who could ruin everything for him. He could tell the world that Hart had hired him to alter Bernard Hart's will. He couldn't risk that. No party will back a candidate with that kind of smear against his name."

"But if Mundy said anything, wouldn't he be at risk of being arrested?" Phyllis asked.

"Perhaps, perhaps not. Mundy's risk was far less than Hart's. All he had to do was leave the country and write a letter to one of Hart's relatives or the newspapers. Neither of them would keep silent. But Hart stood to lose it all if Mundy told what he knew. He had to kill him, and he had to do it quickly."

"Go on, then. Hart follows Mundy from Hanover Square. How does the hansom driver fit in?" Luty asked.

"I know," Betsy volunteered. "Mundy went to Oxford Street and got into a cab, but the street was very congested, so Hart, though on foot, was able to keep him in sight until Mundy's hansom reached Marble Arch. That's when Hart waved one down and told the driver to follow Mundy's cab." She looked at Mrs. Jeffries. "Am I right?"

"Yes. Then Hart compounded his error by not letting the driver stop in front of the Wrexley. He made him pull around the corner to let him out."

"Making sure the cabbie would remember 'im," Smythe muttered. "That was stupid."

"Hart slipped in the back door and up the stairs," Mrs. Jeffries continued. "He raced down the corridor of the first floor to look down at the lobby. He wanted to see which floor Mundy's room was on."

"And that's when the Ottley woman saw him," Mrs. Goodge said. "She claimed he hid his face so she'd not get a good look at him."

"She was right, too. It took me a while to understand this part, but it makes sense when one thinks of it. He watched Mundy start up the stairs. Hart ran for the back stairs and realized that Mundy hadn't come out onto the first-floor rooms. So he went up the back stairs and did the same thing. He waited and saw that Mundy didn't come down that corridor, either."

"So he knew Mundy's room was on the third floor," Ruth said.

"Correct. All he had to do was hide by the back stairs and

see which room Mundy went into. There're only three guest floors in the hotel. From the third floor up, the back stairs lead to the storage rooms and the attic."

"That's where he lost his button." Phyllis looked at Mrs. Jeffries in amazement. "And you realized what he must have done, because Elsie Scott found the button before the murder."

"Correct. His real purpose was locating Mundy's room. He also knew that Mundy's walking stick would make a good weapon. So later that evening, he dressed in dark clothes and came back to the Wrexley. He went to the third floor and hid on the back staircase. Now, remember, this was the same night that Mundy spotted Daniel Wright, the one person he was frightened of. Mundy hurried back to the hotel, had a few words with the ladies in the lobby, and then dashed upstairs to pack. Somehow or other, Hart managed to get into Mundy's room."

"He probably opened the door for him," Hatchet said. "He wasn't frightened of him."

"However he did it, the second Mundy's back was turned, Hart used the walking stick to kill him. If we're right about Mundy using the carpetbag to stash his cash, then Hart found the bag and stole it. He got out the same way he'd come in, only he didn't realize that both Marianne Pelletier and Daniel Wright saw him leave the hotel."

"But they couldn't possibly identify him," Betsy said.

"True, but with both their statements, the carpetbag, and the button, which I suspect will match the buttons on Hart's green coat, there should be enough to get a conviction."

They discussed the case for another hour or two, going over and over the details and enjoying the parts they'd individually played. Betsy and Smythe were the first who had to break up the party. "We've got to get the little one home." She lifted her out of Mrs. Goodge's lap. "She needs her nap."

Ruth got up as well. "Please tell Gerald I'd love him to come to dinner tonight," she said to Mrs. Jeffries. "Seven o'clock. Oh dear, I must run. I've got an executive committee meeting."

Luty and Hatchet left next. "Make sure you send Nicholas over real soon," she told Wiggins.

"But what if the inspector sees him at your 'ouse?" Wiggins asked. Witherspoon was frequently invited to social occasions at the Crookshank home. "Won't he think it odd?"

"Nope, I'll just tell 'im that I heard the boy needed a job and I sent you to git him."

"Don't concern yourself, Wiggins." Hatchet slipped Luty's cloak over her shoulders. "We'll handle it properly if the matter comes up."

Mrs. Jeffries dashed upstairs to air the linen cupboard, and Mrs. Goodge went to her room for a quick lie-down before she started cooking dinner. Just Wiggins and Phyllis were left. She started to get up to clear the tea things off the table.

"Don't get up just yet." Wiggins gave her a shy smile. "I want to talk to you."

She sank back into her chair. "What about? Look, I know I've been a bit rude . . ."

"Not as rude as me," he said. "And I'm so sorry. The truth is, I was a bit jealous. You used to ask me for advice and, you know, for my opinion about things, but you don't anymore. I guess it 'urt my feelings that you don't seem to need me now."

"That's not true. I do need your advice, and I value your opinions." She licked her lips nervously. "But I didn't want you to think of me as such a ninny . . . Oh, I don't know what I mean. I just wanted you to think well of me, and constantly needing help made me sound like such a whiny child."

Wiggins brightened. "You really cared about what I thought of you?"

"Of course, why wouldn't I?" She stared at him in confusion. "You've been very good to me since I came here."

Wiggins wasn't sure what she meant, but at least she wasn't looking daggers at him. "I do think highly of you, and it was right clever you gettin' in and out of the hotel like that."

Phyllis grinned. "Yes, I thought so, too."

Witherspoon was in an excellent mood when he got home late that afternoon. He came into the kitchen while the members of the household were finishing their tea.

"You're home early, sir." Mrs. Jeffries started to rise, but he motioned for her to sit.

"Indeed, we've made an arrest in the Mundy murder. If you don't mind, I think I'll join you." He pulled out a chair and sat down.

"Will you tell us all about it, sir?" Phyllis asked excitedly. She rose to get him a place setting. "Please, sir, you know how we all love hearing about your work."

He laughed. "We've arrested Ronald Hart."

"Ronald Hart?" Mrs. Jeffries pretended to be surprised. "But I thought you were going to arrest Daniel Wright. What on earth happened?"

"It was actually quite extraordinary." He nodded his thanks as the cook handed him a cup. "A few minutes after we got to the station, Ronald Hart's footman, a very young one at that, demanded to see me." He told them about his interview with

Nicholas Foley. They listened carefully, occasionally breaking in to ask a question or make a comment.

Witherspoon started to reach for a second slice of brown bread.

"Don't eat too much, sir. Lady Cannonberry has invited you to dinner tonight if you're free."

"Of course I'm free." He pulled his hand back. "What time?"

"Seven o'clock, sir, but do go on. What happened after you spoke with the footman?"

"After that, things happened very quickly. We'd not finished with the lad when a hansom driver wanted to see me, and he had information about the crime." He continued his narrative, taking his time and pausing occasionally for dramatic effect. When he told them what happened at Ronald Hart's home, the room got so quiet, one could have heard a pin drop. As he finished, he sat back in his chair with a pleased, rather proud expression on his face.

"Oh my gracious, sir, his own butler stopped him from escaping?" Mrs. Jeffries exclaimed.

"Indeed—his servants don't like him very much. Actually, most of them looked quite happy to see him arrested."

"Do you have enough evidence to get a conviction?" Phyllis asked.

"I think so." Witherspoon frowned thoughtfully. "Of course, he'll have the best legal representation money can buy, but we've Elsie Scott's statement about the carpetbag being in Mundy's room, and the footman will testify that he witnessed Hart throwing it in the dustbin the day after the murder. But our best witness will be Josiah Thornquist."

"The elderly man who Hart swore would be dead before the

trial started." Wiggins was a bit worried that Hart might be right. "How old a man is 'e?"

Witherspoon laughed. "We've taken a formal statement from him, but I shouldn't look so concerned, Wiggins. Mr. Thornquist assures us he's in excellent health and that he comes from a long-lived line of people." He rose to his feet. "I think I'll take Fred for a walk, and then I'll have a bit of a rest before I go to dinner." He patted his thigh. "Come on, boy. Let's get your leash and go walkies."

A few minutes later, Mrs. Jeffries and Mrs. Goodge had the kitchen to themselves.

"Did you see the way that Phyllis and Wiggins were smiling at each other?" Mrs. Goodge kept her voice low in case one of them unexpectedly appeared. The maid had gone upstairs to dust the banisters, and Wiggins had gone to finish moving the rest of the bricks into the larder.

"I saw. They seem to have cleared the air, and I'm glad. It'll make our next case easier."

The cook cocked her head to one side and stared off into space. "I'm not so sure it's not going to lead to more problems."

"How so?"

"Wiggins likes her—he likes her a lot—and I mean he likes her as a woman." She frowned. "I'm not so sure how she thinks of him. But if he tries to court her and she still sees him as a brother, he'll get his heart broken."

"Let's not borrow trouble." Mrs. Jeffries chuckled. "We've had enough of that lately. Let's enjoy a few days of peace and quiet."

The cook got up. "You're right—we've had enough on our plate recently. I'm glad this one is over. I have to tell you, Hepzibah, I was a bit worried that you'd got this one wrong."

"So was I," she admitted. She picked up the teapot and carried it to the sink.

"But you got it right in the end." Mrs. Goodge laughed heartily. "And you kept the inspector from doing wrong. Then again, you always do."